JORIS-KARL HUYSMANS was born in Paris in 1848, the only son of a French mother and a Dutch father. After a childhood saddened by his father's death and his mother's speedy re-marriage, he became a junior clerk in the Ministry of the Interior, where he remained for thirty-two years. He spent the first half of the Franco-Prussian War in hospital, suffering from dysentery, and the second half under fire in the besieged capital. When peace returned he went back to the Ministry, and three years later published his first book, *Le Drageoir à épices* (1874), a collection of prose-poems after Baudelaire. He then turned to novel-writing and published *Marthe* (1876), *Les Sœurs Vatard* (1879), *En Ménage* (1881) and *À Vau-l'Eau* (1882). *À Rebours*, published in 1884 and hailed by Arthur Symons as 'the breviary of the Decadence', marked his break with Zola's Médan Group and the beginning of an attempt to widen the scope of the novel. His other novels were *En Rade* (1887), *Là-Bas* (1891), *En Route* (1895), *La Cathédrale* (1898) and *L'Oblat* (1903). He died in 1907.

ROBERT BALDICK, the late co-editor of the Penguin Classics, received his M.A. and D.Phil. from Oxford University, where he was a Fellow of Pembroke College. A Fellow of the Royal Society of Literature, he wrote biographies of J.-K. Huysmans, Frédérick Lemaître and Henry Murger, a study of the Gon-courts, *The Siege of Paris* and *The Duel*. Authors whose work he translated from the French include the Goncourts, Montherlant, Radiguet, Restif de la Bretonne, Sartre, Simenon and Jules Verne. For the Penguin Classics he translated Flaubert's *Three Tales* and *Sentimental Education*, Chateaubriand's *Memoirs* and Huysmans' *Against Nature*. He died in 1972.

J.-K. HUYSMANS

Against Nature

A NEW TRANSLATION OF
À Rebours

BY
ROBERT BALDICK

PENGUIN BOOKS

Penguin Books Ltd, Harmondsworth, Middlesex, England
Penguin Books Inc., 7110 Ambassador Road, Baltimore, Maryland 21207, U.S.A.
Penguin Books Australia Ltd, Ringwood, Victoria, Australia
Penguin Books Canada Ltd, 41 Steelcase Road West, Markham, Ontario, Canada
Penguin Books (N.Z.) Ltd, 182–190 Wairau Road, Auckland 10, New Zealand

—

This translation first published 1959
Reprinted 1966, 1968, 1971, 1973, 1974, 1976

—

Copyright © the Estate of Robert Baldick, 1959

—

Made and printed in Great Britain
by Richard Clay (The Chaucer Press) Ltd,
Bungay, Suffolk
Set in Monotype Garamond

INTRODUCTION

'It was the strangest book that he had ever read. It seemed to him that in exquisite raiment and to the delicate sound of flutes, the sins of the world were passing in dumb show before him. Things that he had dimly dreamed of were suddenly made real to him. Things of which he had never dreamed were gradually revealed.'

Thus Oscar Wilde in The Picture of Dorian Gray, *referring to the yellow-backed French novel lent to his hero by Lord Henry Wotton. In 1895, at the Queensberry trial, Edward Carson cross-examined Wilde as to the identity and morality of this same French novel. Wilde identified it readily enough as Huysmans'* À Rebours, *but he refused to say anything about its morality or immorality; to ask a writer to pass moral judgement on a fellow writer's work was, he said, 'an impertinence and a vulgarity'. The British public, left to draw its own unsavoury conclusions, probably decided that the author of the notorious 'yellow book' must be a wealthy hedonist, a monster of depravity, a nineteenth-century Elagabalus. Only a few people outside France (including, perhaps, Wilde himself) knew that in fact he was a minor civil servant of modest means, living what was as yet a very humdrum life.*

Joris-Karl Huysmans was born in Paris on 5 February 1848, the only son of a French mother and a Dutch father. After a childhood saddened by two major events – his father's death and his mother's speedy remarriage – he became a junior clerk in the Ministry of the Interior, where he was to remain for thirty-two years, writing reports for the Sûreté Générale and novels for himself. For a short period before the Franco-Prussian War he also studied law, without much enthusiasm, and lived with a young soubrette in a somewhat sordid liaison described in his first novel, Marthe. *He spent the first half of the War in hospital, suffering from dysentery, and the second half under fire in the besieged capital; with the return of peace he went back to his office stool, and three years later published his first book.*

This was Le Drageoir à épices *(1874), a collection of highly-coloured prose-poems in the Baudelaire manner, signed with what*

Huysmans supposed was the Dutch form of two of his French names. He then turned to novel-writing, his first three efforts in this genre showing the influence of the three great masters of the contemporary French novel: Edmond de Goncourt, who inspired Marthe (*1876*), reputed to be the first novel dealing with a prostitute in a licensed brothel; Émile Zola, who was the dedicatee of Les Sœurs Vatard (*1879*), a well-documented study of working-class life; and Gustave Flaubert, to whom the delightful but obviously derivative En Ménage (*1881*) was a sort of posthumous tribute. Flaubert's influence can also be seen in the short novel À Vau-l'Eau (*1882*), the tragi-comic story of a little clerk called Jean Folantin, an older, poorer, sicklier Huysmans, who samples the humble pleasures of life as systematically as Flaubert's Bouvard and Pécuchet amassed knowledge, and finally decides to 'ship his oars and drift – downstream'.

So far Huysmans was still regarded by public and critics alike as a faithful member of Zola's Médan Group of young Realists, or rather Naturalists, together with Guy de Maupassant, Henry Céard, Léon Hennique, and Paul Alexis. But there were already disquieting signs that he had no intention of spending the rest of his life producing bleak social documentaries such as Zola urged his disciples to write and carefully avoided writing himself. His style, for one thing, was too colourful, too individual for a good Naturalist, while in his latest works all pretence of objectivity was abandoned and his heroes stood revealed as J.-K. Huysmans in the thinnest of disguises. What is more, these heroes would often admit to odd fancies that seemed even odder in their context; for instance, in the working-class novel Les Sœurs Vatard, Cyprien Tibaille expressed a longing to 'embrace a woman dressed as a rich circus artiste, under a wintry, yellow-grey, snow-laden sky, in a room hung with Japanese silks, while some half-starved beggar emptied the belly of his barrel-organ of the sad waltzes it contained'.

It was clear that Cyprien Tibaille's creator, as one perceptive critic put it, had 'taken a return ticket to Médan'. But Huysmans later claimed that the other members of the Médan Group were almost as tired as he was of following in the Master's footsteps. The novel of the average man, in their opinion, had been done to perfection by Flaubert in his Éducation sentimentale; the novel of adultery had been worked to death by writers great and small; and as for the social documentary, they saw little point in plodding through every trade and

6

profession, one by one, from rat-catcher to stockbroker. 'We began to wonder', writes Huysmans, 'whether Naturalism was not advancing up a blind alley, and whether we might not soon be running our heads into a wall.' While his colleagues hesitated, he himself decided on an ambitious attempt ' to shake off preconceived ideas, to extend the scope of the novel, to introduce into it art, science, history: in a word, to use this form of literature only as a frame in which to insert more serious work'. The result was À Rebours.

This book was originally conceived as an esoteric extension of À Vau-l'Eau. *'I pictured to myself', writes Huysmans, ' a Monsieur Folantin, more cultured, more refined, more wealthy than the first, and who has discovered in artificiality a specific for the disgust inspired by the worries of life and the American manners of his time. I imagined him winging his way to the land of dreams, seeking refuge in extravagant illusions, living alone and apart, far from the present-day world, in an atmosphere suggestive of more cordial epochs and less odious surroundings.' Where poor Folantin had sought satisfaction in the simple, natural things of life, the rich hero of* À Rebours, Duc Jean Floressas des Esseintes, *would resort to the artificial and the exotic; where Folantin had read realistic novels and collected prints of the Dutch masters, Des Esseintes would prefer the poetry of Mallarmé and the pictures of Gustave Moreau; where Folantin had indulged his body in restaurants and brothels, Des Esseintes would use enemas and enjoy ' unnatural loves and perverse pleasures'. But if the clerk and the aesthete went opposite ways in their pursuit of happiness, the result of their quest was to be the same in each case: disgust and disillusionment.*

Des Esseintes was not, of course, just a refined reincarnation of Monsieur Folantin; he owed something to half-a-dozen dandies and aesthetes who were living or only lately dead when Huysmans wrote À Rebours. *Thus there was the ' mad' Ludwig II of Bavaria, who was said to possess an artificial forest inhabited by mechanical animals; there was Charles Baudelaire, who as a young man had furnished his rooms in the Hôtel Lauzun in the same exotic style as Des Esseintes, and Edmond de Goncourt, who in* La Maison d'un artiste *had listed the contents of his Auteuil treasure-house in the same detail; there was the old dandy, Jules Barbey d'Aurevilly, disciple and biographer of Beau Brummel, and the young dandy, Francis Poictevin, a rich friend*

7

of Huysmans' who later used the original title of À Rebours – Seul – for a book of his own; and, last but by no means least, there was Robert, Comte de Montesquiou-Fezensac.

This elegant aristocrat, like Des Esseintes a scion of one of France's oldest families, enjoyed a well deserved reputation for eccentricity. It was rumoured, for instance, that he would sometimes wear a bunch of Parma violets tucked into his shirt in lieu of a cravat, and that he always dressed in colours which he considered matched the tastes and temperament of his host or guest. But these sartorial idiosyncrasies were as nothing compared to the furnishings of his house in the Rue Franklin, which Stéphane Mallarmé visited one evening in 1883. According to Montesquiou, 'he went away in a state of silent exaltation . . . I do not doubt, therefore, that it was in the most admiring, sympathetic and sincere good faith that he retailed to Huysmans what he had seen during the few moments he spent in Ali-Baba's Cave.' Whether it was retailed in good faith or bad, Huysmans certainly made good use of the poet's information, and all the bizarre features of Montesquiou's house – the sledge on a snow-white bearskin, the silk socks displayed in a glass case, the church furniture and the gilded tortoise – eventually appeared, suitably adapted and embellished, in À Rebours. Montesquiou himself was understandably annoyed when the public proceeded to identify him with Huysmans' unhealthy hero; thus there is a story that when he ordered some rare works from one of Huysmans' bookseller friends, and the man, failing to recognize his customer, exclaimed: 'Why, Monsieur, those are books fit for Des Esseintes!' he reacted violently. As the author of some passable verse, he hoped to achieve immortality as a poet, and it must have been galling for him to realize, before he died in 1921, that he was destined to be remembered only as the prototype of Huysmans' Des Esseintes and Proust's Charlus.

In fact, the identity of the models Huysmans used for Des Esseintes is of little importance compared with the inspiration he derived from contemporary literature, and particularly from the works of Baudelaire, Goncourt, and Zola.

Baudelaire's influence on À Rebours is everywhere apparent, from the very title and theme of the book, inspired by the poet's paradoxical praise of artifice and denigration of Nature, to details such as the nightmare finale of Chapter Seven, obviously suggested by the poem

8

Les Métamorphoses du Vampire. *Moreover, the spirit of Baude-*
laire's Correspondances *pervades Huysmans' novel, the concept of*
the interrelation of sense-impressions being pushed to its furthest limits
in the famous episode of the 'mouth organ' – although the actual idea of
the ingenious arrangement of liqueur-casks was taken from an anony-
mous eighteenth-century brochure.

Edmond de Goncourt also had a considerable influence on À
Rebours. *It was from him that Des Esseintes derived many of his*
aesthetic beliefs and literary opinions; it was Goncourt too who, in his
envious anxiety to wean disciples away from Zola, had advised Huys-
mans to abandon the working-class novel in order to study 'cultured
beings and exquisite things', setting him an example with his own most
recent novel, La Faustin. *Huysmans, like Des Esseintes, admired this*
book for what he called its 'subtle and elegant depravity', and in a
significant letter to the author, written in 1882, he had declared that
'this analysis of the sensual and cerebral pleasures of refined and
neurotic creatures opened up to me new, if not unsuspected, horizons'.

As for Zola, who might appear at first to have made no contribu-
tion to À Rebours, *it should be remembered that in many of his*
novels – generally those we most admire today – the poet overrules the
Naturalist and gives free rein to his lyrical genius. Des Esseintes ex-
presses warm admiration for one of these novels, La Faute de l'Abbé
Mouret, *and readers of this book will recall a symphony of flowers*
during the heroine's aromatic death-agony which, like the symphony of
cheeses in Le Ventre de Paris, *foreshadows the symphony of liqueurs*
in À Rebours.

Nor must it be imagined that Huysmans had abjured every article in
the Médan creed; to the end of his life he was to remain faithful to the
Naturalist ideal of careful and conscientious documentation. The sub-
ject and scope of À Rebours *in particular called for detailed research*
in many different spheres. In the first place, it involved some of that
'field-work' to which every Naturalist was accustomed, taking Huys-
mans and his note-book to the Bodega on the corner of the Rue Casti-
glione and the tavern known as Austin's Bar in the Rue d'Amsterdam
that are patronized by Des Esseintes in the course of his ill-starred
London journey; incidentally, the latter establishment still serves
drinks, but the only trace of its English connexion that remains is its
name, now Le Bar Britannia. Then the nature of Des Esseintes' illness

9

necessitated a thorough study of the relevant medical textbooks, and Huysmans later told Zola that he had faithfully followed the works of Bouchut and Axenfeld in his representation of every symptom and phase of his hero's neurosis. And finally, to cover the vast range of Des Esseintes' interests and experiments, Huysmans had to consult countless specialist treatises on subjects as diverse as theology and perfumery, floriculture and furniture, picking out unusual details or startling opinions and recasting them in the mould of his own distinctive style. How successfully he used this technique can be judged from the fact that his chapter on late Latin literature earned him the reputation of a brilliant if perverse scholar, and only years later did he reveal that it had been cunningly adapted from Ebert's Allgemeine Geschichte der Literatur des Mittelalters.

Huysmans had originally intended À Rebours *to be no longer than* À Vau-l'Eau, *but this plan miscarried. In a preface he wrote in 1903 for a limited edition of the novel, he explained that ' the more I thought about it, the more the subject grew, calling for painstaking research; each chapter became the essence of a speciality, the sublimate of a different art'. The result was an encyclopaedic work so far removed from the average novel that, when the author was asked in 1883 how he thought it would be received, he was pessimistic – but unrepentant. ' It will be the biggest fiasco of the year,' he said; ' but I don't care a damn! It will be something nobody has ever done before, and I shall have said what I want to say . . .'*

In fact, when it was published by Charpentier in May 1884, À Rebours *was anything but a fiasco. As Huysmans wrote twenty years later, ' it fell like a meteorite into the literary fairground, provoking anger and stupefaction, especially among the Press'. The critic Francisque Sarcey was moved to declare in a public lecture that ' he'd be hanged if he understood a word of the novel'; Catholic reviewers damned it out of hand as being hostile to religion, while anticlerical writers thought it treated the enemy too sympathetically; Romantics and Parnassians were outraged by the attacks on Hugo and Leconte de Lisle, while the Naturalists were no less offended by the hero's detestation of modern life. As for Zola, he brushed aside Huysmans' well-meant but dishonest hints that the whole thing was just a literary leg-pull, and sadly reproached his former disciple with ' delivering a terrible blow to Naturalism' and ' leading the school astray'.*

On the other hand, the indignation of the novel's critics was more than matched by the enthusiasm of its admirers, both inside and outside France. Thus George Moore called it 'that prodigious book, that beautiful mosaic'; Wilde paid tribute to its potency, declaring that 'the heavy odour of incense seemed to cling about its pages and to trouble the brain'; while Rémy de Gourmont insisted that 'we should never forget what a huge debt we owe to this memorable breviary'.

Certainly these authors and countless others owed a great deal to À Rebours, as any student of modern European literature can testify. Moore's John Norton, in A Mere Accident and Mike Fletcher, copies Des Esseintes in his furnishing schemes, his reading of Schopenhauer, his taste in church music; Wilde's Dorian Gray models his conduct on Des Esseintes' and incidentally explores the subjects of jewellery and tapestry as exhaustively as Huysmans' hero studied perfumery and floriculture; Rémy de Gourmont's Hubert d'Entragues, in Sixtine, repeats both Des Esseintes' literary judgements and his final cry for faith; and Eça de Queiroz's Jacinto, the hero of the great Portuguese novel À cidade e as serras, imitates Des Esseintes in nearly every respect, even organizing a rose-coloured meal as a delicate variation on the latter's notorious black dinner. These are a few of the more obvious instances of À Rebours' influence, but the total number of Des Esseintes' literary progeny is incalculable: almost every unhappy, solitary hero of a twentieth-century novel could probably trace his descent back to Huysmans' great creation.

There are, of course, critics who maintain that Des Esseintes himself was intended to be a caricature of such aesthetes as Montesquiou, just as Amarinth in Robert Hichens' novel The Green Carnation was meant as a satire on Wilde. The flaw in this theory lies in the fact that Des Esseintes is basically a self-portrait, for if Huysmans lacked his hero's wealth and breeding, he shared his neurotic sensibility, his yearning for solitude, his loathing for mediocrity, his passion for novelty.

À Rebours indeed forms an integral and important part of the great spiritual autobiography represented by Huysmans' novels. With the exception of Marthe and Les Sœurs Vatard, all these novels tell the story of the efforts made by one character, under different names, to achieve happiness in various forms of spiritual and physical escapism. Thus in En Ménage he hopes to find content in love-affairs conducted *in his former bachelor establishment; in* À Vau-l'Eau, *in the humbler satisfactions of life and his snugly furnished rooms; in* À Rebours, *in artificial, esoteric pleasures and his 'refined Thebaid'; in* En Rade *(1887), in country life and the dilapidated Château de Lourps where Des Esseintes was born; in* Là-Bas *(1891), in satanism and the bell-ringer's eyrie at Saint-Sulpice; in* En Route *(1895), in monastic life and the Trappist abbey where Huysmans was received back into the Catholic Church; in* La Cathédrale *(1898), in provincial life and the cathedral city of Chartres; in* L'Oblat *(1903), in semi-monastic life and the village where Huysmans spent two years as a Benedictine oblate. All these hopes are disappointed, but in* L'Oblat *Huysmans and his last hero show that they have learnt their lesson; the novel ends with an admission that escapism is not only futile but wrong – that one should accept suffering willingly in expiation of one's own sins and the sins of others. With this statement of the doctrine of mystical substitution, Huysmans' spiritual odyssey as recounted in his novels came to an end; it only remained for him to put the doctrine into effect, as he did in the six months of atrocious agony, heroically borne, that preceded his death from cancer in May 1907.*

It is easy for us today, when reading À Rebours, *to be wise after the event; to see auguries of Huysmans' subsequent conversion in his hero's hankering after 'the impossible belief in a future life' and his despairing appeal to God; to belittle Barbey d'Aurevilly's prescience in telling Huysmans that after writing this novel he would have to choose between 'the muzzle of a pistol and the foot of the Cross'. But it should be remembered that it was seven years before the author of* À Rebours *asked to see a priest and was introduced to the Abbé Mugnier; eight years before he returned to the Church in the course of a retreat at the lonely Abbey of Notre-Dame-d'Igny. Huysmans himself, when he wrote the novel, was totally unaware that he was already treading the road to Rome; as he later pointed out, he had received a secular education, had abandoned his religion in childhood, and knew no priests or practising Catholics; the cry for faith that he put into Des Esseintes' mouth was therefore quite unconscious. Yet, looking back on* À Rebours *in 1903, he recognized that it contained the seeds of his future development, the fruits of his past; the brothel and tavern scenes, for instance, so reminiscent of Degas and Toulouse-Lautrec, might have been taken from* Marthe, *and the passages on church music or monastic*

life from En Route. *The novel is, in fact, the keystone of Huysmans'
life and work.*

It is also, of course, the keystone of the so-called Decadence, that
movement in France and England characterized by a delight in the perverse and artificial, a craving for new and complex sensations, a
desire to extend the boundaries of emotional and spiritual experience.
Huysmans had imagined that he was 'writing for a dozen persons'; he
found instead that he had hundreds of enthusiastic readers who, like
Paul Valéry, made À Rebours *their 'Bible and bedside book' – not
only because it mirrored their 'decadent' ideas and aspirations, but also
because it revealed and consecrated a new and exciting literature, the
literature of Baudelaire, Verlaine, and Mallarmé. Just as in* L'Art
moderne *Huysmans had championed Degas and the Impressionists in
defiance of public and critical opinion, so in* À Rebours, *with the same
unerring skill, he singled out the then neglected authors whom we regard as the most important French writers of his time. Arthur Symons
once aptly described Huysmans' novel as 'the breviary of the Decadence'; but we can see now that it looked beyond the Decadence to Sym-
bolism and Surrealism, and that Rémy de Gourmont has been justified
in his prophetic judgement: 'It is a book which has stated in advance,
and for a long time to come, our loves and hates.'*

The significance of À Rebours, *however, transcends autobiography
and literary history, and Des Esseintes is more than his creator's* alter
ego *and the quintessential Decadent. He is also, and above all else, the
modern man* par excellence, *tortured by that vague longing for an
elusive ideal which we used to call the* mal du siècle; *torn between
desire and satiety, hope and disillusionment; painfully conscious that
his pleasures are finite, his needs infinite.*

Two of Huysmans' contemporaries saw at once that the book epito-
mized the spiritual anguish of modern times: Léon Bloy and Barbey
d'Aurevilly. Bloy declared that 'in this kaleidoscopic review of all that
can possibly interest the modern mind, there is nothing that is not
flouted, stigmatized, vilified, and anathematized by this misanthrope
who refuses to regard the ignoble creatures of our time as the fulfilment
of human destiny, and who clamours distractedly for a God'. Barbey
noted that 'behind the hero's boredom and his futile efforts to conquer
it, there is a spiritual affliction which does even more to exalt the book
than the author's considerable talent'. Both recognized that Huysmans'*

supreme achievement was to have created, out of an extraordinary figure apparently incapable of generalization, a type, representative not simply of a group, or of a generation, but of an entire epoch.

NOTE ON THIS TRANSLATION

I have used Volume VII of Huysmans' Œuvres Complètes (Paris, Crès, 1929), in which certain errors contained in the first edition and in the standard Fasquelle edition have been corrected.

Huysmans' style, which Bloy described as 'continually dragging Mother Image by the hair or the feet down the worm-eaten staircase of terrified Syntax', is one of the strangest literary idioms in existence, packed with purple passages, intricate sentences, weird metaphors, unexpected tense changes, and a vocabulary rich in slang and technical terms. I have tried to achieve the same effect, using the same constituents, in this English translation; and it is only fair to warn the reader that he may find that the resultant mixture, like the French original, is best taken in small doses.

I should like to thank the Delegates of the Clarendon Press for permission to reproduce passages I had already translated in my Life of J.-K. Huysmans *(Oxford, 1955); my long-suffering friends and colleagues for help with the terminology of a wide range of subjects.*

May 1957   R. B.

AGAINST NATURE

*I must rejoice beyond the bounds
of time . . . though the world may shudder at
my joy, and in its coarseness know
not what I mean.*

JAN VAN RUYSBROECK

PROLOGUE

JUDGING by the few portraits preserved in the Château de Lourps, the Floressas des Esseintes family had been composed in olden times of sturdy campaigners with forbidding faces. Imprisoned in old picture-frames which were scarcely wide enough for their broad shoulders, they were an alarming sight with their piercing eyes, their sweeping mustachios, and their bulging chests filling the enormous cuirasses which they wore.

These were the founders of the family; the portraits of their descendants were missing. There was, in fact, a gap in the pictorial pedigree, with only one canvas to bridge it, only one face to join past and present. It was a strange, sly face, with pale, drawn features; the cheekbones were punctuated with cosmetic commas of rouge, the hair was plastered down and bound with a string of pearls, and the thin, painted neck emerged from the starched pleats of a ruff.

In this picture of one of the closest friends of the Duc d'Épernon and the Marquis d'O, the defects of an impoverished stock and the excess of lymph in the blood were already apparent.

Since then, the degeneration of this ancient house had clearly followed a regular course, with the men becoming progressively less manly; and over the last two hundred years, as if to complete the ruinous process, the Des Esseintes had taken to intermarrying among themselves, thus using up what little vigour they had left.

Now, of this family which had once been so large that it occupied nearly every domain in the Île de France and La Brie, only one descendant was still living: the Duc Jean des Esseintes, a frail young man of thirty who was anaemic and highly strung, with hollow cheeks, cold eyes of steely blue, a nose which was turned up but straight, and thin, papery hands.

By some freak of heredity, this last scion of the family bore a striking resemblance to his distant ancestor the court favourite, for he had the same exceptionally fair pointed beard, and the same ambiguous expression, at once weary and wily.

His childhood had been overshadowed by sickness. However, despite the threat of scrofula and recurrent bouts of fever, he had succeeded in clearing the hurdle of adolescence with the aid of good nursing and fresh air; and after this his nerves had rallied, had overcome the languor and lethargy of chlorosis, and had brought his body to its full physical development.

His mother, a tall, pale, silent woman, died of nervous exhaustion. Then it was his father's turn to succumb to some obscure illness when Des Esseintes was nearly seventeen.

There was no gratitude or affection associated with the memories he retained of his parents: only fear. His father, who normally resided in Paris, was almost a complete stranger; and he remembered his mother chiefly as a still, supine figure in a darkened bedroom in the Château de Lourps. It was only rarely that husband and wife met, and all that he could recall of these occasions was a drab impression of his parents sitting facing each other over a table that was lighted only by a deeply shaded lamp, for the Duchess had a nervous attack whenever she was subjected to light or noise. In the semi-darkness they would exchange one or two words at the most, and then the Duke would unconcernedly slip away to catch the first available train.

At the Jesuit school to which Jean was sent to be educated, life was easier and pleasanter. The good Fathers made a point of cosseting the boy, whose intelligence amazed them; but in spite of all their efforts, they could not get him to pursue a regular course of study. He took readily to certain subjects and acquired a precocious proficiency in the Latin tongue; but on the other hand he was absolutely incapable of construing the simplest sentence in Greek, revealed no aptitude whatever for modern languages, and displayed blank incomprehension when anyone tried to teach him the first principles of science.

His family showed little interest in his doings. Occasionally his father would come to see him at school, but all he had to say was: 'Good day, goodbye, be good, and work hard.' The summer holidays he spent at Lourps, but his presence in the Château failed to awaken his mother from her reveries; she scarcely noticed him, or if she did, gazed at him for a few moments with a sad smile and then sank back again into the artificial night which the heavy curtains drawn across the windows created in her bedroom.

The servants were old and tired, and the boy was left to his own devices. On rainy days he used to browse through the books in the library, and when it was fine he would spend the afternoon exploring the local countryside.

His chief delight was to go down into the valley to Jutigny, a village lying at the foot of the hills, a little cluster of cottages wearing thatch bonnets decorated with sprigs of stonecrop and patches of moss. He used to lie down in the meadows, in the shadow of the tall hayricks, listening to the dull rumble of the water-mills and breathing in the fresh breezes coming from the Voulzie. Sometimes he would go as far as the peateries and the hamlet of Longueville with its green and black houses, or else he would scramble up the windswept hillsides from which he could survey an immense prospect. On the one hand he could look down on the Seine valley, winding away into the distance where it merged into the blue sky, and on the other he could see, far away on the horizon, the churches and the great tower of Provins, which seemed to tremble under the sun's rays in a dusty golden haze.

He would spend hours reading or daydreaming, enjoying his fill of solitude until night fell; and by dint of pondering the same thoughts his intelligence grew sharper and his ideas gained in maturity and precision. At the end of every vacation he went back to his masters a more serious and a more stubborn boy. These changes did not escape their notice: shrewd and clear-sighted men, accustomed by their profession to probing the inmost recesses of the human soul, they treated this lively but intractable mind with caution and reserve. They realized that this particular pupil of theirs would never do anything to add to the glory of their house; and as his family was rich and apparently uninterested in his future, they soon gave up any idea of turning his thoughts towards the profitable careers open to their successful scholars. Similarly, although he was fond of engaging with them in argument about theological doctrines whose niceties and subtleties intrigued him, they never even thought of inducing him to enter a religious order, for in spite of all their efforts his faith remained infirm. Finally, out of prudence and fear of the unknown, they let him pursue whatever studies pleased him and neglect the rest, not wishing to turn this independent spirit against them by subjecting him to the sort of irksome discipline imposed by lay tutors.

He therefore lived a perfectly contented life at school, scarcely aware of the priests' fatherly control. He worked at his Latin and French books in his own way and in his own time; and although theology was not one of the subjects in the school syllabus, he finished the apprenticeship to this science which he had begun at the Château de Lourps, in the library left by his great-great-uncle Dom Prosper, a former Prior of the Canons Regular of Saint-Ruf.

The time came, however, to leave the Jesuit establishment, for he was nearly of age and would soon have to take possession of his fortune. When at last he reached his majority, his cousin and guardian, the Comte de Montchevrel, gave him an account of his stewardship. Relations between the two men did not last long, for there could be no point of contact between one so old and one so young. But while they lasted, out of curiosity, as a matter of courtesy, and for want of something to do, Des Esseintes saw a good deal of his cousin's family; and he spent several desperately dull evenings at their townhouse in the Rue de la Chaise, listening to female relatives old as the hills conversing about noble quarterings, heraldic moons and antiquated ceremonial.

Even more than these dowagers, the men gathered round their whist-tables revealed an unalterable emptiness of mind. These descendants of medieval warriors, these last scions of feudal families, appeared to Des Esseintes in the guise of crotchety, catarrhal old men, endlessly repeating insipid monologues and immemorial phrases. The fleur-de-lis, which you find if you cut the stalk of a fern, was apparently also the only thing that remained impressed on the softening pulp inside these ancient skulls.

The young man felt a surge of ineffable pity for these mummies entombed in their Pompadour catafalques behind rococo panelling; these crusty dotards who lived with their eyes forever fixed upon a nebulous Canaan, an imaginary land of promise.

After a few experiences of this kind, he resolved, in spite of all the invitations and reproaches he might receive, never to set foot in this society again.

Instead, he took to mixing with young men of his own age and station.

Some of them, who like himself had been brought up in religious institutions, had been distinctively marked for life by the education they had received. They went to church regularly, took communion at Easter, frequented Catholic societies, and shamefacedly concealed their sexual activities from each other as if they were heinous crimes. For the most part they were docile, good-looking ninnies, congenital dunces who had worn their masters' patience thin, but had none the less satisfied their desire to send pious, obedient creatures out into the world.

The others, who had been educated in state schools or in *lycées*, were less hypocritical and more adventurous, but they were no more interesting and no less narrow-minded than their fellows. These gay young men were mad on races and operettas, lansquenet and baccarat, and squandered fortunes on horses, cards, and all the other pleasures dear to empty minds. After a year's trial, Des Esseintes was overcome by an immense distaste for the company of these men, whose debauchery struck him as being base and facile, entered into without discrimination or desire, indeed without any real stirring of the blood or stimulation of the nerves.

Little by little, he dropped these people and sought the society of men of letters, imagining that theirs must surely be kindred spirits with which his own mind would feel more at ease. A fresh disappointment lay in store for him: he was revolted by their mean, spiteful judgements, their conversation that was as commonplace as a church-door, and the nauseating discussions in which they gauged the merit of a book by the number of editions it went through and the profits from its sale. At the same time, he discovered the free-thinkers, those bourgeois doctrinaires who clamoured for absolute liberty in order to stifle the opinions of other people, to be nothing but a set of greedy, shameless hypocrites whose intelligence he rated lower than the village cobbler's.

His contempt for humanity grew fiercer, and at last he came to realize that the world is made up mostly of fools and scoundrels. It became perfectly clear to him that he could entertain no hope of finding in someone else the same aspirations and antipathies; no hope of linking up with a mind which, like his own, took pleasure in a life of studious decrepitude; no hope of associating an intelligence as sharp and wayward as his own with that of any author or scholar.

He felt irritable and ill at ease; exasperated by the triviality of the ideas normally bandied about, he came to resemble those people mentioned by Nicole who are sensitive to anything and everything. He was constantly coming across some new source of offence, wincing at the patriotic or political twaddle served up in the papers every morning, and exaggerating the importance of the triumphs which an omnipotent public reserves at all times and in all circumstances for works written without thought or style.

Already he had begun dreaming of a refined Thebaid, a desert hermitage equipped with all modern conveniences, a snugly heated ark on dry land in which he might take refuge from the incessant deluge of human stupidity.

One passion and one only – woman – might have arrested the universal contempt that was taking hold of him, but that passion like the rest had been exhausted. He had tasted the sweets of the flesh like a crotchety invalid with a craving for food but a palate which soon becomes jaded. In the days when he had belonged to a set of young men-about-town, he had gone to those unconventional supper-parties where drunken women loosen their dresses at dessert and beat the table with their heads; he had hung around stage-doors, had bedded with singers and actresses, had endured, over and above the innate stupidity of the sex, the hysterical vanity common to women of the theatre. Then he had kept mistresses already famed for their depravity, and helped to swell the funds of those agencies which supply dubious pleasures for a consideration. And finally, weary to the point of satiety of these hackneyed luxuries, these commonplace caresses, he had sought satisfaction in the gutter, hoping that the contrast would revive his exhausted desires and imagining that the fascinating filthiness of the poor would stimulate his flagging senses.

Try what he might, however, he could not shake off the overpowering tedium which weighed upon him. In desperation he had recourse to the perilous caresses of the professional virtuosos, but the only effect was to impair his health and exacerbate his nerves. Already he was getting pains at the back of his neck, and his hands were shaky: he could keep them steady enough when he was gripping a heavy object, but they trembled uncontrollably when holding something light such as a wineglass.

The doctors he consulted terrified him with warnings that it was time he changed his way of life and gave up these practices which were sapping his vitality. For a little while he led a quiet life, but soon his brain took fire again and sent out a fresh call to arms. Like girls who at the onset of puberty hanker after weird or disgusting dishes, he began to imagine and then to indulge in unnatural love-affairs and perverse pleasures. But this was too much for him. His overfatigued senses, as if satisfied that they had tasted every imaginable experience, sank into a state of lethargy; and impotence was not far off.

When he came to his senses again, he found that he was utterly alone, completely disillusioned, abominably tired; and he longed to make an end of it all, prevented only by the cowardice of his flesh.

The idea of hiding away far from human society, of shutting himself up in some snug retreat, of deadening the thunderous din of life's inexorable activity, just as people deadened the noise of traffic by laying down straw outside a sick person's house – this idea tempted him more than ever.

Besides, there was another reason why he should lose no time in coming to a decision: taking stock of his fortune, he discovered to his horror that in extravagant follies and riotous living he had squandered the greater part of his patrimony, and that what remained was invested in land and brought in only a paltry revenue.

He decided to sell the Château de Lourps, which he no longer visited and where he would leave behind him no pleasant memories or fond regrets. He also realized his other assets and with the money he obtained bought sufficient government stocks to assure him of an annual income of fifty thousand francs, keeping back a tidy sum to buy and furnish the little house where he proposed to steep himself in peace and quiet for the rest of his life.

He scoured the suburbs of Paris and eventually discovered a villa for sale on the hillside above Fontenay-aux-Roses, standing in a lonely spot close to the Fort and far from all neighbours. This was the answer to his dreams, for in this district which had so far remained unspoilt by rampaging Parisians, he would be safe from molestation: the wretched state of communications, barely maintained by a comical railway at the far end of the town and a few little trams which came and went as they pleased, reassured him on this point. Thinking of the new existence he was going to fashion for himself, he felt a glow of pleasure at the idea that here he would be too far out for the tidal wave of Parisian life to reach him, and yet near enough for the proximity of the capital to strengthen him in his solitude. For, since a man has only to know he cannot get to a certain spot to be seized with a desire to go there, by not entirely barring the way back he was guarding against any hankering after human society, any nostalgic regrets.

He set the local mason to work on the house he had bought; then suddenly, one day, without telling anyone of his plans, he got rid of his furniture, dismissed his servants, and disappeared without leaving any address with the concierge.

I

OVER two months elapsed before Des Esseintes could immerse himself in the peaceful silence of his house at Fontenay, for purchases of all sorts still kept him perambulating the streets and ransacking the shops from one end of Paris to the other. And this was in spite of the fact that he had already made endless inquiries and given considerable thought to the matter before entrusting his new home to the decorators.

He had long been a connoisseur of colours both simple and subtle. In former years, when he had been in the habit of inviting women to his house, he had fitted out a boudoir with delicate carved furniture in pale Japanese camphor-wood under a sort of canopy of pink Indian satin, so that their flesh borrowed soft warm tints from the light which hidden lamps filtered through the awning.

This room, where mirror echoed mirror, and every wall reflected an endless succession of pink boudoirs, had been the talk of all his mistresses, who loved steeping their nakedness in this warm bath of rosy light and breathing in the aromatic odours given off by the camphor-wood. But quite apart from the beneficial effect which this tinted atmosphere had in bringing a ruddy flush to complexions worn and discoloured by the habitual use of cosmetics and the habitual abuse of the night hours, he himself enjoyed, in this voluptuous setting, peculiar satisfactions – pleasures which were in a way heightened and intensified by the recollection of past afflictions and bygone troubles.

Thus, in hateful and contemptuous memory of his childhood, he had suspended from the ceiling of this room a little silver cage containing a cricket which chirped as other crickets had once chirped among the embers in the fireplaces at the Château de Lourps. Whenever he heard this familiar sound, all the silent evenings of constraint he had spent in his mother's company and all the misery he had endured in the course of a lonely, unhappy childhood came back to haunt him. And when the movements of the woman he was mechanically caressing suddenly dispelled these memories and her words or laughter brought him back to the present reality of the boudoir, then his soul was swept by tumultuous emotions: a longing to take vengeance for the boredom inflicted on him in the past, a craving to sully what memories he retained of his family with acts of sensual depravity, a furious desire to expend his lustful frenzy on cushions of soft flesh and to drain the cup of sensuality to its last and bitterest dregs.

At other times, when he was weighed down by splenetic boredom, and the rainy autumn weather brought on an aversion for the streets, for his house, for the dirty yellow sky and the tar-macadam clouds, then he took refuge in this room, set the cage swinging gently to and fro and watched its movements reflected *ad infinitum* in the mirrors on the walls, until it seemed to his dazed eyes that the cage itself was not moving but that the boudoir was tossing and turning, waltzing round the house in a dizzy whirl of pink.

Then, in the days when he had thought it necessary to advertise his individuality, he had decorated and furnished the public rooms of his house with ostentatious oddity. The drawing-room, for example, had been partitioned off into a series of niches, which were styled to harmonize vaguely, by means of subtly analogous colours that were gay or sombre, delicate or barbarous, with the character of his favourite works in Latin and French. He would then settle down to read in whichever of these niches seemed to correspond most exactly to the peculiar essence of the book which had taken his fancy.

His final caprice had been to fit up a lofty hall in which to receive his tradesmen. They used to troop in and take their places side by side in a row of church stalls; then he would ascend an imposing pulpit and preach them a sermon on dandyism, adjuring his bootmakers and tailors to conform strictly to his encyclicals on matters of cut, and threatening them with pecuniary excommunication if they did not follow to the letter the instructions contained in his monitories and bulls.

By these means he won a considerable reputation as an eccentric – a reputation which he crowned by wearing suits of white velvet with gold-laced waistcoats, by sticking a bunch of Parma violets in his shirt-front in lieu of a cravat, and by entertaining men of letters to dinners which were greatly talked about. One of these meals, modelled on an eighteenth-century original, had been a funeral feast to mark the most ludicrous of personal misfortunes. The dining-room, draped in black, opened out on to a garden metamorphosed for the occasion, the paths being strewn with charcoal, the ornamental pond edged with black basalt and filled with ink, and the shrubberies replanted with cypresses and pines. The dinner itself was served on a black cloth adorned with baskets of violets and scabious; candelabra shed an eerie green light over the table and tapers flickered in the chandeliers.

While a hidden orchestra played funeral marches, the guests were waited on by naked negresses wearing only slippers and stockings in cloth of silver embroidered with tears.

Dining off black-bordered plates, the company had enjoyed turtle soup, Russian rye bread, ripe olives from Turkey, caviare, mullet botargo, black puddings from Frankfurt, game served in sauces the colour of liquorice and boot-polish, truffle jellies, chocolate creams, plum-puddings, nectarines, pears in grape-juice syrup, mulberries, and black heart-cherries. From dark-tinted glasses they had drunk the wines of Limagne and Roussillon, of Tenedos, Valdepeñas, and Oporto. And after coffee and walnut cordial, they had rounded off the evening with kvass, porter, and stout.

On the invitations, which were similar to those sent out before more solemn obsequies, this dinner was described as a funeral banquet in memory of the host's virility, lately but only temporarily deceased.

In time, however, his taste for these extravagant caprices, of which he had once been so proud, died a natural death; and nowadays he shrugged his shoulders in contempt whenever he recalled the puerile displays of eccentricity he had given, the extraordinary clothes he had worn, and the bizarre furnishing schemes he had devised. The new home he was now planning, this time for his own personal pleasure and not to astonish other people, was going to be comfortably though curiously appointed: a peaceful and unique abode specially designed to meet the needs of the solitary life he intended to lead.

When the architect had fitted up the house at Fontenay in accordance with his wishes, and when all that remained was to settle the question of furniture and decoration, Des Esseintes once again gave long and careful consideration to the entire series of available colours.

What he wanted was colours which would appear stronger and clearer in artificial light. He did not particularly care if they looked crude or insipid in daylight, for he lived most of his life at night, holding that night afforded greater intimacy and isolation and that the mind was truly roused and stimulated only by awareness of the dark; moreover he derived a peculiar pleasure from being in a well lighted room when all the surrounding houses were wrapped in sleep and darkness, a sort of enjoyment in which vanity may have played some small part, a very special feeling of satisfaction familiar to those who sometimes work late at night and draw aside the curtains to find that all around them the world is dark, silent, and dead.

Slowly, one by one, he went through the various colours.

Blue, he remembered, takes on an artificial green tint by candlelight; if a dark blue like indigo or cobalt, it becomes black; if pale, it turns to grey; and if soft and true like turquoise, it goes dull and cold. There could, therefore, be no question of making it the keynote of a room, though it might be used to help out another colour.

On the other hand, under the same conditions the iron greys grow sullen and heavy; the pearl greys lose their blue sheen and are metamorphosed into a dirty white; the browns become cold and sleepy; and as for the dark greens such as emperor green and myrtle green, they react like the dark blues and turn quite black. Only the pale greens remained – peacock green, for instance, or the cinnabar and lacquer greens –

but then artificial light kills the blue in them and leaves only the yellow, which for its part lacks clarity and consistency.

Nor was there any point in thinking of such delicate tints as salmon pink, maize, and rose; for their very effeminacy would run counter to his ideas of complete isolation. Nor again was it any use considering the various shades of purple, which with one exception lose their lustre in candlelight. That exception is plum, which somehow survives intact, but then what a muddy reddish hue it is, unpleasantly like lees of wine! Besides, it struck him as utterly futile to resort to this range of tints, in so far as it is possible to see purple by ingesting a specified amount of santonin, and thus it becomes a simple matter for anyone to change the colour of his walls without laying a finger on them.

Having rejected all these colours, he was left with only three: red, orange, and yellow.

Of the three, he preferred orange, so confirming by his own example the truth of a theory to which he attributed almost mathematical validity: to wit, that there exists a close correspondence between the sensual make-up of a person with a truly artistic temperament and whatever colour that person reacts to most strongly and sympathetically.

In fact, leaving out of account the majority of men, whose coarse retinas perceive neither the cadences peculiar to different colours nor the mysterious charm of their gradation; leaving out also those bourgeois optics that are insensible to the pomp and glory of the clear, bright colours; and considering only those people with delicate eyes that have undergone the education of libraries and art-galleries, it seemed to him an undeniable fact that anyone who dreams of the ideal, prefers illusion to reality, and calls for veils to clothe the naked truth, is almost certain to appreciate the soothing caress of blue and its cognates, such as mauve, lilac, and pearl grey, always provided they retain their delicacy and do not pass the point where they change their personalities and turn into pure violets and stark greys.

The hearty, blustering type on the other hand, the handsome, full-blooded sort, the strapping he-men who scorn the formalities of life and rush straight for their goal, losing their heads completely, these generally delight in the vivid glare of the reds and yellows, in the percussion effect of the vermilions and chromes, which blind their eyes and intoxicate their senses.

As for those gaunt, febrile creatures of feeble constitution and nervous disposition whose sensual appetite craves dishes that are smoked and seasoned, their eyes almost always prefer that most morbid and irritating of colours, with its acid glow and unnatural splendour – orange.

There could therefore be no doubt whatever as to Des Esseintes' final choice; but indubitable difficulties still remained to be solved. If red and yellow become more pronounced in artificial light, the same is not true of their compound, orange, which often flares up into a fiery nasturtium red.

He carefully studied all its different shades by candlelight and finally discovered one which he considered likely to keep its balance and answer his requirements.

Once these preliminaries were over, he made every effort to avoid, in his study at any rate, the use of Oriental rugs and fabrics, which had become so commonplace and vulgar now that upstart tradesmen could buy them in the bargain basement of any department-store.

The walls he eventually decided to bind like books in large-grained crushed morocco: skins from the Cape glazed by means of strong steel plates under a powerful press.

When the lining of the walls had been completed, he had the mouldings and the tall plinths lacquered a deep indigo, similar to the colour coachbuilders use for the panels of carriage bodies. The ceiling, which was slightly coved, was also covered in morocco; and set in the middle of the orange leather, like a huge circular window open to the sky, there was a piece of royal-blue silk from an ancient cope on which silver seraphim had been depicted in angelic flight by the weavers' guild of Cologne.

After everything had been arranged according to plan, these various colours came to a quiet understanding with each other at nightfall: the blue of the woodwork was stabilized and, so to speak, warmed up by the surrounding orange tints, which for their part glowed with undiminished brilliance, maintained and in a way intensified by the close proximity of the blue.

As to furniture, Des Esseintes did not have to undertake any laborious treasure-hunts, in so far as the only luxuries he intended to have in this room were rare books and flowers. Leaving himself free to adorn any bare walls later on with a few drawings and paintings, he confined himself for the present to fitting up ebony bookshelves and bookcases round the greater part of the room, strewing tiger skins and blue fox furs about the floor, and installing beside a massive money-changer's table of the fifteenth century, several deep-seated wing-armchairs and an old church lectern of wrought iron, one of those antique singing-desks on which deacons of old used to place the antiphonary and which now supported one of the weighty folios of Du Cange's *Glossarium mediæ et infimæ Latinatis*.

The windows, with panes of bluish crackle-glass or gilded bottle-punts which shut out the view and admitted only a very dim light, were dressed with curtains cut out of old ecclesiastical stoles, whose faded gold threads were almost invisible against the dull red material.

As a finishing touch, in the centre of the chimney-piece, which was likewise dressed in sumptuous silk from a Florentine dalmatic, and flanked by two Byzantine monstrances of gilded copper which had originally come from the Abbaye-au-Bois at Bièvre, there stood a magnificent triptych whose separate panels had been fashioned to resemble lace-work. This now contained, framed under glass, copied on real vellum in exquisite missal lettering and marvellously illuminated, three pieces by Baudelaire: on the right and left, the sonnets *La Mort des amants* and *L'Ennemi*, and in the middle, the prose poem bearing the English title *Anywhere out of the World*.

II

AFTER the sale of his goods, Des Esseintes kept on the two old servants who had looked after his mother and who between them had acted as steward and concierge at the Château de Lourps while it waited, empty and untenanted, for a buyer.

He took with him to Fontenay this faithful pair who had been accustomed to a methodical sickroom routine, trained to administer spoonfuls of physic and medicinal brews at regular intervals, and inured to the absolute silence of cloistered monks, barred from all communication with the outside world and confined to rooms where the doors and windows were always shut.

The husband's duty was to clean the rooms and go marketing; the wife's to do all the cooking. Des Esseintes gave up the first floor of the house to them; but he made them wear thick felt slippers, had the doors fitted with tambours and their hinges well oiled, and covered the floors with long-pile carpeting, to make sure that he never heard the sound of their footsteps overhead.

He also arranged a code of signals with them so that they should know what he needed by the number of long or short peals he rang on his bell; and he appointed a particular spot on his desk where the household account-book was to be left once a month while he was asleep. In short, he did everything he could to avoid seeing them or speaking to them more often than was absolutely necessary.

However, since the woman would have to pass alongside the house occasionally to get to the woodshed, and he had no desire to see her commonplace silhouette through the window, he had a costume made for her of Flemish faille, with a white cap and a great black hood let down on the shoulders, such as the beguines still wear to this day at Ghent. The shadow of this coif gliding past in the twilight produced an impression of convent life, and reminded him of those peaceful, pious communities, those sleepy villages shut away in some hidden corner of the busy, wide-awake city.

He went on to fix his mealtimes according to an unvarying schedule; the meals themselves were necessarily plain and simple, for the feebleness of his stomach no longer allowed him to enjoy heavy or elaborate dishes.

At five o'clock in winter, after dusk had fallen, he ate a light breakfast of two boiled eggs, toast and tea; then he had lunch about eleven, drank coffee or sometimes tea and wine during the night, and finally toyed with a little supper about five in the morning, before going to bed.

These meals, the details and menu of which were decided once for all at the beginning of each season of the year, he ate at a table in the middle of a small room linked to his study by a corridor which was padded and hermetically sealed, to allow neither sound nor smell to pass from one to the other of the two rooms it connected.

This dining-room resembled a ship's cabin, with its ceiling of arched beams, its bulkheads and floorboards of pitch-pine, and the little window-opening let into the wainscoting like a porthole.

Like those Japanese boxes that fit one inside the other, this room had been inserted into a larger one, which was the real dining-room planned by the architect.

This latter room was provided with two windows. One of these was now invisible, being hidden behind the bulkhead; but this partition could be lowered by releasing a spring, so that when fresh air was admitted it not only circulated around the pitch-pine cabin but entered it. The other was visible enough, as it was directly opposite the porthole cut into the wainscoting, but it had been rendered useless by a large aquarium occupying the entire space between the porthole and this real window in the real house-wall. Thus what daylight penetrated into the cabin had first to pass through the outer window, the panes of which had been replaced by a sheet of plate-glass, then through the water, and finally through the fixed bull's-eye in the porthole.

On autumn evenings, when the samovar stood steaming on the table and the sun had almost set, the water in the aquarium, which had been dull and turbid all morning, would turn red like glowing embers and shed a fiery, glimmering light upon the pale walls.

Sometimes of an afternoon, when Des Esseintes happened to be already up and about, he would set in action the system of pipes and conduits which emptied the aquarium and re-filled it with fresh water, and then pour in a few drops of coloured essences, thus producing at will the various tints, green or grey, opaline or silvery, which real rivers take on according to the colour of the sky, the greater or less brilliance of the sun's rays, the more or less imminent threat of rain – in a word, according to the season and the weather.

He could then imagine himself between-decks in a brig, and gazed inquisitively at some ingenious mechanical fishes driven by clockwork, which moved backwards and forwards behind the port-hole window and got entangled in artificial seaweed. At other times, while he was inhaling the smell of tar which had been introduced into the room before he entered it, he would examine a series of colour-prints on the walls, such as you see in packet-boat offices and Lloyd's agencies, representing steamers bound for Valparaiso and the River Plate, alongside framed notices giving the itineraries of the Royal Mail Steam Packet Line and the Lopez and Valéry Companies, as well as the freight charges and ports of call of the transatlantic mail-boats.

Then, when he was tired of consulting these time-tables, he would rest his eyes by looking at the chronometers and compasses, the sextants and dividers, the binoculars and charts scattered about on a side-table which was dominated by a single book, bound in sea-calf leather: the *Narrative of Arthur Gordon Pym*, specially printed for him on laid paper of pure linen, hand picked and bearing a seagull water-mark.

Finally he could take stock of the fishing-rods, the brown-tanned nets, the rolls of russet-coloured sails and the miniature anchor made of cork painted black, all piled higgledy-piggledy beside the door that led to the kitchen by way of a corridor padded, like the passage between dining-room and study, in such a way as to absorb any noises and smells.

By these means he was able to enjoy quickly, almost simultaneously, all the sensations of a long sea-voyage, without ever leaving home; the pleasure of moving from place to place, a pleasure which in fact exists only in recollection of the past and hardly ever in experience of the present, this pleasure he could savour in full and in comfort, without fatigue or worry, in this cabin whose deliberate disorder, impermanent appearance, and makeshift appointments corresponded fairly closely to the flying visits he paid it and the limited time he gave his meals, while it offered a complete contrast to his study, a permanent, orderly, well-established room, admirably equipped to maintain and uphold a stay-at-home existence.

Travel, indeed, struck him as being a waste of time, since he believed that the imagination could provide a more-than-adequate substitute for the vulgar reality of actual experience. In his opinion it was perfectly possible to fulfil those desires commonly supposed to be the most difficult to satisfy under normal conditions, and this by the trifling subterfuge of producing a fair imitation of the object of those desires. Thus it is well known that nowadays, in restaurants famed for the excellence of their cellars, the gourmets go into raptures over rare vintages manufactured out of cheap wines treated according to Monsieur Pasteur's method. Now, whether they are genuine or faked, these wines have the same aroma, the same colour, the same bouquet; and consequently the pleasure experienced in tasting these factitious, sophisticated beverages is absolutely identical with that which would be afforded by the pure, unadulterated wine, now unobtainable at any price.

There can be no doubt that by transferring this ingenious trickery, this clever simulation to the intellectual plane, one can enjoy, just as easily as on the material plane, imaginary pleasures similar in all respects to the pleasures of reality; no doubt, for instance, that anyone can go on long voyages of exploration sitting by the fire, helping out his sluggish or refractory mind, if the need arises, by dipping into some book describing travels in distant lands; no doubt, either, that without stirring out of Paris it is possible to obtain the health-giving impression of sea-bathing – for all that this involves is a visit to the Bain Vigier, an establishment to be found on a pontoon moored in the middle of the Seine.

There, by salting your bath-water and adding sulphate of soda with hydrochlorate of magnesium and lime in the proportions recommended by the Pharmacopoeia; by opening a box with a tight-fitting screw-top and taking out a ball of twine or a twist of rope, bought for the occasion from one of those enormous roperies whose warehouses and cellars reek with the smell of the sea and sea-ports; by breathing in the odours which the twine or the twist of rope is sure to have retained; by consulting a life-like photograph of the casino and zealously reading the *Guide Joanne* describing the beauties of the seaside resort where you would like to be; by letting yourself be lulled by the waves created in your bath by the backwash of the paddle-steamers passing close to the pontoon; by listening to the moaning of the wind as it blows under the arches of the Pont Royal and the dull rumble of the buses crossing the bridge just a few feet over your head; by employing these simple devices, you can produce an illusion of sea-bathing which will be undeniable, convincing, and complete.

The main thing is to know how to set about it, to be able to concentrate your attention on a single detail, to forget yourself sufficiently to bring about the desired hallucination and so substitute the vision of a reality for the reality itself.

As a matter of fact, artifice was considered by Des Esseintes to be the distinctive mark of human genius.

Nature, he used to say, has had her day; she has finally and utterly exhausted the patience of sensitive observers by the revolting uniformity of her landscapes and skyscapes. After all, what platitudinous limitations she imposes, like a tradesman specializing in a single line of business; what petty-minded restrictions, like a shopkeeper stocking one article to the exclusion of all others; what a monotonous store of meadows and trees, what a commonplace display of mountains and seas!

In fact, there is not a single one of her inventions, deemed so subtle and sublime, that human ingenuity cannot manufacture; no moonlit Forest of Fontainebleau that cannot be reproduced by stage scenery under floodlighting; no cascade that cannot be imitated to perfection by hydraulic engineering; no rock that papier-mâché cannot counterfeit; no flower that carefully chosen taffeta and delicately coloured paper cannot match!

There can be no shadow of doubt that with her never-ending platitudes the old crone has by now exhausted the good-humoured admiration of all true artists, and the time has surely come for artifice to take her place whenever possible.

After all, to take what among all her works is considered to be the most exquisite, what among all her creations is deemed to possess the most perfect and original beauty – to wit, woman – has not man for his part, by his own efforts, produced an animate yet artificial creature that is every bit as good from the point of view of plastic beauty? Does there exist, anywhere on this earth, a being conceived in the joys of fornication and born in the throes of motherhood who is more dazzlingly, more outstandingly beautiful than the two locomotives recently put into service on the Northern Railway?

One of these, bearing the name of Crampton, is an adorable blonde with a shrill voice, a long slender body imprisoned in a shiny brass corset, and supple catlike movements; a smart golden blonde whose extraordinary grace can be quite terrifying when she stiffens her muscles of steel, sends the sweat pouring down her steaming flanks, sets her elegant wheels spinning in their wide circles, and hurtles away, full of life, at the head of an express or a boat-train.

The other, Engerth by name, is a strapping saturnine brunette given to uttering raucous, guttural cries, with a thick-set figure encased in armour-plating of cast iron; a monstrous creature with her dishevelled mane of black smoke and her six wheels coupled together low down, she gives an indication of her fantastic strength when, with an effort that shakes the very earth, she slowly and deliberately drags along her heavy train of goods-wagons.

It is beyond question that, among all the fair, delicate beauties and all the dark, majestic charmers of the human race, no such superb examples of comely grace and terrifying force are to be found; and it can be stated without fear of contradiction that in his chosen province man has done as well as the God in whom he believes.

These thoughts occurred to Des Esseintes whenever the breeze carried to his ears the faint whistle of the toy trains that shuttle backwards and forwards between Paris and Sceaux. His house was only about a twenty minutes' walk from the station at Fontenay, but the height at which it stood and its isolated position insulated it from the hullabaloo of the vile hordes that are inevitably attracted on Sundays to the purlieus of a railway station.

As for the village itself, he had scarcely seen it. Only once, looking out of his window one night, had he examined the silent landscape stretching down to the foot of a hill which is surmounted by the batteries of the Bois de Verrières.

In the darkness, on both right and left, rows of dim shapes could be seen lining the hillsides, dominated by other far-off batteries and fortifications whose high retaining-walls looked in the moonlight like silver-painted brows over dark eyes.

The plain, lying partly in the shadow of the hills, appeared to have shrunk in size; and in the middle it seemed as if it were sprinkled with face-powder and smeared with cold-cream. In the warm breeze that fanned the colourless grass and scented the air with cheap spicy perfumes, the moon-bleached trees rustled their pale foliage and with their trunks drew a shadow-pattern of black stripes on the white-washed earth, littered with pebbles that glinted like fragments of broken crockery.

On account of its artificial, made-up appearance, Des Esseintes found this landscape not unattractive; but since that first afternoon he had spent house-hunting in the village of Fontenay, he had never once set foot in its streets by day. The greenery of this part of the country had no appeal whatever for him, lacking as it did even that languid, melancholy charm possessed by the pitiful, sickly vegetation clinging pathetically to life on the suburban rubbish-heaps near the ramparts. And then, on that same day, in the village itself, he had caught sight of bewhiskered bourgeois with protuberant paunches and mustachioed individuals in fancy dress, whom he took to be magistrates and army officers, carrying their heads as proudly as a priest would carry a monstrance; and after that experience his detestation of the human face had grown even fiercer than before.

During the last months of his residence in Paris, at a time when, sapped by disillusionment, depressed by hypochondria and weighed down by spleen, he had been reduced to such a state of nervous sensitivity that the sight of a disagreeable person or thing was deeply impressed upon his mind and it took several days even to begin removing the imprint, the human face as glimpsed in the street had been one of the keenest torments he had been forced to endure.

It was a fact that he suffered actual pain at the sight of certain physiognomies, that he almost regarded the benign or crabbed expressions on some faces as personal insults, and that he felt sorely tempted to box the ears of, say, one worthy he saw strolling along with his eyes shut in donnish affectation, another who smiled at his reflection as he minced past the shop-windows, and yet another who appeared to be pondering a thousand-and-one weighty thoughts as he knit his brows over the rambling articles and sketchy news-items in his paper.

He could detect such inveterate stupidity, such hatred of his own ideas, such contempt for literature and art and everything he held dear, implanted and rooted in these mean mercenary minds, exclusively preoccupied with thoughts of swindling and money-grubbing and accessible only to that ignoble distraction of mediocre intellects, politics, that he would go home in a fury and shut himself up with his books.

Last but not least, he hated with all the hatred that was in him the rising generation, the appalling boors who find it necessary to talk and laugh at the top of their voices in restaurants and cafés, who jostle you in the street without a word of apology, and who, without expressing or even indicating regret, drive the wheels of a baby-carriage into your legs.

III

ONE section of the bookshelves lining the walls of Des Esseintes' blue and orange study was filled with nothing but Latin works – works which minds drilled into conformity by repetitious university lectures lump together under the generic name of 'the Decadence'.

The truth was that the Latin language, as it was written during the period which the academics still persist in calling the Golden Age, held scarcely any attraction for him. That restricted idiom with its limited stock of almost invariable constructions; without suppleness of syntax, without colour, without even light and shade; pressed flat along all its seams and stripped of the crude but often picturesque expressions of earlier epochs – that idiom could, at a pinch, enunciate the pompous platitudes and vague commonplaces endlessly repeated by the rhetoricians and poets of the time, but it was so tedious and unoriginal that in the study of linguistics you had to come down to the French style current in the age of Louis XIV to find another idiom so wilfully debilitated, so solemnly tiresome and dull.

Among other authors, the gentle Virgil, he whom the schoolmastering fraternity call the Swan of Mantua, presumably because that was not his native city, impressed him as being one of the most appalling pedants and one of the most deadly bores that Antiquity ever produced; his well-washed, beribboned shepherds taking it in turns to empty over each other's heads jugs of icy-cold sententious verse, his Orpheus whom he compares to a weeping nightingale, his Aristæus who blubbers about bees, and his Æneas, that irresolute, garrulous individual who strides up and down like a puppet in a shadow-theatre, making wooden gestures behind the ill-fitting, badly oiled screen of the poem, combined to irritate Des Esseintes. He might possibly have tolerated the dreary nonsense these marionettes spout into the wings; he might

40

even have excused the impudent plagiarizing of Homer, Theocritus, Ennius, and Lucretius, as well as the outright theft Macrobius has revealed to us of the whole of the Second Book of the *Æneid*, copied almost word for word from a poem of Pisander's; he might in fact have put up with all the indescribable fatuity of this rag-bag of vapid verses; but what utterly exasperated him was the shoddy workmanship of the tinny hexameters, with their statutory allotment of words weighed and measured according to the unalterable laws of a dry, pedantic prosody; it was the structure of the stiff and starchy lines in their formal attire and their abject subservience to the rule of grammar; it was the way in which each and every line was mechanically bisected by the inevitable caesura and finished off with the invariable shock of dactyl striking spondee.

Borrowed as it was from the system perfected by Catullus, that unchanging prosody, unimaginative, inexorable, stuffed full of useless words and phrases, dotted with pegs that fitted only too foreseeably into corresponding holes, that pitiful device of the Homeric epithet, used time and again without ever indicating or describing anything, and that poverty-stricken vocabulary with its dull, dreary colours, all caused him unspeakable torment.

It is only fair to add that, if his admiration for Virgil was anything but excessive and his enthusiasm for Ovid's limpid effusions exceptionally discreet, the disgust he felt for the elephantine Horace's vulgar twaddle, for the stupid patter he keeps up as he simpers at his audience like a painted old clown, was absolutely limitless.

In prose, he was no more enamoured of the long-winded style, the redundant metaphors and the rambling digressions of old Chick-Pea; the bombast of his apostrophes, the wordiness of his patriotic perorations, the pomposity of his harangues, the heaviness of his style, well-fed and well-covered, but weak-boned and running to fat, the intolerable insignificance of his long introductory adverbs, the monotonous uniformity of his adipose periods clumsily tied together with conjunctions, and finally his wearisome predilection for tautology, all signally failed to endear him to Des Esseintes. Nor was Caesar, with his reputation for laconism, any more to his taste than Cicero; for he went to the other extreme, and offended by his pop-gun pithiness, his jotting-pad brevity, his unforgivable, unbelievable constipation.

The fact of the matter was that he could find mental pabulum neither among these writers nor among those who for some reason are the delight of dilettante scholars: Sallust who is at least no more insipid than the rest, Livy who is pompous and sentimental, Seneca who is turgid and colourless, Suetonius who is larval and lymphatic, and Tacitus, who with his studied concision is the most virile, the most biting, the most sinewy of them all. In poetry, Juvenal, despite a few vigorous lines, and Persius, for all his mysterious innuendoes, both left him cold. Leaving aside Tibullus and Propertius, Quintilian and the two Plinys, Statius, Martial of Bilbilis, Terence even and Plautus, whose jargon with its plentiful neologisms, compounds, and diminutives attracted him, but whose low wit and salty humour repelled him, Des Esseintes only began to take an interest in the Latin language when he came to Lucan, in whose hands it took on new breadth, and became brighter and more expressive. The fine craftsmanship of Lucan's enamelled and jewelled verse won his admiration; but the poet's exclusive preoccupation with form, bell-like stridency and metallic brilliance did not entirely hide from his eyes the bombastic blisters disfiguring the *Pharsalia*, or the poverty of its intellectual content.

The author he really loved, and who made him abandon Lucan's resounding tirades for good, was Petronius.

Petronius was a shrewd observer, a delicate analyst, a marvellous painter; dispassionately, with an entire lack of prejudice or animosity, he described the everyday life of Rome, recording the manners and morals of his time in the lively little chapters of the *Satyricon*.

Noting what he saw as he saw it, he set forth the day-to-day existence of the common people, with all its minor events, its bestial incidents, its obscene antics.

Here we have the Inspector of Lodgings coming to ask for

the names of any travellers who have recently arrived; there, a brothel where men circle round naked women standing beside placards giving their price, while through half-open doors couples can be seen disporting themselves in the bedrooms. Elsewhere, in villas full of insolent luxury where wealth and ostentation run riot, as also in the mean inns described throughout the book, with their unmade trestle beds swarming with fleas, the society of the day has its fling – depraved ruffians like Ascyltus and Eumolpus, out for what they can get; unnatural old men with their gowns tucked up and their cheeks plastered with white lead and acacia rouge; catamites of sixteen, plump and curly-headed; women having hysterics; legacy-hunters offering their boys and girls to gratify the lusts of rich testators, all these and more scurry across the pages of the *Satyricon*, squabbling in the streets, fingering one another in the baths, beating one another up like characters in a pantomime.

All this is told with extraordinary vigour and precise colouring, in a style that makes free of every dialect, that borrows expressions from all the languages imported into Rome, that extends the frontiers and breaks the fetters of the so-called Golden Age, that makes every man talk in his own idiom – uneducated freedmen in vulgar Latin, the language of the streets; foreigners in their barbaric lingo, shot with words and phrases from African, Syrian, and Greek; and stupid pedants, like the Agamemnon of the book, in a rhetorical jargon of invented words. There are lightning sketches of all these people, sprawled round a table, exchanging the vapid pleasantries of drunken revellers, trotting out mawkish maxims and stupid saws, their heads turned towards Trimalchio, who sits picking his teeth, offers the company chamber-pots, discourses on the state of his bowels, farts to prove his point, and begs his guests to make themselves at home.

This realistic novel, this slice cut from Roman life in the raw, with no thought, whatever people may say, of reforming or satirizing society, and no need to fake a conclusion or point a moral; this story with no plot or action in it, simply relating the erotic adventures of certain sons of Sodom, analysing with smooth finesse the joys and sorrows of these loving couples, depicting in a splendidly wrought style, without affording a single glimpse of the author, without any comment whatever, without a word of approval or condemnation of his characters' thoughts and actions, the vices of a decrepit civilization, a crumbling Empire – this story fascinated Des Esseintes; and in its subtle style, acute observation, and solid construction he could see a curious similarity, a strange analogy with the few modern French novels he could stomach.

Naturally enough he bitterly regretted the loss of the *Eustion* and the *Albutia*, those two works by Petronius mentioned by Planciades Fulgentius which have vanished for ever; but the bibliophile in him consoled the scholar, as he reverently handled the superb copy he possessed of the *Satyricon*, in the octavo edition of 1585 printed by J. Dousa at Leyden.

After Petronius, his collection of Latin authors came to the second century of the Christian era, skipped tub-thumping Fronto with his old-fashioned expressions, clumsily restored and unsuccessfully renovated, passed over the *Noctes Atticae* of his friend and disciple Aulus Gellius, a sagacious and inquisitive mind, but a writer bogged down in a glutinous style, and stopped only for Apuleius, whose works he had in the editio princeps, in folio, printed at Rome in 1469.

This African author gave him enormous pleasure. The Latin language reached the top of the tide in his *Metamorphoses*, sweeping along in a dense flood fed by tributary waters from every province, and combining them all in a bizarre, exotic, almost incredible torrent of words; new mannerisms and new details of Latin society found expression in neologisms called into being to meet conversational requirements in an obscure corner of Roman Africa. What was more, Des Esseintes was amused by Apuleius' exuberance and joviality – the exuberance of a southerner and the joviality of a man who was beyond all question fat. He had the air of a lecherous boon companion compared with the Christian apologists living in the same century – the soporific Minucius Felix for instance, a pseudo-classic in whose *Octavius* Cicero's oily phrases have grown thicker and heavier, and even Tertullian, whom he kept more perhaps for the sake of the Aldine edition of his works than for the works themselves.

Although he was perfectly at home with theological problems, the Montanist wrangles with the Catholic Church and the polemics against Gnosticism left him cold; so, despite the interest of Tertullian's style, a compact style full of amphibologies, built on participles, shaken by antitheses, strewn with puns, and speckled with words borrowed from the language of jurisprudence or the Fathers of the Greek Church, he now scarcely ever opened the *Apologeticus* or the *De Patientia*; at the very most he sometimes read a page or two of the *De Cultu Feminarum* where Tertullian exhorts women not to adorn their persons with jewels and precious stuffs, and forbids them to use cosmetics because these attempt to correct and improve on Nature.

These ideas, diametrically opposed to his own, brought a smile to his lips, and he recalled the part played by Tertullian as Bishop of Carthage, a role which he considered pregnant with pleasant day-dreams. It was, in fact, the man more than his works that attracted him.

Living in times of appalling storm and stress, under Caracalla, under Macrinus, under the astonishing high-priest of Emesa, Elagabalus, he had gone on calmly writing his sermons, his dogmatic treatises, his apologies and homilies, while the Roman Empire tottered, and while the follies of Asia and the vices of paganism swept all before them. With perfect composure he had gone on preaching carnal abstinence, frugality of diet, sobriety of dress, at the same time as Elagabalus was treading in silver dust and sand of gold, his head crowned with a tiara and his clothes studded with jewels, working at women's tasks in the midst of his eunuchs, calling himself Empress and bedding every night with a new Emperor, picked for choice from among his barbers, scullions, and charioteers.

This contrast delighted Des Esseintes. He knew that this was the point at which the Latin language, which had attained supreme maturity in Petronius, began to break up; the literature of Christianity was asserting itself, matching its novel

45

ideas with new words, unfamiliar constructions, unknown verbs, adjectives of super-subtle meaning, and finally abstract nouns, which had hitherto been rare in the Roman tongue and which Tertullian had been one of the first to use.

However, this deliquescence, which was carried on after Tertullian's death by his pupil St Cyprian, by Arnobius, by the obscure Lactantius, was an unattractive process. It was a slow and partial decay, retarded by awkward attempts to return to the emphasis of Cicero's periods; as yet it had not acquired that special gamy flavour which in the fourth century – and even more in the following centuries – the odour of Christianity was to give to the pagan tongue as it decomposed like venison, dropping to pieces at the same time as the civilization of the Ancient World, falling apart while the Empires succumbed to the barbarian onslaught and the accumulated pus of ages.

The art of the third century was represented in his library by a single Christian poet, Commodian of Gaza. His *Carmen Apologeticum*, written in the year 259, is a collection of moral maxims twisted into acrostics, composed in rude hexameters, divided by a caesura after the fashion of heroic verse, written without any respect for quantity or hiatus, and often provided with the sort of rhymes of which church Latin could later offer numerous examples.

This strained, sombre verse, this mild, uncivilized poetry, full of everyday expressions and words robbed of their original meaning, appealed to him; it interested him even more than the already over-ripe, delightfully decadent style of the historians Ammianus Marcellinus and Aurelius Victor, the letter-writer Symmachus and the compilator and grammarian Macrobius, and he even preferred it to the properly scanned verse and the superbly variegated language of Claudian, Rutilius, and Ausonius.

These last were in their day the masters of their art; they filled the dying Empire with their cries – the Christian Ausonius with his *Cento Nuptialis* and his long, elaborate poem on the Moselle; Rutilius with his hymns to the glory of Rome, his anathemas against the Jews and the monks, and his account of a journey across the Alps into Gaul, in which he sometimes manages to convey certain visual impressions, the landscapes hazily reflected in water, the mirage effect of the vapours, the mists swirling round the mountain tops.

As for Claudian, he appears as a sort of avatar of Lucan, dominating the entire fourth century with the tremendous trumpeting of his verse; a poet hammering out a brilliant, sonorous hexameter on his anvil, beating out each epithet with a single blow amid showers of sparks, attaining a certain grandeur, filling his work with a powerful breath of life. With the Western Empire crumbling to its ruin all about him, amid the horror of the repeated massacres occurring on every side, and under the threat of invasion by the barbarians now pressing in their hordes against the creaking gates of the Empire, he calls Antiquity back to life, sings of the Rape of Proserpine, daubs his canvas with glowing colours, and goes by with all his lights blazing through the darkness closing in upon the world.

Paganism lives again in him, sounding its last proud fanfare, lifting its last great poet high above the floodwaters of Christianity which are henceforth going to submerge the language completely and hold absolute and eternal sway over literature – with Paulinus, the pupil of Ausonius; with the Spanish priest Juvencus, who paraphrases the Gospels in verse; with Victorinus, author of the *Machabœi*; with Sanctus Burdigalensis, who in an eclogue imitated from Virgil makes the herdsmen Egon and Buculus bewail the maladies afflicting their flocks. Then there are the saints, a whole series of saints – Hilary of Poitiers, who championed the faith of Nicaea and was called the Athanasius of the West; Ambrosius, the author of indigestible homilies, the tiresome Christian Cicero; Damasus, the manufacturer of lapidary epigrams; Jerome, the translator of the Vulgate; and his adversary Vigilantius of Comminges, who attacks the cult of the saints, the abuse of miracles, the practice of fasting, and already preaches against monastic vows and the celibacy of the priesthood, using arguments that will be repeated down the ages.

Finally, in the fifth century, there comes Augustine, Bishop

47

of Hippo. Him Des Esseintes knew only too well, for he was the most revered of all ecclesiastical writers, the founder of Christian orthodoxy, the man whom pious Catholics regard as an oracle, a sovereign authority. The natural consequence was that he never opened his books any more, even though he had proclaimed his loathing for this world in his *Confessions*, and, in his *De Civitate Dei*, to the accompaniment of pious groans, had tried to assuage the appalling distress of his time with sedative promises of better things to come in the after-life. Even in his younger days, when he was studying theology, Des Esseintes had become sick and tired of Augustine's sermons and jeremiads, his theories on grace and predestination, his fights against the schismatic sects.

He was much happier dipping into the *Psychomachia* of Prudentius, the inventor of the allegorical poem, a genre destined to enjoy uninterrupted favour in the Middle Ages, or the works of Sidonius Apollinaris, whose correspondence, sprinkled with quips and sallies, archaisms and enigmas, captivated him. He always enjoyed re-reading the panegyrics in which the good Bishop invokes the pagan deities in support of his pompous praises; and in spite of himself, he had to admit to a weakness for the conceits and innuendoes in these poems, turned out by an ingenious mechanic who takes good care of his machine, keeps its component parts well oiled, and if need be can invent new parts which are both intricate and useless.

After Sidonius, he kept up his acquaintance with the panegyrist Merobaudes; with Sedulius, the author of rhymed poems and alphabetical hymns of which the Church has appropriated certain parts for use in her offices; with Marius Victor, whose gloomy treatise *De Perversis Moribus* is lit up here and there by lines that shine like phosphorus; with Paulinus of Pella, who composed that icy poem the *Eucharisticon*; and with Orientius, Bishop of Auch, who in the distichs of his *Monitoria* inveighs against the licentiousness of women, whose faces, he declares, bring down disaster upon the peoples of the world.

Des Esseintes lost nothing of his interest in the Latin

language now that it was rotten through and through and hung like a decaying carcase, losing its limbs, oozing pus, barely keeping, in the general corruption of its body, a few sound parts, which the Christians removed in order to preserve them in the pickling brine of their new idiom.

The second half of the fifth century had arrived, the awful period when appalling shocks convulsed the world. The barbarians were ravaging Gaul while Rome, sacked by the Visigoths, felt the chill of death invade her paralysed body and saw her extremities, the East and the West, thrashing about in pools of blood and growing weaker day by day.

Amid the universal dissolution, amid the assassinations of Caesars occurring in rapid succession, amid the uproar and carnage covering Europe from end to end, a terrifying hurrah was suddenly heard which stilled every other noise, silenced every other voice. On the banks of the Danube, thousands of men wrapped in ratskin cloaks and mounted on little horses, hideous Tartars with enormous heads, flat noses, hairless, jaundiced faces, and chins furrowed with gashes and scars, rode hell-for-leather into the territories of the Lower Empire, sweeping all before them in their whirlwind advance.

Civilization disappeared in the dust of their horses' hooves, in the smoke of the fires they kindled. Darkness fell upon the world and the peoples trembled in consternation as they listened to the dreadful tornado pass by with a sound like thunder. The horde of Huns swept over Europe, threw itself on Gaul, and was only halted on the plains of Châlons, where Ætius smashed it in a fearful encounter. The earth, gorged with blood, looked like a sea of crimson froth; two hundred thousand corpses barred the way and broke the impetus of the invading avalanche which, turned from its path, fell like a thunderbolt on Italy, whose ruined cities burned like blazing hay-ricks.

The Western Empire crumbled under the shock; the doomed life it had been dragging out in imbecility and corruption was extinguished. It even looked as if the end of the universe were also at hand, for the cities Attila had overlooked were decimated by famine and plague. And the Latin language, like everything else, seemed to vanish from sight beneath the ruins of the old world.

Years went by, and eventually the barbarian idioms began to acquire a definite shape, to emerge from their rude gangues, to grow into true languages. Meanwhile Latin, saved by the monasteries from death in the universal debacle, was confined to the cloister and the presbytery. Even so, a few poets appeared here and there to keep the flame burning, albeit slowly and dully – the African Dracontius with his *Hexameron*, Claudius Mamert with his liturgical poems, and Avitus of Vienne. Then there were biographers such as Ennodius, who recounts the miracles of St Epiphanius, that shrewd and revered diplomatist, that upright and vigilant pastor, or Eugippius, who has recorded for us the incomparable life of St Severinus, that mysterious anchorite and humble ascetic who appeared like an angel of mercy to the peoples of his time, frantic with fear and suffering; writers such as Veranius of the Gévaudan, who composed a little treatise on the subject of continence, or Aurelian and Ferreolus, who compiled ecclesiastical canons; and finally historians such as Rotherius of Agde, famed for a history of the Huns which is now lost.

There were far fewer works from the following centuries in Des Esseintes' library. Still, the sixth century was represented by Fortunatus, Bishop of Poitiers, whose hymns and *Vexilla Regis*, carved out of the ancient carcase of the Latin language and spiced with the aromatics of the Church, haunted his thoughts on certain days; also by Boethius, Gregory of Tours, and Jornandes. As for the seventh and eighth centuries, apart from the Low Latin of such chroniclers as Fredegarius and Paul the Deacon, or of the poems contained in the Bangor Antiphonary, one of which – an alphabetical, monorhymed hymn in honour of St Comgall – he sometimes glanced at, literary output was restricted almost exclusively to Lives of the Saints, notably the legend of St Columban by the cenobite Jonas and that of Blessed Cuthbert compiled by the Venerable Bede from the notes of an anonymous monk of Lindisfarne. The result was that he confined himself to dipping at odd moments into the works of these hagiographers and re-reading passages from the Lives of St Rusticula and St Radegonde, the former related by Defensorius, a Ligugé synodist, the latter by the naïve and modest Baudonivia, a Poitiers nun.

However, he found certain remarkable Latin works of Anglo-Saxon origin more to his taste: to wit, the whole series of enigmas by Aldhelm, Tatwin, and Eusebius, those literary descendants of Symphosius, and above all the enigmas composed by St Boniface in acrostics where the answer was provided by the initial letters of each stanza.

His predilection for Latin literature grew feebler as he neared the end of these two centuries, and he could summon up little enthusiasm for the turgid prose of the Carolingian Latinists, the Alcuins and the Eginhards. As specimens of the language of the ninth century, he contented himself with the chronicles by Freculf, Reginon, and the anonymous writer of Saint-Gall; with the poem on the Siege of Paris contrived by Abbo le Courbé; and with the *Hortulus*, the didactic poem by the Benedictine Walafrid Strabo, whose canto devoted to the glorification of the pumpkin as a symbol of fecundity tickled his sense of humour. Another work he appreciated was the poem by Ermold le Noir celebrating the exploits of Louis le Débonnaire, a poem written in regular hexameters, in an austere, even sombre style, an iron idiom chilled in monastic waters but with flaws in the hard metal where feeling showed through; and another, a poem by Macer Floridus, *De Viribus Herbarum*, which he particularly enjoyed for its poetic recipes and the remarkable virtues it attributed to certain plants and flowers – to the aristolochia, for instance, which mixed with beef and laid on a pregnant woman's abdomen invariably results in the birth of a male child, or borage, which served as a cordial makes the gloomiest guest merry, or the peony, whose powdered root is a lasting cure for epilepsy, or fennel, which applied to a woman's bosom clears her urine and stimulates her sluggish periods.

Except for a few special books which had not been classified; certain undated or modern texts; some ˙ cabbalistic, medical, or botanical works; sundry odd volumes of Migne's patrology, containing Christian poems to be found nowhere else, and of Wernsdorff's anthology of the minor Latin poets; except for Meursius, Forberg's manual of classical erotology, the moechialogy and the diaconals intended for the use of father-confessors, which he took down and dusted off at long intervals, his collection of Latin works stopped at the beginning of the tenth century.

By that time, after all, the peculiar originality and elaborate simplicity of Christian Latinity had likewise come to an end. Henceforth the gibble-gabble of the philosophers and the scholiasts, the logomachy of the Middle Ages, would reign supreme. The sooty heaps of chronicles and history books, the leaden masses of cartularies, would steadily pile up, while the stammering grace, the often exquisite clumsiness of the monks, stirring the poetical left-overs of Antiquity into a pious stew, were already things of the past; the workshop turning out verbs of refined sweetness, substantives smelling of incense, and strange adjectives crudely fashioned out of gold in the delightfully barbaric style of Gothic jewellery, had already closed down. The old editions so beloved of Des Esseintes tailed away to nothing – and making a prodigious jump of several centuries, he stacked the rest of his shelves with modern books which, without regard to the intermediate ages, brought him right down to the French language of the present day.

IV

A CARRIAGE drew up late one afternoon outside the house at Fontenay. As Des Esseintes never had any visitors and the postman did not so much as approach this uninhabited region, since there were no newspapers, reviews, or letters to be delivered, the servants hesitated, wondering whether they should answer the door or not. But when the bell was sent jangling violently against the wall, they ventured so far as to uncover the spy-hole let into the door, and beheld a gentleman whose entire breast was covered, from neck to waist, by a huge buckler of gold.

They informed their master, who was at breakfast.

'Yes indeed,' he said; 'show the gentleman in' – for he remembered having once given his address to a lapidary so that the man might deliver an article he had ordered.

The gentleman bowed his way in, and on the pitch-pine floor of the dining-room he deposited his golden buckler, which rocked backwards and forwards, rising a little from the ground and stretching out at the end of a snake-like neck a tortoise's head which, in a sudden panic, it drew back under its carapace.

This tortoise was the result of a fancy which had occurred to him shortly before leaving Paris. Looking one day at an Oriental carpet aglow with iridescent colours, and following with his eyes the silvery glints running across the weft of the wool, which was a combination of yellow and plum, he had thought what a good idea it would be to place on this carpet something that would move about and be dark enough to set off these gleaming tints.

Possessed by this idea, he had wandered at random through the streets as far as the Palais-Royal, where he glanced at Chevet's display and suddenly struck his forehead – for there in the window was a huge tortoise in a tank. He had bought the creature; and once it had been left to itself on the carpet, he had sat down and subjected it to a long scrutiny, screwing up his eyes in concentration.

Alas, there could be no doubt about it: the nigger-brown tint, the raw Sienna hue of the shell, dimmed the sheen of the carpet instead of bringing out its colours; the predominating gleams of silver had now lost nearly all their sparkle and matched the cold tones of scraped zinc along the edges of this hard, lustreless carapace.

He bit his nails, trying to discover a way of resolving the marital discord between these tints and preventing an absolute divorce. At last he came to the conclusion that his original idea of using a dark object moving to and fro to stir up the fires within the woollen pile was mistaken. The fact of the matter was that the carpet was still too bright, too garish, too new looking; its colours had not yet been sufficiently toned down and subdued. The thing was to reverse his first plan and to deaden those colours, to dim them by the contrast of a brilliant object that would kill everything around it, drowning the gleams of silver in a golden radiance. Stated in these terms, the problem was easier to solve; and Des Esseintes accordingly decided to have his tortoise's buckler glazed with gold.

Back from the workshop where the gilder had given it board and lodging, the reptile blazed as brightly as any sun, throwing out its rays over the carpet, whose tints turned pale and weak, and looking like a Visigothic shield tegulated with shining scales by a barbaric artist.

At first, Des Esseintes was delighted with the effect he had achieved; but soon it struck him that this gigantic jewel was only half-finished and that it would not be really complete until it had been encrusted with precious stones.

From a collection of Japanese art he selected a drawing representing a huge bunch of flowers springing from a single slender stalk, took it to a jeweller's, sketched out a border to enclose this bouquet in an oval frame, and informed the astonished lapidary that the leaves and petals of each and every flower were to be executed in precious stones and mounted on the actual shell of the tortoise.

Choosing the stones gave him pause. The diamond, he told

himself, has become terribly vulgar now that every business-man wears one on his little finger; Oriental emeralds and rubies are not so degraded and they dart bright tongues of fire, but they are too reminiscent of the green and red eyes of certain Paris buses fitted with headlamps in the selfsame colours; as for topazes, whether pink or yellow, they are cheap stones, dear to people of the small shopkeeper class who long to have a few jewel-cases to lock up in their mirror wardrobes. Similarly, although the Church has helped the amethyst to retain something of a sacerdotal character, at once unctuous and solemn, this stone too has been debased by use in the red ears and on the tubulous fingers of butchers' wives whose ambition it is to deck themselves out at little cost with genuine, heavy jewels. Alone among these stones, the sapphire has kept its fires inviolate, unsullied by contact with commercial and financial stupidity. The glittering sparks playing over its cold, limpid water have as it were protected its discreet and haughty nobility against any defilement. But unfortunately in artificial light its bright flames lose their brilliance; the blue water sinks low and seems to go to sleep, to wake and sparkle again only at daybreak.

It was clear that none of these stones satisfied Des Esseintes' requirements; besides, they were all too civilized, too familiar. Instead he turned his attention to more startling and unusual gems; and after letting them trickle through his fingers, he finally made a selection of real and artificial stones which in combination would result in a fascinating and disconcerting harmony.

He made up his bouquet in this way: the leaves were set with gems of a strong and definite green – asparagus-green chrysoberyls, leek-green peridots, olive-green olivines – and these sprang from twigs of almandine and uvarovite of a purplish red, which threw out flashes of harsh, brilliant light like the scales of tartar that glitter on the insides of wine-casks.

For the flowers which stood out from the stem a long way from the foot of the spray, he decided on a phosphate blue; but he absolutely refused to consider the Oriental turquoise which is used for brooches and rings, and which, together with the banal pearl and the odious coral, forms the delight of the common herd.

He chose only turquoises from the West – stones which, strictly speaking, are simply a fossil ivory impregnated with coppery substances and whose celadon blue looks thick, opaque, and sulphurous, as if jaundiced with bile.

This done, he could now go on to encrust the petals of such flowers as were in full bloom in the middle of his spray, those closest to the stem, with translucent minerals that gleamed with a glassy, sickly light and glinted with fierce, sharp bursts of fire.

For this purpose he used only Ceylon cat's-eyes, cymophanes, and sapphirines – three stones which all sparkled with mysterious, deceptive flashes, painfully drawn from the icy depths of their turbid water: the cat's-eye of a greenish grey streaked with concentric veins which seem to shift and change position according to the way the light falls; the cymophane with blue waterings rippling across the floating, milky-coloured centre; the sapphirine which kindles bluish, phosphorescent fires against a dull, chocolate-brown background.

The lapidary took careful notes as it was explained to him exactly where each stone was to be let in.

'What about the edging of the shell?' he then asked Des Esseintes.

The latter had originally thought of a border of opals and hydrophanes. But these stones, interesting though they may be on account of their varying colour and vacillating fire, are too unstable and unreliable to be given serious consideration; the opal, in fact, has a positively rheumatic sensitivity, the play of its rays changing in accordance with changes in moisture or temperature, while the hydrophane will burn only in water and refuses to light up its grey fires unless it is wetted.

He finally decided on a series of stones with contrasting colours – the mahogany-red hyacinth of Compostella followed by the sea-green aquamarine, the vinegar-pink balas ruby by the pale slate-coloured Sudermania ruby. Their feeble lustre would be sufficient to set off the dark shell but not enough to detract from the bunch of jewelled flowers which they were to frame in a slender garland of subdued brilliance.

Now Des Esseintes sat gazing at the tortoise where it lay huddled in a corner of the dining-room, glittering brightly in the half-light.

He felt perfectly happy, his eyes feasting on the splendour of these jewelled corollas, ablaze with colour against a golden background. Suddenly he had a craving for food, unusual for him, and soon he was dipping slices of toast spread with superlative butter in a cup of tea, an impeccable blend of Si-a-Fayoun, Mo-you-Tann, and Khansky – yellow teas brought from China into Russia by special caravans.

He drank this liquid perfume from cups of that Oriental porcelain known as egg-shell china, it is so delicate and diaphanous; and just as he would never use any but these adorably dainty cups, so he insisted on plates and dishes of genuine silver-gilt, slightly worn so that the silver showed a little where the thin film of gold had been rubbed off, giving it a charming old-world look, a fatigued appearance, a moribund air.

After swallowing his last mouthful he went back to his study, instructing his manservant to bring along the tortoise, which was still obstinately refusing to budge.

Outside the snow was falling. In the lamplight icy leaf-patterns could be seen glittering on the blue-black windows, and hoar-frost sparkled like melted sugar in the hollows of the bottle-glass panes, all spattered with gold.

The little house, lying snug and sleepy in the darkness, was wrapped in a deep silence.

Des Esseintes sat dreaming of one thing and another. The burning logs piled high in the fire-basket filled the room with hot air, and eventually he got up and opened the window a little way.

Like a great canopy of counter-ermine, the sky hung before him, a black curtain spattered with white.

Suddenly an icy wind blew up which drove the dancing snowflakes before it and reversed this arrangement of colours. The sky's heraldic trappings were turned round to reveal a true ermine, white dotted with black where pinpricks of darkness showed through the curtain of falling snow.

He shut the window again. This quick change, straight from the torrid heat of the room to the biting cold of midwinter had taken his breath away; and curling up beside the fire again, it occurred to him that a drop of spirits would be the best thing to warm him up.

He made his way to the dining-room, where there was a cupboard built into one of the walls containing a row of little barrels, resting side-by-side on tiny sandalwood stands and each broached at the bottom with a silver spigot.

This collection of liqueur casks he called his mouth organ.

A rod could be connected to all the spigots, enabling them to be turned by one and the same movement, so that once the apparatus was in position it was only necessary to press a button concealed in the wainscoting to open all the conduits simultaneously and so fill with liqueur the minute cups underneath the taps.

The organ was then open. The stops labelled 'flute', 'horn', and 'vox angelica' were pulled out, ready for use. Des Esseintes would drink a drop here, another there, playing internal symphonies to himself, and providing his palate with sensations analogous to those which music dispenses to the ear.

Indeed, each and every liqueur, in his opinion, corresponded in taste with the sound of a particular instrument. Dry curaçao, for instance, was like the clarinet with its piercing, velvety note; kümmel like the oboe with its sonorous, nasal timbre; crème de menthe and anisette like the flute, at once sweet and tart, soft and shrill. Then to complete the orchestra there was kirsch, blowing a wild trumpet blast; gin and whisky raising the roof of the mouth with the blare of their cornets and trombones; marc-brandy matching the tubas with its deafening din; while peals of thunder came from the cymbal and the bass drum, which arak and mastic were banging and beating with all their might.

He considered that this analogy could be pushed still further and that string quartets might play under the palatal arch, with the violin represented by an old brandy, choice and heady, biting and delicate; with the viola simulated by rum, which was stronger, heavier, and quieter; with vespetro as poignant, drawn-out, sad, and tender as a violoncello; and with the double-bass a fine old bitter, full-bodied, solid, and dark. One might even form a quintet, if this were thought desirable, by adding a fifth instrument, the harp, imitated to near perfection by the vibrant savour, the clear, sharp, silvery note of dry cumin.

The similarity did not end there, for the music of liqueurs had its own scheme of interrelated tones; thus, to quote only one example, Benedictine represents, so to speak, the minor key corresponding to the major key of those alcohols which wine-merchants' scores indicate by the name of green Chartreuse.

Once these principles had been established, and thanks to a series of erudite experiments, he had been able to perform upon his tongue silent melodies and mute funeral marches; to hear inside his mouth crème-de-menthe solos and rum-and-vespetro duets.

He even succeeded in transferring specific pieces of music to his palate, following the composer step by step, rendering his intentions, his effects, his shades of expression, by mixing or contrasting related liqueurs, by subtle approximations and cunning combinations.

At other times he would compose melodies of his own, executing pastorals with the sweet blackcurrant liqueur that filled his throat with the warbling song of a nightingale; or with the delicious cacaochouva that hummed sugary bergerets like the *Romances of Estelle* and the '*Ah! vous dirai-je, maman*' of olden days.

But tonight Des Esseintes had no wish to listen to the taste of music; he confined himself to removing one note from the keyboard of his organ, carrying off a tiny cup which he had filled with genuine Irish whiskey.

He settled down in his armchair again and slowly sipped this fermented spirit of oats and barley, a pungent odour of creosote spreading through his mouth.

Little by little, as he drank, his thoughts followed the re-newed reactions of his palate, caught up with the savour of the whiskey, and were reminded by a striking similarity of smell of memories which had lain dormant for years.

The acrid, carbolic bouquet forcibly recalled the identical scent of which he had been all too conscious whenever a dentist had been at work on his gums.

Once started on this track, his recollections, ranging at first over all the different practitioners he had known, finally gathered together and converged on one of these men whose distinctive method had been graven with particular force upon his memory.

This had happened three years ago: afflicted in the middle of the night with an abominable toothache, he had plugged his cheek with cotton-wool and paced up and down his room like a madman, blundering into the furniture in his pain.

It was a molar that had already been filled and was now past cure; the only possible remedy lay in the dentist's forceps. In a fever of agony he waited for daylight, resolved to bear the most atrocious operation if only it would put an end to his sufferings.

Nursing his jawbone, he asked himself exactly what he should do when morning came. The dentists he usually con-sulted were well-to-do businessmen who could not be seen at short notice; appointments had to be made in advance and times agreed.

'That's out of the question,' he told himself. 'I can't wait any longer.'

He made up his mind to go and see the first dentist he could find, to resort to a common, lower-class tooth-doctor, one of those iron-fisted fellows who, ignorant though they may be of the useless art of treating decay and filling cavities, know how to extirpate the most stubborn of stumps with unparal-leled speed. Their doors are always open at daybreak, and their customers are never kept waiting.

Seven o'clock struck at last. He rushed out of doors, and remembering the name of a mechanic who called himself a dentist and lived in a corner house by the river, he hurried in that direction, biting on a handkerchief and choking back his tears.

Soon he arrived at the house, which was distinguished by an enormous wooden placard bearing the name 'Gatonax' spread out in huge yellow letters on a black ground, and by two little glass-fronted cases displaying neat rows of false teeth set in pink wax gums joined together with brass springs. He stood there panting for breath, with sweat pouring down his forehead; a horrid fear gripped him, a cold shiver ran over his body – and then came sudden relief, the pain vanished, the tooth stopped aching.

After staying for a while in the street, wondering what to do, he finally mastered his fears and climbed the dark staircase, taking four steps at a time as far as the third floor. There he came up against a door with an enamel plaque repeating the name he had seen on the placard outside. He rang the bell; then, terrified by the sight of great splashes of blood and spittle on the steps, he suddenly turned tail, resolved to go on suffering from toothache for the rest of his life, when a piercing scream came from behind the partition, filling the well of the staircase and nailing him to the spot with sheer horror. At that very moment a door opened and an old woman asked him to come in.

Shame overcame fear, and he let her show him into what appeared to be a dining-room. Another door banged open, admitting a great, strapping fellow dressed in a frock-coat and trousers that seemed carved in wood. Des Esseintes followed him into an inner sanctum.

His recollections of what happened after that were somewhat confused. He vaguely remembered dropping into an armchair facing a window, putting a finger on the offending tooth, and stammering out:

'It has been filled before. I'm afraid there's nothing can be done this time.'

The man promptly put a stop to this explanation by inserting an enormous forefinger into his mouth; then, muttering to himself behind his curly waxed moustaches, he picked up an instrument from a table.

At this point the drama really began. Clutching the arms of the chair, Des Esseintes felt the cold touch of metal inside his cheek, then saw a whole galaxy of stars, and in unspeakable agony started stamping his feet and squealing like a stuck pig.

There was a loud crack as the molar broke on its way out. By now it seemed as if his head were being pulled off and his skull smashed in; he lost all control of himself and screamed at the top of his voice, fighting desperately against the man, who bore down on him again as if he wanted to plunge his arm into the depths of his belly. Suddenly the fellow took a step backwards, lifted his patient bodily by the refractory tooth and let him fall back into the chair, while he stood there blocking the window, puffing and blowing as he brandished at the end of his forceps a blue tooth tipped with red.

Utterly exhausted, Des Esseintes had spat out a basinful of blood, waved away the old woman who came in to offer him his tooth, which she was prepared to wrap up in a piece of newspaper, and after paying two francs had fled, adding his contribution to the bloody spittle on the stairs. But out in the street he had recovered his spirits, feeling ten years younger and taking an interest in the most insignificant things.

'Ugh!' he said to himself, shuddering over these gruesome recollections. He got to his feet to break the horrid fascination of his nightmare vision, and coming back to present-day preoccupations he felt suddenly uneasy about the tortoise.

It was still lying absolutely motionless. He touched it; it was dead. Accustomed no doubt to a sedentary life, a modest existence spent in the shelter of its humble carapace, it had not been able to bear the dazzling luxury imposed upon it, the glittering cape in which it had been clad, the precious stones which had been used to decorate its shell like a jewelled ciborium.

V

TOGETHER with the desire to escape from a hateful period of sordid degradation, the longing to see no more pictures of the human form toiling in Paris between four walls or roaming the streets in search of money had taken an increasing hold on him.

Once he had cut himself off from contemporary life, he had resolved to allow nothing to enter his hermitage which might breed repugnance or regret; and so he had set his heart on finding a few pictures of subtle, exquisite refinement, steeped in an atmosphere of ancient fantasy, wrapped in an aura of antique corruption, divorced from modern times and modern society.

For the delectation of his mind and the delight of his eyes, he had decided to seek out evocative works which would transport him to some unfamiliar world, point the way to new possibilities, and shake up his nervous system by means of erudite fancies, complicated nightmares, suave and sinister visions.

Among all the artists he considered, there was one who sent him into raptures of delight, and that was Gustave Moreau. He had bought Moreau's two masterpieces, and night after night he would stand dreaming in front of one of them, the picture of Salome.

This painting showed a throne like the high altar of a cathedral standing beneath a vaulted ceiling – a ceiling crossed by countless arches springing from thick-set, almost Roman-esque columns, encased in polychromic brickwork, encrusted with mosaics, set with lapis lazuli and sardonyx – in a palace which resembled a basilica built in both the Moslem and the Byzantine styles.

In the centre of the tabernacle set on the altar, which was approached by a flight of recessed steps in the shape of a semi-circle, the Tetrarch Herod was seated, with a tiara on his head, his legs close together and his hands on his knees.

63

His face was yellow and parchment-like, furrowed with wrinkles, lined with years; his long beard floated like a white cloud over the jewelled stars that studded the gold-laced robe moulding his breast.

Round about this immobile, statuesque figure, frozen like some Hindu god in a hieratic pose, incense was burning, sending up clouds of vapour through which the fiery gems set in the sides of the throne gleamed like the phosphorescent eyes of wild animals. The clouds rose higher and higher, swirling under the arches of the roof, where the blue smoke mingled with the gold dust of the great beams of sunlight slanting down from the domes.

Amid the heady odour of these perfumes, in the overheated atmosphere of the basilica, Salome slowly glides forward on the points of her toes, her left arm stretched out in a commanding gesture, her right bent back and holding a great lotus-blossom beside her face, while a woman squatting on the floor strums the strings of a guitar.

With a withdrawn, solemn, almost august expression on her face, she begins the lascivious dance which is to rouse the aged Herod's dormant senses; her breasts rise and fall, the nipples hardening at the touch of her whirling necklaces; the strings of diamonds glitter against her moist flesh; her bracelets, her belts, her rings all spit out fiery sparks; and across her triumphal robe, sewn with pearls, patterned with silver, spangled with gold, the jewelled cuirass, of which every chain is a precious stone, seems to be ablaze with little snakes of fire, swarming over the mat flesh, over the tea-rose skin, like gorgeous insects with dazzling shards, mottled with carmine, spotted with pale yellow, speckled with steel blue, striped with peacock green.

Her eyes fixed in the concentrated gaze of a sleepwalker, she sees neither the Tetrarch, who sits there quivering, nor her mother, the ferocious Herodias, who watches her every movement, nor the hermaphrodite or eunuch who stands sabre in hand at the foot of the throne, a terrifying creature, veiled as far as the eyes and with its sexless dugs hanging like gourds under its orange-striped tunic.

The character of Salome, a figure with a haunting fascination for artists and poets, had been an obsession with him for years. Time and again he had opened the old Bible of Pierre Variquet, translated by the Doctors of Theology of the University of Louvain, and read the Gospel of St Matthew which recounts in brief, naïve phrases the beheading of the Precursor; time and again he had mused over these lines:

'But when Herod's birthday was kept, the daughter of Herodias danced before them, and pleased Herod.

'Whereupon, he promised with an oath to give her whatsoever she would ask.

'And she, being before instructed of her mother, said, "Give me here John Baptist's head in a charger."

'And here the king was sorry: nevertheless, for the oath's sake, and them which sat with him at meat, he commanded it to be given her.

'And he sent, and beheaded John in the prison.

'And his head was brought in a charger, and given to the damsel: and she brought it to her mother.'

But neither St Matthew, nor St Mark, nor St Luke, nor any of the other sacred writers had enlarged on the maddening charm and potent depravity of the dancer. She had always remained a dim and distant figure, lost in a mysterious ecstasy far off in the mists of time, beyond the reach of punctilious, pedestrian minds, and accessible only to brains shaken and sharpened and rendered almost clairvoyant by neurosis; she had always repelled the artistic advances of fleshly painters, such as Rubens who travestied her as a Flemish butcher's wife; she had always passed the comprehension of the writing fraternity, who never succeeded in rendering the disquieting delirium of the dancer, the subtle grandeur of the murderess.

In Gustave Moreau's work, which in conception went far beyond the data supplied by the New Testament, Des Esseintes saw realized at long last the weird and superhuman Salome of his dreams. Here she was no longer just the dancing-girl who extorts a cry of lust and lechery from an old man by the lascivious movements of her loins; who saps the morale and breaks the will of a king with the heaving of her breasts, the twitching of her belly, the quivering of her thighs. She had become, as it were, the symbolic incarnation of undying Lust, the Goddess of immortal Hysteria, the accursed Beauty exalted above all other beauties by the catalepsy that hardens her flesh and steels her muscles, the monstrous Beast, indifferent, irresponsible, insensible, poisoning, like the Helen of ancient myth, everything that approaches her, everything that sees her, everything that she touches.

Viewed in this light, she belonged to the theogonies of the Far East; she no longer had her origin in Biblical tradition; she could not even be likened to the living image of Babylon, the royal harlot of Revelations, bedecked like herself with precious stones and purple robes, with paint and perfume, for the whore of Babylon was not thrust by a fateful power, by an irresistible force, into the alluring iniquities of debauch.

Moreover, the painter seemed to have wished to assert his intention of remaining outside the bounds of time, of giving no precise indication of race or country or period, setting as he did his Salome inside this extraordinary palace with its grandiose, heterogeneous architecture, clothing her in sumptuous, fanciful robes, crowning her with a nondescript diadem like Salammbo's, in the shape of a Phoenician tower, and finally putting in her hand the sceptre of Isis, the sacred flower of both Egypt and India, the great lotus-blossom.

Des Esseintes puzzled his brains to find the meaning of this emblem. Had it the phallic significance which the primordial religions of India attributed to it? Did it suggest to the old Tetrarch a sacrifice of virginity, an exchange of blood, an impure embrace asked for and offered on the express condition of a murder? Or did it represent the allegory of fertility, the Hindu myth of life, an existence held between the fingers of woman and clumsily snatched away by the fumbling hands of man, who is maddened by desire, crazed by a fever of the flesh?

Perhaps, too, in arming his enigmatic goddess with the revered lotus-blossom, the painter had been thinking of the dancer, the mortal woman, the soiled vessel, ultimate cause of every sin and every crime; perhaps he had remembered the sepulchral rites of ancient Egypt, the solemn ceremonies of embalmment, when practitioners and priests lay out the dead woman's body on a slab of jasper, then with curved needles extract her brains through the nostrils, her entrails through an opening made in the left side, and finally, before gilding her nails and her teeth, before anointing the corpse with oils and spices, insert into her sexual parts, to purify them, the chaste petals of the divine flower.

Be that as it may, there was some irresistible fascination exerted by this painting; but the water-colour entitled *The Apparition* created perhaps an even more disturbing impression.

In this picture, Herod's palace rose up like some Alhambra on slender columns iridescent with Moresque tiles, which appeared to be bedded in silver mortar and gold cement; arabesques started from lozenges of lapis lazuli to wind their way right across the cupolas, whose mother-of-pearl marquetry gleamed with rainbow lights and flashed with prismatic fires.

The murder had been done; now the executioner stood impassive, his hands resting on the pommel of his long, blood-stained sword.

The Saint's decapitated head had left the charger where it lay on the flagstones and risen into the air, the eyes staring out from the livid face, the colourless lips parted, the crimson neck dripping tears of blood. A mosaic encircled the face, and also a halo of light whose rays darted out under the porticoes, emphasized the awful elevation of the head, and kindled a fire in the glassy eyeballs, which were fixed in what happened to be agonized concentration on the dancer.

With a gesture of horror, Salome tries to thrust away the terrifying vision which holds her nailed to the spot, balanced on the tips of her toes, her eyes dilated, her right hand clawing convulsively at her throat.

She is almost naked; in the heat of the dance her veils have fallen away and her brocade robes slipped to the floor, so that now she is clad only in wrought metals and translucent gems. A gorgerin grips her waist like a corselet, and like an outsize clasp a wondrous jewel sparkles and flashes in the cleft between her breasts; lower down, a girdle encircles her hips, hiding the upper part of her thighs, against which dangles a gigantic pendant glistening with rubies and emeralds; finally, where the body shows bare between gorgerin and girdle, the belly bulges out, dimpled by a navel which resembles a graven seal of onyx with its milky hues and its rosy finger-nail tints.

Under the brilliant rays emanating from the Precursor's head, every facet of every jewel catches fire; the stones burn brightly, outlining the woman's figure in flaming colours, indicating neck, legs, and arms with points of light, red as burning coals, violet as jets of gas, blue as flaming alcohol, white as moonbeams.

The dreadful head glows eerily, bleeding all the while, so that clots of dark red form at the ends of hair and beard. Visible to Salome alone, it embraces in its sinister gaze neither Herodias, musing over the ultimate satisfaction of her hatred, nor the Tetrarch, who, bending forward a little with his hands on his knees, is still panting with emotion, maddened by the sight and smell of the woman's naked body, steeped in musky scents, anointed with aromatic balms, impregnated with incense and myrrh.

Like the old King, Des Esseintes invariably felt overwhelmed, subjugated, stunned when he looked at this dancing-girl, who was less majestic, less haughty, but more seductive than the Salome of the oil-painting.

In the unfeeling and unpitying statue, in the innocent and deadly idol, the lusts and fears of common humanity had been awakened; the great lotus-blossom had disappeared, the goddess vanished; a hideous nightmare now held in its choking grip an entertainer, intoxicated by the whirling movement of the dance, a courtesan, petrified and hypnotized by terror.

Here she was a true harlot, obedient to her passionate and cruel female temperament; here she came to life, more refined yet more savage, more hateful yet more exquisite than before; here she roused the sleeping senses of the male more powerfully, subjugated his will more surely with her charms – the charms of a great venereal flower, grown in a bed of sacrilege, reared in a hot-house of impiety.

It was Des Esseintes' opinion that never before, in any

period, had the art of water-colour produced such brilliant hues; never before had an aquarellist's wretched chemical pigments been able to make paper sparkle so brightly with precious stones, shine so colourfully with sunlight filtered through stained-glass windows, glitter so splendidly with sumptuous garments, glow so warmly with exquisite flesh-tints.

Deep in contemplation, he would try to puzzle out the ante-cedents of this great artist, this mystical pagan, this illuminee who could shut out the modern world so completely as to behold, in the heart of present-day Paris, the awful visions and magical apotheoses of other ages.

Des Esseintes found it hard to say who had served as his models; here and there, he could detect vague recollections of Mantegna and Jacopo de Barbari; here and there, confused memories of Da Vinci and feverish colouring reminiscent of Delacroix. But on the whole the influence of these masters on his work was imperceptible, the truth being that Gustave Moreau was nobody's pupil. With no real ancestors and no possible descendants, he remained a unique figure in contemporary art. Going back to the beginning of racial tradition, to the sources of mythologies whose bloody enigmas he compared and unravelled; joining and fusing in one those legends which had originated in the Middle East only to be metamorphosed by the beliefs of other peoples, he could cite these researches to justify his architectonic mixtures, his sumptuous and unexpected combinations of dress materials, and his hieratic allegories whose sinister quality was heightened by the morbid perspicuity of an entirely modern sensibility. He himself remained downcast and sorrowful, haunted by the symbols of superhuman passions and superhuman perversities, of divine debauches perpetrated without enthusiasm and without hope.

His sad and scholarly works breathed a strange magic, an incantatory charm which stirred you to the depths of your being like the sorcery of certain of Baudelaire's poems, so that you were left amazed and pensive, disconcerted by this art which crossed the frontiers of painting to borrow from the writer's art its most subtly evocative suggestions, from the enameller's art its most wonderfully brilliant effects, from the lapidary's and etcher's art its most exquisitely delicate touches. These two pictures of Salome, for which Des Esseintes' admiration knew no bounds, lived constantly before his eyes, hung as they were on the walls of his study, on panels reserved for them between the bookcases.

But these were by no means the only pictures he had bought in order to adorn his retreat. True, none were needed for the first and only upper storey of his house, since he had given it over to his servants and did not use any of its rooms; but the ground floor by itself demanded a good many to cover its bare walls.

This ground floor was divided as follows: a dressing-room, communicating with the bedroom, occupied one corner of the building; from the bedroom you went into the library, and from the library into the dining-room, which occupied another corner.

These rooms, making up one side of the house, were set in a straight line, with their windows overlooking the valley of Aunay.

The other side of the building consisted of four rooms corresponding exactly to the first four in their lay-out. Thus the corner kitchen matched the dining-room, a big entrance-hall the library, a sort of boudoir the bedroom, and the closets the dressing-room.

All these latter rooms looked out on the opposite side to the valley of Aunay, towards the Tour du Croy and Châtillon.

As for the staircase, it was built against one end of the house, on the outside, so that the noise the servants made as they pounded up and down the steps was deadened and barely reached Des Esseintes' ears.

He had had the boudoir walls covered with bright red tapestry and all round the room he had hung ebony-framed prints by Jan Luyken, an old Dutch engraver who was almost unknown in France.

He possessed a whole series of studies by this artist in lugubrious fantasy and ferocious cruelty: his *Religious Persecu-*

tions, a collection of appalling plates displaying all the tortures which religious fanaticism has invented, revealing all the agonizing varieties of human suffering – bodies roasted over braziers, heads scalped with swords, trepanned with nails, lacerated with saws, bowels taken out of the belly and wound on to bobbins, finger-nails slowly removed with pincers, eyes put out, eyelids pinned back, limbs dislocated and carefully broken, bones laid bare and scraped for hours with knives.

These pictures, full of abominable fancies, reeking of burnt flesh, dripping with blood, echoing with screams and curses, made Des Esseintes' flesh creep whenever he went into the red boudoir, and he remained rooted to the spot, choking with horror.

But over and above the shudders they provoked, over and above the frightening genius of the man and the extraordinary life he put into his figures, there were to be found in his astonishing crowd-scenes, in the hosts of people he sketched with a dexterity reminiscent of Callot but with a vigour that amusing scribbler never attained, remarkable reconstructions of other places and periods: buildings, costumes, and manners in the days of the Maccabees, in Rome during the persecutions of the Christians, in Spain under the Inquisition, in France during the Middle Ages and at the time of the St Bartholomew massacres and the Dragonnades, were all observed with meticulous care and depicted with wonderful skill.

These prints were mines of interesting information and could be studied for hours on end without a moment's boredom; extremely thought-provoking as well, they often helped Des Esseintes to kill time on days when he did not feel in the mood for reading.

The story of Luyken's life also attracted him and incidentally explained the hallucinatory character of his work. A fervent Calvinist, a fanatical sectary, a zealot for hymns and prayers, he composed and illustrated religious poems, paraphrased the Psalms in verse, and immersed himself in Biblical study, from which he would emerge haggard and enraptured, his mind haunted by bloody visions, his mouth twisted by the maledictions of the Reformation, by its songs of terror and anger.

71

What is more, he despised the world, and this led him to give all he possessed to the poor, living on a crust of bread himself. In the end he had put to sea with an old maidservant who was fanatically devoted to him, landing wherever his boat came ashore, preaching the Gospel to all and sundry, trying to live without eating – a man with little or nothing to distinguish him from a lunatic or a savage.

In the larger adjoining room, the vestibule, which was panelled in cedar-wood the colour of a cigar-box, other prints, other weird drawings hung in rows along the walls.

One of these was Bresdin's *Comedy of Death*. This depicts an improbable landscape which bristles with trees, coppices, and thickets in the shape of demons or phantoms and full of birds with rats' heads and vegetable tails. From the ground, which is littered with vertebrae, ribs, and skulls, there spring gnarled and shaky willow-trees, in which skeletons are perched, waving bouquets and chanting songs of victory, while a Christ flies away into a mackerel sky; a hermit meditates, with his head in his hands, at the back of a grotto; and a beggar dies of privation and hunger, stretched out on his back, his feet pointing to a stagnant pool.

Another was *The Good Samaritan* by the same artist, a lithograph of a huge pen-and-ink drawing. Here the scene is a fantastic tangle of palms, service-trees, and oaks, growing all together in defiance of season and climate; a patch of virgin forest packed with monkeys, owls, and screech-owls, and cumbered with old tree-stumps as unshapely as mandrake roots; a magic wood with a clearing in the centre affording a distant glimpse, first of the Samaritan and the wounded man, then of a river, and finally of a fairytale city climbing up to the horizon to meet a strange sky dotted with birds, flecked with foaming billows, swelling, as it were, with cloudy waves.

It looked rather like the work of a primitive or an Albert Dürer of sorts, composed under the influence of opium; but much as Des Esseintes admired the delicacy of detail and the impressive power of this plate, he paused more often in front of the other pictures that decorated the room. These were all signed Odilon Redon.

In their narrow gold-rimmed frames of unpainted pearwood, they contained the most fantastic of visions: a Merovingian head balanced on a cup; a bearded man with something of the bonze about him and something of the typical speaker at public meetings, touching a colossal cannon-ball with one finger; a horrible spider with a human face lodged in the middle of its body. There were other drawings which plunged even deeper into the horrific realms of bad dreams and fevered visions. Here there was an enormous dice blinking a mournful eye; there, studies of bleak and arid landscapes, of burnt-up plains, of earth heaving and erupting into fiery clouds, into livid and stagnant skies. Sometimes Redon's subjects actually seemed to be borrowed from the nightmares of science, to go back to prehistoric times: a monstrous flora spread over the rocks, and among the ubiquitous boulders and glacier mud-streams wandered bipeds whose apish features – the heavy jaws, the protruding brows, the receding forehead, the flattened top of the skull – recalled the head of our ancestors early in the Quaternary Period, when man was still fructivorous and speechless, a contemporary of the mammoth, the woolly rhinoceros, and the cave-bear. These drawings defied classification, most of them exceeding the bounds of pictorial art and creating a new type of fantasy, born of sickness and delirium.

In fact, there were some of these faces, dominated by great wild eyes, and some of these bodies, magnified beyond measure or distorted as if seen through a carafe of water, that evoked in Des Esseintes' mind recollections of typhoid fever, memories which had somehow stayed with him of the feverish nights and frightful nightmares of his childhood.

Overcome by an indefinable malaise at the sight of these drawings – the same sort of malaise he experienced when he looked at certain rather similar *Proverbs* by Goya or read some of Edgar Allan Poe's stories, whose terrifying or hallucinating effects Odilon Redon seemed to have transposed into a different art – he would rub his eyes and turn to gaze at a radiant figure which, in the midst of all these frenzied pictures, stood out calm and serene: the figure of Melancholy, seated on some rocks before a disk-like sun, in a mournful and despondent attitude.

His gloom would then be dissipated, as if by magic; a sweet sadness, an almost languorous sorrow would gently take possession of his thoughts, and he would meditate for hours in front of this work, which, with its splashes of gouache amid the heavy pencil-lines, introduced a refreshing note of liquid green and pale gold into the unbroken black of all these charcoal drawings and etchings.

Besides this collection of Redon's works, covering nearly every panel in the vestibule, he had hung in his bedroom an extravagant sketch by Theotocopuli, a study of Christ in which the drawing was exaggerated, the colouring crude and bizarre, the general effect one of frenzied energy, an example of the painter's second manner, when he was obsessed by the idea of avoiding any further resemblance to Titian.

This sinister picture, with its boot-polish blacks and cadaverous greens, fitted in with certain ideas Des Esseintes held on the subject of bedroom furniture and decoration.

There were, in his opinion, only two ways of arranging a bedroom: you could either make it a place for sensual pleasure, for nocturnal delectation, or else you could fit it out as a place for sleep and solitude, a setting for quiet meditation, a sort of oratory.

In the first case, the Louis-Quinze style was the obvious choice for people of delicate sensibility, exhausted by mental stimulation above all else. The eighteenth century is, in fact, the only age which has known how to envelop woman in a wholly depraved atmosphere, shaping its furniture on the model of her charms, imitating her passionate contortions and spasmodic convulsions in the curves and convolutions of wood and copper, spicing the sugary languor of the blonde with its bright, light furnishings, and mitigating the salty savour of the brunette with tapestries of delicate, watery, almost insipid hues.

In his Paris house he had had a bedroom decorated in just this style, and furnished with the great white lacquered bed which provides that added titillation, that final touch of depravity so precious to the experienced voluptuary, excited by the spurious chastity and hypocritical modesty of the Greuze figures, by the pretended purity of a bed of vice apparently designed for innocent children and young virgins.

In the other case – and now that he meant to break with the irritating memories of his past life, this was the only one for him – the bedroom had to be turned into a facsimile of a monastery cell. But here difficulties piled up before him, for as far as he was concerned, he categorically refused to put up with the austere ugliness that characterizes all penitential prayer-houses.

After turning the question over in his mind, he eventually came to the conclusion that what he should try to do was this: to employ cheerful means to attain a drab end, or rather, to impress on the room as a whole, treated in this way, a certain elegance and distinction, while yet preserving its essential ugliness. He decided, in fact, to reverse the optical illusion of the stage, where cheap finery plays the part of rich and costly fabrics; to achieve precisely the opposite effect, by using magnificent materials to give the impression of old rags; in short, to fit up a Trappist's cell that would look like the genuine article, but would of course be nothing of the sort.

He set about it in the following way: to imitate the yellow distemper beloved by church and state alike, he had the walls hung with saffron silk; and to represent the chocolate-brown dado normally found in this sort of room, he covered the lower part of the walls with strips of kingwood, a dark-brown wood with a purple sheen. The effect was delightful, recalling – though not too clearly – the unattractive crudity of the model he was copying and adapting. The ceiling was similarly covered with white holland, which had the appearance of plaster without its bright, shiny look; as for the cold tiles of the floor, he managed to hit them off quite well, thanks to a carpet patterned in red squares, with the wood dyed white in places where sandals and boots could be supposed to have left their mark.

He furnished this room with a little iron bedstead, a mock hermit's bed, made of old wrought iron, but highly polished and set off at head and foot with an intricate design of tulips and vine-branches intertwined, a design taken from the balustrade of the great staircase of an old mansion.

By way of a bedside table, he installed an antique priedieu, the inside of which could hold a chamber-pot while the top supported a euchologion; against the opposite wall he set a churchwardens' pew, with a great openwork canopy and misericords carved in the solid wood; and to provide illumination, he had some altar candlesticks fitted with real wax tapers which he bought from a firm specializing in ecclesiastical requirements, for he professed a genuine antipathy to all modern forms of lighting, whether paraffin, shale-oil, stearin candles or gas, finding them all too crude and garish for his liking.

Before falling asleep in the morning, as he lay in bed with his head on the pillow, he would gaze at his Theotocopuli, whose harsh colouring did something to dampen the gaiety of the yellow silk hangings and put them in a graver mood; and at these times he found it easy to imagine that he was living hundreds of miles from Paris, far removed from the world of men, in the depths of some secluded monastery.

After all, it was easy enough to sustain this particular illusion, in that the life he was leading was very similar to the life of a monk. He thus enjoyed all the benefits of cloistered confinement while avoiding the disadvantages – the army-style discipline, the lack of comfort, the dirt, the promiscuity, the monotonous idleness. Just as he had made his cell into a warm, luxurious bedroom, so he had ensured that his everyday existence should be pleasant and comfortable, sufficiently occupied and in no way restricted.

Like an eremite, he was ripe for solitude, exhausted by life and expecting nothing more of it; like a monk again, he was overwhelmed by an immense weariness, by a longing for peace and quiet, by a desire to have no further contact with the heathen, who in his eyes comprised all utilitarians and fools.

In short, although he had no vocation for the state of grace, he was conscious of a genuine fellow-feeling for those who

76

were shut up in religious houses, persecuted by a vindictive society that cannot forgive either the proper contempt they feel for it or their averred intention of redeeming and expiating by years of silence the ever-increasing licentiousness of its silly, senseless conversations.

VI

Buried deep in a vast wing-chair, his feet resting on the pear-shaped, silver-gilt supports of the andirons, his slippers toasting in front of the crackling logs that shot out bright tongues of flame as if they felt the furious blast of a bellows, Des Esseintes put the old quarto he had been reading down on a table, stretched himself, lit a cigarette, and gave himself up to a delicious reverie. His mind was soon going full tilt in pursuit of certain recollections which had lain low for months, but which had suddenly been started by a name recurring, for no apparent reason, to his memory.

Once again he could see, with surprising clearness, his friend D'Aigurande's embarrassment when he had been forced to confess to a gathering of confirmed bachelors that he had just completed the final arrangements for his wedding. There was a general outcry, and his friends tried to dissuade him with a frightening description of the horrors of sharing a bed. But it was all in vain: he had taken leave of his senses, believed that his future wife was a woman of intelligence, and maintained that he had discovered in her quite exceptional qualities of tenderness and devotion.

Des Esseintes had been the only one among all these young men to encourage him in his resolve, and this he did as soon as he learnt that his friend's fiancée wanted to live on the corner of a newly constructed boulevard, in one of those modern flats built on a circular plan.

Persuaded of the merciless power of petty vexations, which can have a more baneful effect on sanguine souls than the great tragedies of life, and taking account of the fact that D'Aigurande had no private means, while his wife's dowry was practically non-existent, he saw in this innocent whim an endless source of ridiculous misfortunes.

As he had foreseen, D'Aigurande proceeded to buy rounded pieces of furniture – console-tables sawn away at the back to

78

form a semi-circle, curtain-poles curved like bows, carpets cut on a crescent pattern – until he had furnished the whole flat with things made to order. He spent twice as much as anybody else; and then, when his wife, finding herself short of money for new dresses, got tired of living in this rotunda, and took herself off to a flat with ordinary square rooms at a lower rent, not a single piece of furniture would fit in or stand up properly. Soon the bothersome things were giving rise to endless annoyances; the bond between husband and wife, already worn thin by the inevitable irritations of a shared life, grew more tenuous week by week; and there were angry scenes and mutual recriminations as they came to realize the impossibility of living in a sitting-room where sofas and console-tables would not go against the walls and wobbled at the slightest touch, however many blocks and wedges were used to steady them. There was not enough money to pay for alterations, and even if there had been, these would have been almost impossible to carry out. Everything became a ground for high words and squabbles, from the drawers that had stuck in the rickety furniture to the petty thefts of the maidservant, who took advantage of the constant quarrels between her master and mistress to raid the cash-box. In short, their life became unbearable; he went out in search of amusement, while she looked to adultery to provide compensation for the drizzly dreariness of her life. Finally, by mutual consent, they cancelled their lease and petitioned for a legal separation.

'My plan of campaign was right in every particular,' Des Esseintes had told himself on hearing the news, with the satisfaction of a strategist whose manoeuvres, worked out long beforehand, have resulted in victory.

Now, sitting by his fireside and thinking about the break-up of this couple whose union he had encouraged with his good advice, he threw a fresh armful of wood into the hearth and promptly started dreaming again.

More memories, belonging to the same order of ideas, now came crowding in on him.

Some years ago, he remembered he had been walking along the Rue de Rivoli one evening, when he had come across a young scamp of sixteen or so, a peaky-faced, sharp-eyed child, as attractive in his way as any girl. He was sucking hard at a cigarette, the paper of which had burst where bits of the coarse tobacco were poking through. Cursing away, the boy was striking kitchen matches on his thigh; not one of them would light and soon he had used them all up. Catching sight of Des Esseintes, who was standing watching him, he came up, touched his cap, and politely asked for a light. Des Esseintes offered him some of his own scented Dubèques, got into conversation with the boy, and persuaded him to tell the story of his life.

Nothing could have been more banal: his name was Auguste Langlois, he worked for a cardboard-manufacturer, he had lost his mother, and his father beat him black and blue.

Des Esseintes listened thoughtfully.

'Come and have a drink,' he said, and took him to a café where he regaled him with a few glasses of heady punch. These the boy drank without a word.

'Look here,' said Des Esseintes suddenly; 'how would you like a bit of fun tonight? I'll foot the bill, of course.' And he had taken the youngster off to an establishment on the third floor of a house in the Rue Mosnier, where a certain Madame Laure kept an assortment of pretty girls in a series of crimson cubicles furnished with circular mirrors, couches, and wash-basins.

There a wonderstruck Auguste, twisting his cap in his hands, had stood gaping at a battalion of women whose painted mouths opened all together to exclaim:

'What a duck! Isn't he sweet!'

'But dearie, you're not old enough,' said a big brunette, a girl with prominent eyes and a hook nose who occupied at Madame Laure's the indispensable position of the handsome Jewess.

Meanwhile Des Esseintes, who was obviously quite at home in this place, had made himself comfortable and was quietly chatting with the mistress of the house. But he broke off for a moment to speak to the boy.

'Don't be so scared, stupid,' he said. 'Go on, take your pick – remember this is on me.'

He gave a gentle push to the lad, who flopped on to a divan between two of the women. At a sign from Madame Laure, they drew a little closer together, covering Auguste's knees with their peignoirs and cuddling up to him so that he breathed in the warm, heady scent of their powdered shoulders. He was sitting quite still now, flushed and dry-mouthed, his downcast eyes darting from under their lashes inquisitive glances that were all directed at the upper part of the girls' thighs.

Vanda, the handsome Jewess, suddenly gave him a kiss and a little good advice, telling him to do whatever his parents told him, while all the time her hands were wandering over the boy's body; his expression changed and he lay back in a kind of swoon, with his head on her breast.

'So it's not on your own account that you've come here tonight,' said Madame Laure to Des Esseintes. 'But where the devil did you get hold of that baby?' she added, as Auguste disappeared with the handsome Jewess.

'Why, in the street, my dear.'

'But you're not tight,' muttered the old lady. Then, after a moment's thought, she gave an understanding, motherly smile.

'Ah, now I see! You rascal, so you like 'em young, do you?'

Des Esseintes shrugged his shoulders.

'No, you're wide of the mark there,' he said; 'very wide of the mark. The truth is that I'm simply trying to make a murderer of the boy. See if you can follow my line of argument. The lad's a virgin and he's reached the age where the blood starts coming to the boil. He could, of course, just run after the little girls of his neighbourhood, stay decent and still have his bit of fun, enjoy his little share of the tedious happiness open to the poor. But by bringing him here, by plunging him into luxury such as he's never known and will never forget, and by giving him the same treat every fortnight, I hope to get him into the habit of these pleasures which he can't afford. Assuming that it will take three months for them to become absolutely indispensable to him – and by spacing them out as I do, I avoid the risk of jading his appetite – well, at the end of those three months, I stop the little allowance I'm going to pay you in advance for being nice to the boy. And to get the money to pay for his visits here, he'll turn burglar, he'll do anything if it helps him on to one of your divans in one of your gaslit rooms.

'Looking on the bright side of things, I hope that, one fine day, he'll kill the gentleman who turns up unexpectedly just as he's breaking open his desk. On that day my object will be achieved: I shall have contributed, to the best of my ability, to the making of a scoundrel, one enemy the more for the hideous society which is bleeding us white.'

The woman gazed at him with open-eyed amazement.

'Ah, there you are!' he exclaimed, as he caught sight of Auguste sneaking back into the room, all red and sheepish, and hiding behind his Jewess. 'Come on, my boy, it's getting late. Say good night to the ladies.'

Going downstairs, he explained to him that once a fortnight he could pay a visit to Madame Laure's without spending a sou. And then as they stood outside on the pavement, he looked the bewildered child in the face and said:

'We shan't see each other again. Hurry off home to your father, whose hand must be itching for work to do, and re-member this almost evangelic dictum: Do unto others as you would not have them do unto you.'

'Good night, sir.'

'One other thing. Whatever you do, show a little gratitude for what I've done for you, and let me know as soon as you can how you're getting on – preferably through the columns of the Police Gazette.'

Now, sitting by the fire and stirring the glowing embers, he muttered to himself:

'The little Judas! To think that I've never once seen his name in the papers! It's true, of course, that I haven't been able to play a close game, in that I couldn't guard against cer-tain obvious contingencies – the danger of old mother Laure swindling me, pocketing the money and not delivering the goods; the chance of one of the women taking a fancy to

Auguste, so that when his three months were up she let him have his fun on the nod; and even the possibility that the handsome Jewess's exotic vices had already scared the boy, who may have been too young and impatient to bear her slow preliminaries or enjoy her savage climaxes. So unless he's been up against the law since I came to Fontenay and stopped reading the papers, I've been diddled.'

He got to his feet and took a few turns round the room.

'That would be a pity, all the same,' he went on, 'because all I was doing was parabolizing secular instruction, allegorizing universal education, which is well on the way to turning everybody into a Langlois: instead of permanently and mercifully putting out the eyes of the poor, it does its best to force them wide open, so that they may see all around them lives of less merit and greater comfort, pleasures that are keener and more voluptuous, and therefore sweeter and more desirable.

'And the fact is,' he added, following this line of thought still further, 'the fact is that, pain being one of the consequences of education, in that it grows greater and sharper with the growth of ideas, it follows that the more we try to polish the minds and refine the nervous systems of the under-privileged, the more we shall be developing in their hearts the atrociously active germs of hatred and moral suffering.'

The lamps were smoking. He turned them up and looked at his watch. It was three o'clock in the morning. He lit a cigarette and gave himself up again to the perusal, interrupted by his dreaming, of the old Latin poem, *De Laude Castitatis*, written in the reign of Gondebald by Avitus, Metropolitan Bishop of Vienne.

VII

BEGINNING on the night when, for no apparent reason, he had conjured up the melancholy memory of Auguste Langlois, Des Esseintes lived his whole life over again.

He found he was now incapable of understanding a single word of the volumes he consulted; his very eyes stopped reading, and it seemed as if his mind, gorged with literature and art, refused to absorb any more.

He had to live on himself, to feed on his own substance, like those animals that lie torpid in a hole all winter. Solitude had acted on his brain like a narcotic, first exciting and stimulating him, then inducing a languor haunted by vague reveries, vitiating his plans, nullifying his intentions, leading a whole cavalcade of dreams to which he passively submitted, without even trying to get away.

The confused mass of reading and meditation on artistic themes that he had accumulated since he had been on his own like a barrage to hold back the current of old memories, had suddenly been carried away, and the flood was let loose, sweeping away the present and the future, submerging everything under the waters of the past, covering his mind with a great expanse of melancholy, on the surface of which there drifted, like ridiculous bits of flotsam, trivial episodes of his existence, absurdly insignificant incidents.

The book he happened to be holding would fall into his lap, and he would give himself up to a fearful and disgusted review of his dead life, the years pivoting round the memory of Auguste and Madame Laure as around a solid fact, a stake planted in the midst of swirling waters. What a time that had been! – a time of elegant parties, of race-meetings and card-games, of love-potions ordered in advance and served punctually on the stroke of midnight in his pink boudoir! Faces, looks, meaningless words came back to him with the haunting persistence of those popular tunes you suddenly find yourself humming and just as suddenly and unconsciously you forget.

This phase lasted only a little while and then his memory took a siesta. He took advantage of this respite to immerse himself once more in his Latin studies, in the hope of effacing every sign, every trace of these recollections. But it was too late to call a halt; a second phase followed almost immediately on the first, a phase dominated by memories of his youth, and particularly the years he had spent with the Jesuit Fathers.

These memories were of a more distant period, yet they were clearer than the others, engraved more deeply and enduringly in his mind; the thickly wooded park, the long paths, the flower-beds, the benches – all the material details were conjured up before him.

Then the gardens filled up, and he heard the shouting of the boys at play, and the laughter of their masters as they joined in, playing tennis with their cassocks hitched up in front, or else chatting with their pupils under the trees without the slightest affectation or pomposity, just as if they were talking to friends of their own age.

He recalled that paternal discipline which deprecated any form of punishment, declined to inflict impositions of five hundred or a thousand lines, was content with having unsatisfactory work done over again while the others were at recreation, resorted more often than not to a mere reprimand, and kept the child under active but affectionate surveillance, forever trying to please him, agreeing to whatever walks he suggested on Wednesday afternoons, seizing the opportunity afforded by all the minor feast-days of the Church to add cakes and wine to the ordinary bill of fare or to organize a picnic in the country – a discipline which consisted of reasoning with the pupil instead of brutalizing him, already treating him like a grown man yet still coddling him like a spoilt child.

In this way the Fathers managed to gain a real hold upon their pupils, to mould to some extent the minds they cultivated, to guide them in certain specific directions, to inculcate particular notions, and to ensure the desired development of their ideas by means of an insinuating, ingratiating technique which they continued to apply in after-years, doing their best to keep track of their charges in adult life, backing them up in their careers, and writing them affectionate letters such as the Dominican Lacordaire wrote to his former pupils at Sorrèze.

Des Esseintes was well aware of the sort of conditioning to which he had been subjected, but he felt sure that in his case it had been without effect. In the first place, his captious and inquisitive character, his refractory and disputatious nature had saved him from being moulded by the good Fathers' discipline or indoctrinated by their lessons. Then, once he had left school, his scepticism had grown more acute; his experience of the narrow-minded intolerance of Legitimist society, and his conversations with unintelligent churchwardens and uncouth priests whose blunders tore away the veil the Jesuits had so cunningly woven, had still further fortified his spirit of independence and increased his distrust of any and every form of religious belief.

He considered, in fact, that he had shaken off all his old ties and fetters, and that he differed from the products of *lycées* and lay boarding-schools in only one respect, namely that he retained pleasant memories of his school and his schoolmasters. And yet, now that he examined his conscience, he began to wonder whether the seed which had fallen on apparently barren ground was not showing signs of germinating.

As a matter of fact, for some days he had been in an indescribably peculiar state of mind. For a brief instant he would believe, and turn instinctively to religion; then, after a moment's thought, his longing for faith would vanish, though he remained perplexed and uneasy.

Yet he was well aware, on looking into his heart, that he could never feel the humility and contrition of a true Christian; he knew beyond all doubt that the moment of which Lacordaire speaks, that moment of grace 'when the last ray of light enters the soul and draws together to a common centre all the truths that lie scattered therein', would never come for him. He felt nothing of that hunger for mortification and prayer without which, if we are to believe the majority of priests, no conversion is possible; nor did he feel any desire to

86

invoke a God whose mercy struck him as extremely problematical. At the same time the affection he still had for his old masters led him to take an interest in their works and doctrines; and the recollection of those inimitable accents of conviction, the passionate voices of those highly intelligent men, made him doubt the quality and strength of his own intellect. The lonely existence he was leading, with no fresh food for thought, no novel experiences, no replenishment of ideas, no exchange of impressions received from the outside world, from mixing with other people and sharing in their life, this unnatural isolation which he stubbornly maintained, encouraged the re-emergence in the form of irritating problems of all manner of questions he had disregarded when he was living in Paris.

Reading the Latin works he loved, works almost all written by bishops and monks, had doubtless done something to bring on this crisis. Steeped in a monastic atmosphere and intoxicated by the fumes of incense, he had become over-excited, and by a natural association of ideas, these books had ended up by driving back the recollections of his life as a young man and bringing out his memories of the years he had spent as a boy with the Jesuit Fathers.

'There's no doubt about it,' Des Esseintes said to himself, after a searching attempt to discover how the Jesuit element had worked its way to the surface at Fontenay; 'ever since boyhood, and without my knowing it, I've had this leaven inside me, ready to ferment; the taste I've always had for religious objects may be proof of this.'

However, he tried his hardest to persuade himself of the contrary, annoyed at finding that he was no longer master in his own house. Hunting for more acceptable explanations of his ecclesiastical predilections, he told himself he had been obliged to turn to the Church, in that the Church was the only body to have preserved the art of past centuries, the lost beauty of the ages. She had kept unchanged, even in shoddy modern reproductions, the goldsmiths' traditional forms; preserved the charm of chalices as slender as petunias, of pyxes simply and exquisitely styled; retained, even in aluminium, in fake enamel, in coloured glass, the grace of the patterns of olden days. Indeed, most of the precious objects which were kept in the Cluny Museum, and which by some miracle had escaped the bestial savagery of the sansculottes, came from the old abbeys of France. Just as in the Middle Ages the Church saved philosophy, history, and literature from barbarism, so she had safeguarded the plastic arts and brought down to modern times those marvellous examples of costume and jewellery which present-day ecclesiastical furnishers did their best to spoil, though they could never quite succeed in destroying the original qualities of form and style. There was therefore no cause for surprise in the fact that he had hunted eagerly for these antique curios, and that like many another collector he had bought relics of this sort from Paris antiquaries and country dealers.

But however much he dwelt on these motives, he could not quite manage to convince himself. It was true that, after careful thought, he still regarded the Christian religion as a superb legend, a magnificent imposture; and yet, in spite of all his excuses and explanations, his scepticism was beginning to crack.

Odd as it might seem, the fact remained that he was not as self-confident now as in his youth, when the Jesuits' supervision had been direct and their teaching inescapable, when he had been entirely in their hands, belonging to them body and soul, without any family ties or outside influences to counteract their ascendancy. What is more, they had implanted in him a certain taste for things supernatural which had slowly and imperceptibly taken root in his soul, was now blossoming out in these secluded conditions, and was inevitably having an effect on his silent mind, tied to the treadmill of certain fixed ideas.

By dint of examining his thought-processes, of trying to join together the threads of his ideas and trace them back to their sources, he came to the conclusion that his activities in the course of his social life had all originated in the education he had received. Thus his penchant for artificiality and his love of eccentricity could surely be explained as the results of sophistical studies, super-terrestrial subtleties, semi-theological speculations; fundamentally, they were ardent aspirations towards an ideal, towards an unknown universe, towards a distant beatitude, as utterly desirable as that promised by the Scriptures.

He pulled himself up short, and broke this chain of reflections.

'Come, now,' he told himself angrily. 'I've got it worse than I thought: here I am arguing with myself like a casuist.'

He remained pensive, troubled by a nagging fear. Obviously, if Lacordaire's theory was correct, he had nothing to worry about, seeing that the magic of conversion was not worked at a single stroke; to produce the explosion the ground had to be patiently and thoroughly mined. But if the novelists talked about love at first sight, there were also a number of theologians who spoke of conversion as of something equally sudden and overwhelming. Supposing that they were right, it followed that nobody could be sure he would never succumb. There was no longer any point in practising self-analysis, paying attention to presentiments or taking preventive measures: the psychology of mysticism was non-existent. Things happened because they happened, and that was the end of it.

'Dammit, I'm going crazy,' Des Esseintes said to himself. 'My dread of the disease will bring on the disease itself if I keep this up.'

He managed to shake off this fear to some extent, and his memories of boyhood faded away; but other morbid symptoms supervened. Now it was the subjects of theological disputations that haunted him to the exclusion of everything else. The school garden, the lessons, the Jesuits might never have been, his mind was so completely dominated by abstractions; in spite of himself, he began pondering over some of the contradictory interpretations of dogma and the long-forgotten apostasies recorded in Father Labbe's work on the Councils of the Church. Odd scraps of these schisms and heresies, which for centuries had divided the Western and Eastern Churches, came back to mind. Here, for instance, was

Nestorius denying Mary's right to the title of Mother of God because, in the mystery of the Incarnation, it was not the God but the man she had carried in her womb; and there was Eutyches maintaining that Christ could not have looked like other men, since the Godhead had elected domicile in his body and had thereby changed his nature utterly and completely. Then there were some other quibblers asserting that the Redeemer had had no body at all and that references to his body in the Holy Books should be understood figuratively; Tertullian could be heard positing his famous quasi-materialistic axiom: 'Anything which lacks a body does not exist; everything which exists has a body of its own'; and finally that hoary old question debated year after year came up again: 'Was Christ alone nailed to the cross, or did the Trinity, one in three persons, suffer in its triple hypostasis on the gibbet of Calvary?' All these problems teased and tormented him; and automatically, as if he were repeating a lesson he had learnt by heart, he kept asking himself the questions and responding with the answers.

For several days in succession, his brain was a seething mass of paradoxes and sophisms, a tangle of split hairs, a maze of rules as complicated as the clauses of a law, open to every conceivable interpretation and every kind of quibble, and leading up to a system of celestial jurisprudence of positively baroque subtlety. Then these abstract obsessions left him, and a whole series of plastic impressions took their place, under the influence of the Gustave Moreau pictures hanging on the walls.

He saw a procession of prelates passing before his eyes, a line of archimandrites and patriarchs lifting their golden arms to bless the kneeling multitudes, or wagging their white beards as they read or prayed aloud; he saw silent penitents filing into crypts; he saw great cathedrals rising up with white-robed monks thundering from their pulpits. Just as De Quincey, after a dose of opium, had only to hear the words 'Consul Romanus' to conjure up whole pages of Livy, to see the consuls coming forward in solemn procession or witness the Roman legions moving off in pompous array, so Des

Esseintes would be left gasping with amazement as some theological expression evoked visions of surging multitudes and episcopal figures silhouetted against the fiery windows of their basilicas. Apparitions like these kept him entranced, hurrying in imagination from age to age, and coming down at last to the religious ceremonies of modern times, to the accompaniment of endless waves of music, mournful and tender.

Here there was no longer any room for argument or discussion; there was no denying that he had an indefinable feeling of veneration and fear, that his artistic sense was subjugated by the nicely calculated scenes of Catholic ceremonial. His nerves shuddered at these memories, and then, in a sudden mood of revolt, a swift volte-face, ideas of monstrous depravity came to him – thoughts of the profanities foreseen in the Confessors' Manual, of the impure and ignominious ways in which holy water and consecrated oil could be abused. An omnipotent God was now confronted by the upright figure of a powerful adversary, the Devil; and it seemed to Des Esseintes that a frightful glory must result from any crime committed in open church by a believer filled with dreadful merriment and sadistic joy, bent on blasphemy, resolved to desecrate and befoul the objects of veneration. The mad rites of magical ceremonies, black masses, and witches' sabbaths, together with the horrors of demonic possession and exorcism, were enacted before his mind's eye; and he began to wonder if he were not guilty of sacrilege in possessing articles which had once been solemnly consecrated, such as altar cards, chasubles, and custodials. This idea, that he was possibly living in a state of sin, filled him with a certain pride and satisfaction, not unmixed with delight in these sacrilegious acts – which might not be sacrilegious at all, and in any case were not very serious offences, seeing that he really loved these articles and did not put them to any depraved uses. He beguiled himself in this way with prudent, cowardly thoughts, the uncertainty of his soul preventing him from perpetrating overt crimes, robbing him of the necessary courage to commit real sins of real iniquity with real intent.

Eventually, little by little, this casuistic spirit left him. He then looked out, as it were, from the summit of his mind, over the panorama of the Church and her hereditary influence on humanity down the ages; he pictured her to himself in all her melancholy grandeur, proclaiming to mankind the horror of life, the inclemency of fate; preaching patience, contrition, the spirit of self-sacrifice; endeavouring to salve the sores of men by pointing to the bleeding wounds of Christ; guaranteeing divine privileges and promising the better part of paradise to the afflicted; exhorting the human creature to suffer, to offer to God as a holocaust his tribulations and his offences, his vicissitudes and his sorrows. He saw her become truly eloquent, speaking words full of sympathy for the poor, full of pity for the oppressed, full of menace for tyrants and oppressors.

At this point, Des Esseintes found his footing again. It is true that this admission of social corruption had his entire approval, but on the other hand, his mind revolted against the vague remedy of hope in a future life. Schopenhauer, in his opinion, came nearer to the truth. His doctrine and the Church's started from a common point of view; he too took his stand on the iniquity and rottenness of the world; he too cried out in anguish with the *Imitation of Christ*: 'Verily it is a pitiful thing to live on earth!' He too preached the nullity of existence, the advantages of solitude, and warned humanity that whatever it did, whichever way it turned, it would always remain unhappy – the poor because of the sufferings born of privation, the rich because of the unconquerable boredom engendered by abundance. The difference between them was that he offered you no panacea, beguiled you with no promises of a cure for your inevitable ills.

He did not drum into your ears the revolting dogma of original sin; he did not try to convince you of the superlative goodness of a God who protects the wicked, helps the foolish, crushes the young, brutalizes the old, and chastises the innocent; he did not extol the benefits of a Providence which has invented the useless, unjust, incomprehensible, and inept abomination that is physical pain. Indeed, far from endeavouring, like the Church, to justify the necessity of trials and torments, he exclaimed in his compassionate indignation: 'If a God has made this world, I should hate to be that God, for the misery of the world would break my heart.'

Yes, it was undoubtedly Schopenhauer who was in the right. What, in fact, were all the evangelical pharmacopoeias compared with his treatises on spiritual hygiene? He claimed no cures, offered the sick no compensation, no hope; but when all was said and done, his theory of Pessimism was the great comforter of superior minds and lofty souls; it revealed society as it was, insisted on the innate stupidity of women, pointed out the pitfalls of life, saved you from disillusionment by teaching you to expect as little as possible, to expect nothing at all if you were sufficiently strong-willed, indeed, to consider yourself lucky if you were not constantly visited by some unforeseen calamity.

Setting off from the same starting-point as the *Imitation*, but without losing itself in mysterious mazes and unlikely by-paths, this theory reached the same conclusion, an attitude of resignation and drift.

However, if this resignation, frankly based on the recognition of a deplorable state of affairs and the impossibility of effecting any change, was accessible to the rich in intellect, that made it all the more difficult of attainment for the poor, whose clamorous wrath was more easily appeased by the kindly voice of religion.

These reflections took a load off Des Esseintes' mind; the great German's aphorisms calmed the tumult of his thoughts, while at the same time the points of contact between the two doctrines helped each to remind him of the other. Nor could he forget the poetic and poignant atmosphere of Catholicism in which he had been steeped as a boy, and whose essence he had absorbed through every pore.

These recurrences of belief, these fearful intimations of faith had been troubling him more particularly since his health had begun to deteriorate; they coincided with certain nervous disorders that had recently arisen.

Ever since his earliest childhood, he had been tormented by inexplicable revulsions, by shuddering fits which chilled him to the marrow and set his teeth on edge whenever, for instance, he saw a maid wringing out some wet linen. These instinctive reactions had continued down the years, and to this day it still caused him real suffering to hear a piece of stuff being torn in two, to rub his finger over a bit of chalk, to feel the surface of watered silk.

The excesses of his bachelor days and the abnormal strains put on his brain had aggravated his neurosis to an astonishing degree and still further diluted the impoverished blood of his race. In Paris he had been obliged to have hydropathic treatment for trembling of the hands and for atrocious neuralgic pains that seemed to cut his face in two, hammered away at his temples, stabbed at his eyelids, and brought on fits of nausea he could only overcome by lying flat on his back in the dark.

These troubles had gradually disappeared, thanks to the steadier, quieter life he was leading; but now they were coming back in a different form and affecting every part of his body. The pains left his head to attack his stomach, which was hard and swollen, searing his innards with a red-hot iron and stimulating his bowels to no effect. Then a nervous cough, a dry, racking cough, always beginning at the same time and lasting precisely the same number of minutes, woke him as he lay in his bed, seizing him by the throat and nearly choking him. Finally he lost his appetite completely; the hot, gassy fires of heartburn flared up inside his body; he felt swollen and stifled, and could not bear the constriction of trouser-buttons or waistcoat-buckles after a meal.

He gave up drinking spirits, coffee, and tea, put himself on a milk diet, tried applying cold water to his body, stuffed himself with asafoetida, valerian, and quinine. He even went so far as to leave the house and go for strolls in the country, where the rainy weather had established peace and quiet, forcing himself to keep walking and take exercise. As a last resort, he laid aside his books for the time being; and the result was such surpassing boredom that he decided to occupy the idle hours with carrying out a project he had put off time and again since coming to Fontenay, partly out of laziness and partly out of dislike of the trouble involved.

No longer able to intoxicate himself afresh with the magical charms of style, to thrill to the delicious sorcery of the unusual epithet which, while retaining all its precision, opens up infinite perspectives to the imagination of the initiate, he made up his mind to complete the interior decoration of his thebaid by filling it with costly hothouse flowers, and so provide himself with a material occupation that would distract his thoughts, soothe his nerves, and rest his brain. He also hoped that the sight of their strange and splendid colours would compensate him to some extent for the loss of those real or fancied nuances of style which, on account of his literary dieting, he would now have to forget for a little while or for ever.

VIII

DES ESSEINTES had always been excessively fond of flowers,
but this passion of his, which at Jutigny had originally
embraced all flowers without distinction of species or genus,
had finally become more discriminating, limiting itself to
a single caste.

For a long time now he had despised the common, everyday varieties that blossom on the Paris market-stalls, in wet
flower-pots, under green awnings or red umbrellas.

At the same time that his literary tastes and artistic preferences had become more refined, recognizing only such works
as had been sifted and distilled by subtle and tormented minds,
and at the same time that his distaste for accepted ideas had
hardened into disgust, his love of flowers had rid itself of
its residuum, its lees, had been clarified, so to speak, and
purified.

It amused him to liken a horticulturist's shop to a micro-
cosm in which every social category and class was represented – poor, vulgar slum-flowers, the gilliflower for instance,
that are really at home only on the window-sill of a garret,
with their roots squeezed into milk-cans or old earthenware
pots; then pretentious, conventional, stupid flowers such as
the rose, whose proper place is in pots concealed inside porcelain vases painted by nice young ladies; and lastly, flowers of
charm and tremulous delicacy, exotic flowers exiled to Paris
and kept warm in palaces of glass, princesses of the vegetable
kingdom, living aloof and apart, having nothing whatever in
common with the popular plants or the bourgeois blooms.

Now, he could not help feeling a certain interest, a certain
pity for the lower-class flowers, wilting in the slums under the
foul breath of sewers and sinks; on the other hand, he loathed
those that go with the cream-and-gold drawing-rooms in new
houses; he kept his admiration, in fact, for the rare and aristocratic plants from distant lands, kept alive with cunning

attention in artificial tropics created by carefully regulated stoves.

But this deliberate choice he had made of hothouse flowers had itself been modified under the influence of his general ideas, of the definite conclusions he had now arrived at on all matters. In former days, in Paris, his inborn taste for the artificial had led him to neglect the real flower for its copy, faithfully and almost miraculously executed in indiarubber and wire, calico and taffeta, paper and velvet.

As a result, he possessed a wonderful collection of tropical plants, fashioned by the hands of true artists, following Nature step by step, repeating her processes, taking the flower from its birth, leading it to maturity, imitating it even to its death, noting the most indefinable nuances, the most fleeting aspects of its awakening or its sleep, observing the pose of its petals, blown back by the wind or crumpled up by the rain, sprinkling its unfolding corolla with dewdrops of gum, and adapting its appearance to the time of year – in full bloom when branches are bent under the weight of sap, or with a shrivelled cupula and a withered stem when petals are dropping off and leaves are falling.

This admirable artistry had long enthralled him, but now he dreamt of collecting another kind of flora: tired of artificial flowers aping real ones, he wanted some natural flowers that would look like fakes.

He applied his mind to this problem, but did not have to search for long or go far afield, seeing that his house was in the very heart of the district which had attracted all the great flower-growers. He went straight off to visit the hothouses of Châtillon and the valley of Aunay, coming home tired out and cleaned out, wonder-struck at the floral follies he had seen, thinking of nothing but the varieties he had bought, haunted all the while by memories of bizarre and magnificent blooms.

Two days later the waggons arrived. List in hand, Des Esseintes called the roll, checking his purchases one by one.

First of all the gardeners unloaded from their carts a collection of Caladiums, whose swollen, hairy stems supported

97

huge heart-shaped leaves; though they kept a general air of kinship, no two of them were alike.

There were some remarkable specimens – some a pinkish colour like the Virginale, which seemed to have been cut out of oilskin or sticking-plaster; some all white like the Albane, which looked as if it had been fashioned out of the pleura of an ox or the diaphanous bladder of a pig. Others, especially the one called Madame Mame, seemed to be simulating zinc, parodying bits of punched metal coloured emperor green and spattered with drops of oil-paint, streaks of red lead and white. Here, there were plants like the Bosphorus giving the illusion of starched calico spotted with crimson and myrtle green; there, others such as the Aurora Borealis flaunted leaves the colour of raw meat, with dark-red ribs and purplish fibrils, puffy leaves that seemed to be sweating blood and wine.

Between them, the Albane and Aurora Borealis represented the two temperamental extremes, apoplexy and chlorosis, in this particular family of plants.

The gardeners brought in still more varieties, this time affecting the appearance of a factitious skin covered with a network of counterfeit veins. Most of them, as if ravaged by syphilis or leprosy, displayed livid patches of flesh mottled with roseola, damasked with dartre; others had the bright pink colour of a scar that is healing or the brown tint of a scab that is forming; others seemed to have been puffed up by cauteries, blistered by burns; others again revealed hairy surfaces pitted with ulcers and embossed with chancres; and last of all there were some which appeared to be covered with dressings of various sorts, coated with black mercurial lard, plastered with green belladonna ointment, dusted over with the yellow flakes of iodoform powder.

Gathered together, these sickly blooms struck Des Esseintes as even more monstrous than when he had first come upon them, mixed up with others like hospital patients inside the glass walls of their conservatory wards.

'Sapristi!' he exclaimed, in an access of enthusiasm.

Another plant, of a type similar to the Caladiums, the *Alocasia Metallica*, roused him to still greater admiration.

Covered with a coat of greenish bronze shot with glints of silver, it was the supreme masterpiece of artifice; anyone would have taken it for a bit of stove-pipe cut into a pike-head pattern by the makers.

Next the men unloaded several bunches of lozenge-shaped leaves, bottle-green in colour; from the midst of each bunch rose a stiff stem on top of which trembled a great ace of hearts, as glossy as a pepper; and then, as if in defiance of all the familiar aspects of plant life, there sprang from the middle of this bright vermilion heart a fleshy, downy tail, all white and yellow, straight in some cases, corkscrewing above the heart like a pig's tail in others.

This was the Anthurium, an aroid recently imported from Colombia; it belonged to a section of the same family as a certain Amorphophallus, a plant from Cochin-China with leaves the shape of fish-slices and long black stalks crisscrossed with scars like the limbs of a negro slave.

Des Esseintes could scarcely contain himself for joy.

Now they were getting a fresh batch of monstrosities down from the carts – the Echinopsis, thrusting its ghastly pink blossoms out of cotton-wool compresses, like the stumps of amputated limbs; the Nidularium, opening its sword-shaped petals to reveal gaping flesh-wounds; the *Tillandsia Lindeni*, trailing its jagged plough-shares the colour of wine-must; and the Cypripedium, with its complex, incoherent contours devised by some demented draughtsman. It looked rather like a clog or a tidy, and on top was a human tongue bent back with the string stretched tight, just as you may see it depicted in the plates of medical works dealing with diseases of the throat and mouth; two little wings, of a jujube red, which might almost have been borrowed from a child's toy windmill, completed this baroque combination of the underside of a tongue, the colour of wine lees and slate, and a glossy pocket-case with a lining that oozed drops of viscous paste.

He could not take his eyes off this unlikely-looking orchid from India, and the gardeners, irritated by all these delays, began reading out themselves the labels stuck in the pots they were bringing in.

Des Esseintes watched them open-mouthed, listening in amazement to the forbidding names of the various herbaceous plants – the *Encephalartos horridus*, a gigantic artichoke, an iron spike painted a rust colour, like the ones they put on park gates to keep trespassers from climbing over; the *Cocos Micania*, a sort of palm-tree, with a slim, indented stem, surrounded on all sides with tall leaves like paddles and oars; the *Zamia Lehmanni*, a huge pineapple, a monumental Cheshire cheese stuck in heath-mould and bristling on top with barbed javelins and native arrows; and the *Cibotium Spectabile*, challenging comparison with the weirdest nightmare and outdoing even its congeners in the craziness of its formation, with an enormous orang-outang's tail poking out of a cluster of palm-leaves – a brown, hairy tail twisted at the tip into the shape of a bishop's crozier.

But he did not linger over these plants, as he was waiting impatiently for the series which particularly fascinated him, those vegetable ghouls the carnivorous plants – the downy-rimmed Fly-trap of the Antilles, with its digestive secretions and its curved spikes that interlock to form a grille over any insect it imprisons; the Drosera of the peat-bogs, flaunting a set of glandulous hairs; the Sarracena and the Cephalothus, opening voracious gullets capable of consuming and digesting whole chunks of meat; and finally the Nepenthes, which in shape and form passes all the bounds of eccentricity.

With unwearying delight he turned in his hands the pot in which this floral extravaganza was quivering. It resembled the gum-tree in its long leaves of a dark, metallic green; but from the end of each leaf there hung a green string, an umbilical cord carrying a greenish-coloured pitcher dappled with purple markings, a sort of German pipe in porcelain, a peculiar kind of bird's nest that swayed gently to and fro, displaying an interior carpeted with hairs.

'That really is a beauty,' murmured Des Esseintes.

But he had to cut short his display of pleasure, for now the gardeners, in a hurry to get away, were rapidly unloading the last of their plants, jumbling up tuberous Begonias and black Crotons flecked with spots of red lead like old iron.

Then he noticed that there was still one name left on his list, the Cattleya of New Granada. They pointed out to him a little winged bell-flower of a pale lilac, an almost imperceptible mauve; he went up, put his nose to it, and started back – for it gave out a smell of varnished deal, a toy-box smell that brought back horrid memories of New Year's Day when he was a child. He decided he had better be wary of it, and almost regretted having admitted among all the scentless plants he possessed this orchid with its unpleasantly reminiscent odour.

Once he was alone again, he surveyed the great tide of vegetation that had flooded into his entrance-hall, the various species all intermingling, crossing swords, creeses, or spears with one another, forming a mass of green weapons, over which floated, like barbarian battle-flags, flowers of crude and dazzling colours.

The air in the room was getting purer, and soon, in a dark corner, down by the floor, a soft white light appeared. He went up to it and discovered that it came from a clump of Rhizomorphs which, as they breathed, shone like tiny night-lights.

'These plants are really astounding,' he said to himself, stepping back to appraise the entire collection. Yes, his object had been achieved: not one of them looked real; it was as if cloth, paper, porcelain, and metal had been lent by man to Nature to enable her to create these monstrosities. Where she had not found it possible to imitate the work of human hands, she had been reduced to copying the membranes of animals' organs, to borrowing the vivid tints of their rotting flesh, the hideous splendours of their gangrened skin.

'It all comes down to syphilis in the end,' Des Esseintes reflected, as his gaze was drawn and held by the horrible markings of the Caladiums, over which a shaft of daylight was playing. And he had a sudden vision of the unceasing torments inflicted on humanity by the virus of distant ages. Ever since the beginning of the world, from generation to generation, all living creatures had handed down the inexhaustible heritage, the everlasting disease that ravaged the ancestors of man and even ate into the bones of the old fossils that were being dug up at the present time.

Without ever abating, it had travelled down the ages, still raging to this day in the form of surreptitious pains, in the disguise of headaches or bronchitis, hysteria or gout. From time to time it came to the surface, generally singling out for attack ill-to-do, ill-fed people, breaking out in spots like pieces of gold, ironically crowning the poor devils with an almeh's diadem of sequins, adding insult to injury by stamping their skin with the very symbol of wealth and well-being.

And now here it was again, reappearing in all its pristine splendour on the brightly coloured leaves of these plants!

'It is true,' continued Des Esseintes, going back to the starting point of his argument, 'it is true that most of the time Nature is incapable of producing such depraved, unhealthy species alone and unaided; she supplies the raw materials, the seed and the soil, the nourishing womb and the elements of the plant, which man rears, shapes, paints, and carves afterwards to suit his fancy.

'Stubborn, muddle-headed, and narrow-minded though she is, she has at last submitted, and her master has succeeded in changing the soil components by means of chemical reactions, in utilizing slowly matured combinations, carefully elaborated crossings, in employing cuttings and graftings skilfully and methodically, so that now he can make her put forth blossoms of different colours on the same branch, invents new hues for her, and modifies at will the age-old shapes of her plants. In short, he rough-hews her blocks of stone, finishes off her sketches, signs them with his stamp, impresses on them his artistic hall-mark.

'There's no denying it,' he concluded; 'in the course of a few years man can operate a selection which easy-going Nature could not conceivably make in less than a few centuries; without the shadow of a doubt, the horticulturists are the only true artists left to us nowadays.'

He was a little tired and felt stifled in this hothouse atmosphere; all the outings he had had in the last few days had exhausted him; the transition between the immobility of a sequestered life and the activity of an outdoor existence had been too sudden. He left the hall and went to lie down on his bed; but, engrossed in a single subject, as if wound up by a spring, his mind went on paying out its chain even in sleep, and he soon fell victim to the sombre fantasies of a nightmare.

He was walking along the middle of a path through a forest at dusk, beside a woman he had never met, never even seen before. She was tall and thin, with tow-like hair, a bulldog face, freckled cheeks, irregular teeth projecting under a snub nose; she was wearing a maid's white apron, a long scarlet kerchief draped across her breast, a Prussian soldier's half-boots, a black bonnet trimmed with ruches and a cabbage-bow.

She looked rather like a booth-keeper at a fair, or a member of some travelling circus.

He asked himself who this woman was whom he felt to have been deeply and intimately associated with his life for a long time, and he tried to remember her origins, her name, her occupation, her significance – but all in vain, for no recollection came to him of this inexplicable yet undeniable liaison.

He was still searching his memory when suddenly a strange figure appeared before them on horseback, went ahead for a minute at a gentle trot, then turned round in the saddle.

His blood froze and he stood rooted to the spot in utter horror. The rider was an equivocal, sexless creature with a green skin and terrifying eyes of a cold, clear blue shining out from under purple lids; there were pustules all round its mouth; two amazingly thin arms, like the arms of a skeleton, bare to the elbows and shaking with fever, projected from its ragged sleeves, and its fleshless thighs twitched and shuddered in jack-boots that were far too wide for them.

Its awful gaze was fixed on Des Esseintes, piercing him, freezing him to the marrow, while the bulldog woman, even more terrified than he was, clung to him and howled blue murder, her head thrown back and her neck rigid.

At once he understood the meaning of the dreadful vision. He had before his eyes the image of the Pox.

Utterly panic-stricken, beside himself with fear, he dashed down a side path and ran for dear life until he got to a summer-house standing on the left among some laburnums. Safely inside, he dropped into a chair in the passage.

A few moments later, just as he was beginning to get his breath back, the sound of sobbing made him look up. The bull-dog woman stood before him, a grotesque and pitiful sight. She was weeping bitterly, complaining that she had lost her teeth in her flight, and, taking a number of clay pipes out of her apron pocket, she proceeded to smash them up and stuff bits of the white stems into the holes in her gums.

'But she's mad!' Des Esseintes said to himself; 'those bits of stem will never hold' – and, true enough, they all came dropping out of her jaws, one after the other.

At that moment a galloping horse was heard approaching. Terror seized Des Esseintes and his legs went limp under him. But as the sound of hoofs came nearer, despair stung him to action like the crack of a whip; he flung himself upon the woman, who was now stamping on the pipe bowls, begging her to be quiet and not to betray them both by the noise of her boots. She struggled furiously, and he had to drag her to the end of the passage, throttling her to stop her crying out. Then, all of a sudden, he noticed a tap-room door with green-painted shutters and saw that it was unlatched; he pushed it open, dashed through – and stopped dead.

In front of him, in the middle of a vast clearing, enormous white pierrots were jumping about like rabbits in the moonlight.

Tears of disappointment welled up in his eyes; he would never, no, never be able to cross the threshold of that door.

'I'd be trampled to death if I tried,' he told himself – and as if to confirm his fears, the number of giant pierrots kept increasing; their bounds now filled the whole horizon and the whole sky, so that they bumped alternately against heaven and earth with their heads and their heels.

Just then the sound of the horse's hoofs stopped. It was there in the passage, behind a little round window; more dead than alive, Des Esseintes turned round and saw through the circular opening two pricked ears, a set of yellow teeth, a pair of nostrils breathing twin jets of vapour that stank of phenol.

He sank to the ground, giving up all thought of resistance or flight; and he shut his eyes so as not to meet the dreadful gaze of the Pox, glaring at him from behind the wall, though even so he felt it forcing its way under his closed eyelids, gliding down his clammy back, and travelling over the whole of his body, the hairs of which stood on end in pools of cold sweat. He was prepared for almost anything to happen and even hoped for the *coup de grâce* to make an end of it all. What seemed like a century, and was probably a minute, went by; then he opened his eyes again with a shudder of apprehension.

Everything had vanished without warning; and like some transformation scene, some theatrical illusion, a hideous mineral landscape now lay before him, a wan, gullied landscape stretching away into the distance without a sign of life or movement. This desolate scene was bathed in light: a calm, white light, reminiscent of the glow of phosphorus dissolved in oil.

Suddenly, down on the ground, something stirred – something which took the form of an ashen-faced woman, naked but for a pair of green silk stockings.

He gazed at her inquisitively. Like horsehair crimped by over-hot irons, her hair was frizzy, with broken ends; two Nepenthes pitchers hung from her ears; tints of boiled veal showed in her half-opened nostrils. Her eyes gleaming ecstatically, she called to him in a low voice.

He had no time to answer, for already the woman was changing; glowing colours lit up her eyes; her lips took on the fierce red of the Anthuriums; the nipples of her bosom shone as brightly as two red peppers.

A sudden intuition came to him, and he told himself that this must be the Flower. His reasoning mania persisted even in this nightmare; and as in the daytime, it switched from vegetation to the Virus.

He now noticed the frightening irritation of the mouth and breasts, discovered on the skin of the body spots of bistre and copper, and recoiled in horror; but the woman's eyes fascinated him, and he went slowly towards her, trying to dig his heels into the ground to hold himself back, and falling over deliberately, only to pick himself up again and go on. He was almost touching her when black Amorphophalli sprang up on every side and stabbed at her belly, which was rising and falling like a sea. He thrust them aside and pushed them back, utterly nauseated by the sight of these hot, firm stems twisting and turning between his fingers. Then, all of a sudden, the odious plants had disappeared and two arms were trying to enfold him. An agony of fear set his heart pounding madly, for the eyes, the woman's awful eyes, had turned a clear, cold blue, quite terrible to see. He made a superhuman effort to free himself from her embrace, but with an irresistible movement she clutched him and held him, and pale with horror, he saw the savage Nidularium blossoming between her uplifted thighs, with its swordblades gaping open to expose the bloody depths.

His body almost touching the hideous flesh-wound of this plant, he felt life ebbing away from him – and awoke with a start, choking, frozen, crazy with fear.

'Thank God,' he sobbed, 'it was only a dream.'

IX

THESE nightmares recurred again and again, until he was afraid to go to sleep. He spent hours lying on his bed, sometimes the victim of persistent insomnia and feverish restlessness, at other times a prey to abominable dreams that were interrupted only when the dreamer was shocked into wakefulness by losing his footing, falling all the way downstairs, or plunging helplessly into the depths of an abyss.

His neurosis, which had been lulled to sleep for a few days, gained the upper hand again, showing itself more violent and more stubborn than ever, and taking on new forms.

Now it was the bedclothes that bothered him; he felt stifled under the sheets, his whole body tingled unpleasantly, his blood boiled and his legs itched. To these symptoms were soon added a dull aching of the jaws and a feeling as if his temples were being squeezed in a vice.

His anxiety and depression grew worse, and unfortunately the means of mastering this inexorable illness were lacking. He had tried to install a set of hydropathic appliances in his dressing-room, but without success: the impossibility of bringing water as high up the hill as his house, not to mention the difficulty of getting water in sufficient quantity in a village where the public fountains only produced a feeble trickle at fixed hours, thwarted this particular plan. Cheated of the jets of water which, shot at close range at the disks of his vertebral column, formed the only treatment capable of overcoming his insomnia and bringing back his peace of mind, he was reduced to brief aspersions in his bath or in his tub, mere cold affusions followed by an energetic rub-down that his valet gave him with a horse-hair glove.

But these substitute douches were far from checking the progress of his neurosis; at the very most they gave him a few hours' relief, and dear-bought relief at that, considering that his nervous troubles soon returned to the attack with renewed vigour and violence.

His boredom grew to infinite proportions. The pleasure he had felt in the possession of astonishing flowers was exhausted; their shapes and colours had already lost the power to excite him. Besides, in spite of all the care he lavished on them, most of his plants died; he had them removed from his rooms, but his irritability had reached such a pitch that he was exasperated by their absence and his eye continually offended by the empty spaces they had left.

To amuse himself and while away the interminable hours, he turned to his portfolios of prints and began sorting out his Goyas. The first states of certain plates of the *Caprices*, proof engravings recognizable by their reddish tone, which he had bought long ago in the sale-room at ransom prices, put him in a good humour again; and he forgot everything else as he followed the strange fancies of the artist, delighting in his breathtaking pictures of bandits and succubi, devils and dwarfs, witches riding on cats and women trying to pull out the dead man's teeth after a hanging.

Next, he went through all the other series of Goya's etchings and aquatints, his macabre *Proverbs*, his ferocious war-scenes, and finally his *Garrotting*, a plate of which he possessed a magnificent trial proof printed on thick, unsized paper, with the wire-marks clearly visible.

Goya's savage verve, his harsh, brutal genius, captivated Des Esseintes. On the other hand, the universal admiration his works had won rather put him off, and for years he had refrained from framing them, for fear that if he hung them up, the first idiot who saw them might feel obliged to dishonour them with a few inanities and go into stereotyped ecstasies over them.

He felt the same about his Rembrandts, which he examined now and then on the quiet; and it is of course true that, just as the loveliest melody in the world becomes unbearably vulgar once the public start humming it and the barrel-organs playing it, so the work of art that appeals to charlatans, endears itself to fools, and is not content to arouse the enthusiasm of a few connoisseurs, is thereby polluted in the eyes of the initiate and becomes commonplace, almost repulsive.

This sort of promiscuous admiration was in fact one of the most painful thorns in his flesh, for unaccountable vogues had utterly spoilt certain books and pictures for him that he had once held dear; confronted with the approbation of the mob, he always ended up by discovering some hitherto imperceptible blemish, and promptly rejected them, at the same time wondering whether his flair was not deserting him, his taste getting blunted.

He shut his portfolios and once more fell into a mood of splenetic indecision. To change the trend of his thoughts, he began a course of emollient reading; tried to cool his brain with some of the solanaceae of literature; read those books that are so charmingly adapted for convalescents and invalids, whom more tetanic or phosphatic works would only fatigue: the novels of Charles Dickens.

But the Englishman's works produced the opposite effect from what he had expected: his chaste lovers and his puritanical heroines in their all-concealing draperies, sharing ethereal passions and just fluttering their eyelashes, blushing coyly, weeping for joy and holding hands, drove him to distraction. This exaggerated virtue made him react in the contrary direction; by virtue of the law of contrasts, he jumped from one extreme to the other, recalled scenes of full-blooded, earthy passion, and thought of common amorous practices such as the hybrid kiss, or the columbine kiss as ecclesiastical modesty calls it, where the tongue is brought into play.

He put aside the book he was reading, put from him all thoughts of strait-laced Albion, and let his mind dwell on the salacious seasoning, the prurient peccadilloes of which the Church disapproves. Suddenly he felt an emotional disturbance; his sexual insensibility of brain and body, which he had supposed to be complete and absolute, was shattered. Solitude was again affecting his tortured nerves, but this time it was not religion that obsessed him but the naughty sins religion condemns. The habitual subject of its threats and obsecrations was now the only thing that tempted him; the carnal side of his nature, which had lain dormant for months, had first been disturbed by his reading of pious works, then roused to wakefulness in an attack of nerves brought on by the English writer's cant, and was now all attention. With his stimulated senses carrying him back down the years, he had soon begun wallowing in the memory of his old dissipations.

He got up, and with a certain sadness he opened a little silver-gilt box with a lid studded with aventurines.

This box was full of purple bonbons. He took one out and idly fingered it, thinking about the strange properties of these sweets with their frosty coating of sugar. In former days, when his impotency had been established beyond doubt and he could think of woman without bitterness, regret, or desire, he would place one of these bonbons on his tongue and let it melt; then, all of a sudden, and with infinite tenderness, he would be visited by dim, faded recollections of old debauches.

These bonbons, invented by Siraudin and known by the ridiculous name of 'Pearls of the Pyrenees', consisted of a drop of schoenanthus scent or female essence crystallized in pieces of sugar; they stimulated the papillae of the mouth, evoking memories of water opalescent with rare vinegars and lingering kisses fragrant with perfume.

Ordinarily he would smilingly drink in this amorous aroma, this shadow of former caresses which installed a little female nudity in a corner of his brain and revived for a second the savour of some woman, a savour he had once adored. But today the bonbons were no longer gentle in their effect and no longer confined themselves to evoking memories of distant, half-forgotten dissipations; on the contrary, they tore the veils down and thrust before his eyes the bodily reality in all its crudity and urgency.

Heading the procession of mistresses that the taste of the bonbon helped to define in detail was a woman who paused in front of him, a woman with long white teeth, a sharp nose, mouse-coloured eyes, and short-cropped yellow hair.

This was Miss Urania, an American girl with a supple figure, sinewy legs, muscles of steel, and arms of iron.

She had been one of the most famous acrobats at the Circus,

where Des Esseintes had followed her performance night after night. The first few times, she had struck him as being just what she was, a strapping, handsome woman, but he had felt no desire to approach her; she had nothing to recommend her to the tastes of a jaded sophisticate, and yet he found himself returning to the Circus, drawn by some mysterious attraction, impelled by some indefinable urge.

Little by little, as he watched her, curious fancies took shape in his mind. The more he admired her suppleness and strength, the more he thought he saw an artificial change of sex operating in her; her mincing movements and feminine affectations became ever less obtrusive, and in their place there developed the agile, vigorous charms of a male. In short, after being a woman to begin with, then hesitating in a condition verging on the androgynous, she seemed to have made up her mind and become an integral, unmistakable man.

'In that case,' Des Esseintes said to himself, 'just as a great strapping fellow often falls for a slip of a girl, this hefty young woman should be instinctively attracted to a feeble, broken-down, short-winded creature like myself.'

By dint of considering his own physique and arguing from analogy, he got to the point of imagining that he for his part was turning female; and at this point he was seized with a definite desire to possess the woman, yearning for her just as a chlorotic girl will hanker after a clumsy brute whose embrace could squeeze the life out of her.

This exchange of sex between Miss Urania and himself had excited him tremendously. The two of them, so he said, were made for each other; and added to this sudden admiration for brute strength, a thing he had hitherto detested, there was also that extravagant delight in self-abasement which a common prostitute shows in paying dearly for the loutish caresses of a pimp.

Meanwhile, before deciding to seduce the acrobat and see if his dreams could be made reality, he sought confirmation of these dreams in the facial expressions she unconsciously assumed, reading his own desires into the fixed, unchanging smile she wore on her lips as she swung on the trapeze.

At last, one fine evening, he sent her a message by one of the circus attendants. Miss Urania deemed it necessary not to surrender without a little preliminary courting; however, she was careful not to appear over-shy, having heard that Des Esseintes was rich and that his name could help a woman in her career.

But when at last his wishes were granted, he suffered immediate and immeasurable disappointment. He had imagined the American girl would be as blunt-witted and brutish as a fairground wrestler, but he found to his dismay that her stupidity was of a purely feminine order. It is true that she lacked education and refinement, possessed neither wit nor common-sense, and behaved with bestial greed at table, but at the same time she still displayed all the childish foibles of a woman; she loved tittle-tattle and gewgaws as much as any petty-minded trollop, and it was clear that no transmutation of masculine ideas into her feminine person had occurred.

What is more, she was positively puritanical in bed and treated Des Esseintes to none of those rough, athletic caresses he at once desired and dreaded; she was not subject, as he had for a moment hoped she might be, to sexual fluctuations. Perhaps, if he had probed deep into her unfeeling nature, he might yet have discovered a penchant for some delicate, slightly-built bedfellow with a temperament diametrically opposed to her own; but in that case it would have been a preference, not for a young girl, but for a merry little shrimp of a man, a spindle-shanked, funny-faced clown.

There was nothing Des Esseintes could do but resume the man's part he had momentarily forgotten; his feelings of femininity, of frailty, of dependence, of fear even, all disappeared. He could no longer shut his eyes to the truth, that Miss Urania was a mistress like any other, offering no justification for the cerebral curiosity she had aroused.

Although, at first, her firm flesh and magnificent beauty had surprised Des Esseintes and held him spellbound, he was soon impatient to end their liaison and broke it off in a hurry, for his premature impotence was getting worse as a result of the woman's icy caresses and prudish passivity.

Nevertheless, of all the women in this unending procession of lascivious memories, she was the first to halt in front of him; but the fact was that if she had made a deeper impression on his memory than a host of others whose charms had been less fallacious and whose endearments had been less limited, that was because of the healthy, wholesome animal smell she exuded; her superabundant health was the very antipode of the anaemic, scented savour he could detect in the dainty Siraudin sweet.

With her antithetical fragrance, Miss Urania was bound to take first place in his recollections, but almost immediately Des Esseintes, shaken for a moment by the impact of a natural, unsophisticated aroma, returned to more civilized scents and inevitably started thinking about his other mistresses. These now came crowding in on his memory, but with one woman standing out above the rest: the woman whose monstrous speciality had given him months of wonderful satisfaction.

She was a skinny little thing, a dark-eyed brunette with greasy hair parted on one side near the temple like a boy's, and plastered down so firmly that it looked as if it had been painted on to her head. He had come across her at a café where she entertained the customers with demonstrations of ventriloquism.

To the amazement of a packed audience that was half-frightened by what it heard, she took a set of cardboard puppets perched on chairs like a row of Pandean pipes and gave a voice to each in turn; she conversed with dummies that seemed almost alive, while in the auditorium itself flies could be heard buzzing around and the silent spectators noisily whispering among themselves; finally, she had a line of non-existent carriages rolling up the room from the door to the stage, and passing so close to the audience that they instinctively started back and were momentarily surprised to find themselves sitting indoors.

Des Esseintes had been fascinated, and a whole crop of new ideas sprouted in his brain. First of all he lost no time in firing off a broadside of banknotes to subjugate the ventriloquist, who attracted him by the very fact of the contrast she presented to the American girl. The brunette reeked of skilfully contrived scents, heady and unhealthy perfumes, and she burned like the crater of a volcano. In spite of all his subterfuges, Des Esseintes had worn himself out in a few hours; yet he none the less allowed her to go on fleecing him, for it was not so much the woman as the artiste that appealed to him. Besides, the plans he had in view were ripe for execution, and he decided it was time to carry out a hitherto impracticable project.

One night he had a miniature sphinx brought in, carved in black marble and couched in the classic pose, its paws stretched out and its head held rigidly upright, together with a chimera in coloured terra-cotta, flaunting a bristling mane, darting ferocious glances from its eyes, and lashing flanks as swollen as a blacksmith's bellows with its tail. He placed one of these mythical beasts at either end of the bedroom and put out the lamps, leaving only the red embers glowing in the hearth, to shed a dim light that would exaggerate the size of objects almost submerged in the semi-darkness. This done, he lay down on the bed beside the ventriloquist, whose set face was lit up by the glow of a half-burned log, and waited.

With strange intonations that he had made her rehearse beforehand for hours, she gave life and voice to the monsters, without so much as moving her lips, without even looking in their direction.

There and then, in the silence of the night, began the marvellous dialogue of the Chimera and the Sphinx, spoken in deep, guttural voices, now raucous, now piercingly clear, like voices from another world.

'Here, Chimera, stop!'

'No, that I will never do.'

Spellbound by Flaubert's wonderful prose, he listened in breathless awe to the terrifying duet, shuddering from head to foot when the Chimera pronounced the solemn and magical sentence:

'I seek new perfumes, larger blossoms, pleasures still untasted.'

Ah! it was to him that this voice, as mysterious as an incantation, was addressed; it was to him that it spoke of the feverish desire for the unknown, the unsatisfied longing for an ideal, the craving to escape from the horrible realities of life, to cross the frontiers of thought, to grope after a certainty, albeit without finding one, in the misty upper regions of art! The paltriness of his own efforts was borne in upon him and cut him to the heart. He clasped the woman beside him in a gentle embrace, clinging to her like a child wanting to be comforted, never even noticing the sullen expression of the actress forced to play a scene, to practise her profession, at home, in her leisure moments, far from the footlights.

Their liaison continued, but before long Des Esseintes' sexual fiascos became more frequent; the effervescence of his mind could no longer melt the ice in his body, his nerves would no longer heed the commands of his will, and he was obsessed by the lecherous vagaries common in old men. Feeling more and more doubtful of his sexual powers when he was with this mistress of his, he had recourse to the most effective adjuvant known to old and undependable voluptuaries – fear.

As he lay holding the woman in his arms, a husky, drunken voice would roar from behind the door:

'Open up, damn you! I know you've got a cully in there with you! But just you wait a minute, you slut, and you'll get what's coming to you!'

Straight away, like those lechers who are stimulated by the fear of being caught *flagrante delicto* in the open air, on the river bank, in the Tuileries Gardens, in a public lavatory or on a park bench, he would temporarily recover his powers and hurl himself upon the ventriloquist, whose voice went blustering on outside the room. He derived extraordinary pleasure from this panic-stricken hurry of a man running a risk, interrupted and hustled in his fornication.

Unfortunately these special performances soon came to an end; in spite of the fantastic fees he paid her, the ventriloquist sent him packing, and the very same night gave herself to a fellow with less complicated whims and more reliable loins.

Des Esseintes had been sorry to lose her, and the memory of her artifices made other women seem insipid; even the corrupt graces of depraved children appeared tame in comparison, and he came to feel such contempt for their monotonous grimaces that he could not bring himself to tolerate them any longer.

Brooding over these disappointments one day as he was walking by himself along the Avenue de Latour-Maubourg, he was accosted near the Invalides by a youth who asked him which was the quickest way to get to the Rue de Babylone. Des Esseintes showed him which road to take, and as he was crossing the esplanade too, they set off together.

The young fellow's voice, as with unreasonable persistence he asked for fuller instructions – 'So you think if I went to the left it would take longer; but I was told that if I cut across the Avenue I'd get there sooner' – was both timid and appealing, very low and very gentle.

Des Esseintes ran his eyes over him. He looked as though he had just left school, and was poorly clad in a little cheviot jacket too tight round the hips and barely reaching below the small of the back, a pair of close-fitting black breeches, a turn-down collar and a flowing cravat, dark-blue with thin white stripes, tied in a loose bow. In his hand he was carrying a stiff-backed school-book, and on his head was perched a brown, flat-brimmed bowler.

The face was somewhat disconcerting; pale and drawn, with fairly regular features topped by long black hair, it was lit up by two great liquid eyes, ringed with blue and set close to the nose, which was dotted with a few golden freckles; the mouth was small, but spoilt by fleshy lips with a line dividing them in the middle like a cherry.

They gazed at each other for a moment; then the young man dropped his eyes and came closer, brushing his companion's arm with his own. Des Esseintes slackened his pace, taking thoughtful note of the youth's mincing walk.

From this chance encounter there had sprung a mistrustful friendship that somehow lasted several months. Des Esseintes could not think of it now without a shudder; never had he submitted to more delightful or more stringent exploitation, never had he run such risks, yet never had he known such satisfaction mingled with distress.

Among the memories that visited him in his solitude, the recollection of this mutual attachment dominated all the rest. All the leaven of insanity that a brain over-stimulated by neurosis can contain was fermenting within him; and in his pleasurable contemplation of these memories, in his morose delectation, as the theologians call this recurrence of past iniquities, he added to the physical visions spiritual lusts kindled by his former readings of what such casuists as Busenbaum and Diana, Liguori and Sanchez had to say about sins against the sixth and ninth commandments.

While implanting an extra-human ideal in this soul of his, which it had thoroughly impregnated and which a hereditary tendency dating from the reign of Henri III had possibly preconditioned, the Christian religion had also instilled an unlawful ideal of voluptuous pleasure; licentious and mystical obsessions merged together to haunt his brain, which was affected with a stubborn longing to escape the vulgarities of life and, ignoring the dictates of consecrated custom, to plunge into new and original ecstasies, into paroxysms celestial or accursed, but equally exhausting in the waste of phosphorus they involved.

At present, when he came out of one of these reveries, he felt worn out, completely shattered, half dead; and he promptly lit all the candles and lamps, flooding the room with light, imagining that like this he would hear less distinctly than in the dark the dull, persistent, unbearable drum-beat of his arteries, pounding away under the skin of his neck.

X

In the course of that peculiar malady which ravages effete, enfeebled races, the crises are succeeded by sudden intervals of calm. Though he could not understand why, Des Esseintes awoke one fine morning feeling quite fit and well; no hacking cough, no wedges being hammered into the back of his neck, but instead an ineffable sensation of well-being; his head had cleared and his thoughts too, which had been dull and opaque but were now turning bright and iridescent, like delicately coloured soap-bubbles.

This state of affairs lasted some days; then all of a sudden, one afternoon, hallucinations of the sense of smell began to affect him.

Noticing a strong scent of frangipane in the room, he looked to see if a bottle of the perfume was lying about unstoppered, but there was nothing of the sort to be seen. He went into his study, then into the dining-room; the smell went with him.

He rang for his servant.

'Can't you smell something?' he asked.

The man sniffed and said that he smelt nothing unusual. There was no doubt about it: his nervous trouble had returned in the form of a new sort of sensual illusion.

Irritated by the persistence of this imaginary aroma, he decided to steep himself in some real perfumes, hoping that this nasal homoeopathy might cure him or at least reduce the strength of the importunate frangipane.

He went into his dressing-room. There, beside an ancient font that he used as a wash-basin, and under a long looking-glass in a wrought-iron frame that held the mirror imprisoned like still green water inside the moon-silvered curb-stone of a well, bottles of all shapes and sizes were ranged in rows on ivory shelves.

He placed them on a table and divided them into two categories: first, the simple perfumes, in other words the pure spirits and extracts; and secondly, the compound scents known by the generic name of *bouquets*.

Sinking into an armchair, he gave himself up to his thoughts.

For years now he had been an expert in the science of perfumes; he maintained that the sense of smell could procure pleasures equal to those obtained through sight or hearing, each of the senses being capable, by virtue of a natural aptitude supplemented by an erudite education, of perceiving new impressions, magnifying these tenfold, and co-ordinating them to compose the whole that constitutes a work of art. After all, he argued, it was no more abnormal to have an art that consisted of picking out odorous fluids than it was to have other arts based on a selection of sound waves or the impact of variously coloured rays on the retina of the eye; only, just as no one, without a special intuitive faculty developed by study, could distinguish a painting by a great master from a paltry daub, or a Beethoven theme from a tune by Clapisson, so no one, without a preliminary initiation, could help confusing at first a *bouquet* created by a true artist with a potpourri concocted by a manufacturer for sale in grocers' shops and cheap bazaars.

One aspect of this art of perfumery had fascinated him more than any other, and that was the degree of accuracy it was possible to reach in imitating the real thing.

Hardly ever, in fact, are perfumes produced from the flowers whose names they bear; and any artist foolish enough to take his raw materials from Nature alone would get only a hybrid result, lacking both conviction and distinction, for the very good reason that the essence obtained by distillation from the flower itself cannot possibly offer more than a very distant, very vulgar analogy with the real aroma of the living flower, rooted in the ground and spreading its effluvia through the open air.

Consequently, with the solitary exception of the inimitable jasmine, which admits of no counterfeit, no likeness, no approximation even, all the flowers in existence are represented to perfection by combinations of alcoholates and essences, extracting from the model its distinctive personality and adding that little something, that extra tang, that heady savour, that rare touch which makes a work of art.

In short, the artist in perfumery completes the original natural odour, which, so to speak, he cuts and mounts as a jeweller improves and brings out the water of a precious stone.

Little by little the arcana of this art, the most neglected of them all, had been revealed to Des Esseintes, who could now decipher its complex language that was as subtle as any human tongue, yet wonderfully concise under its apparent vagueness and ambiguity.

To do this he had first had to master the grammar, to understand the syntax of smells, to get a firm grasp on the rules that govern them, and, once he was familiar with this dialect, to compare the works of the great masters, the Atkinsons and Lubins, the Chardins and Violets, the Legrands and Piesses, to analyse the construction of their sentences, to weigh the proportion of their words, to measure the arrangement of their periods.

The next stage in his study of this idiom of essences had been to let experience come to the aid of theories that were too often incomplete and commonplace.

Classical perfumery was indeed little diversified, practically colourless, invariably cast in a mould fashioned by chemists of olden times; it was still drivelling away, still clinging to its old alembics, when the Romantic epoch dawned and, no less than the other arts, modified it, rejuvenated it, made it more malleable and more supple.

Its history followed that of the French language step by step. The Louis XIII style in perfumery, composed of the elements dear to that period – orris-powder, musk, civet, and myrtle-water, already known by the name of angel-water – was scarcely adequate to express the cavalierish graces, the rather crude colours of the time which certain sonnets by Saint-Amand have preserved for us. Later on, with the aid of myrrh and frankincense, the potent and austere scents of religion, it became almost possible to render the stately pomp of the age of Louis XIV, the pleonastic artifices of classical oratory, the ample, sustained, wordy style of Bossuet and the other masters of the pulpit. Later still, the blasé, sophisticated graces of French society under Louis XV found their interpreters more easily in frangipane and *maréchale*, which offered in a way the very synthesis of the period. And then, after the indifference and incuriosity of the First Empire, which used eau-de-Cologne and rosemary to excess, perfumery followed Victor Hugo and Gautier and went for inspiration to the lands of the sun; it composed its own Oriental verses, its own highly spiced salaams, discovered new intonations and audacious antitheses, sorted out and revived forgotten nuances which it complicated, subtilized and paired off, and in short resolutely repudiated the voluntary decrepitude to which it had been reduced by its Malesherbes, its Boileaus, its Andrieux, its Baour-Lormians, the vulgar distillers of its poems.

But the language of scents had not remained stationary since the 1830 epoch. It had continued to develop, had followed the march of the century, had advanced side-by-side with the other arts. Like them, it had adapted itself to the whims of artists and connoisseurs, joining in the cult of things Chinese and Japanese, inventing scented albums, imitating the flower-posies of Takeoka, mingling lavender and clove to produce the perfume of the Rondeletia, marrying patchouli and camphor to obtain the singular aroma of China ink, combining citron, clove, and neroli to arrive at the odour of the Japanese Hovenia.

Des Esseintes studied and analysed the spirit of these compounds and worked on an interpretation of these texts; for his own personal pleasure and satisfaction he took to playing the psychologist, to dismantling the mechanism of a work and re-assembling it, to unscrewing the separate pieces forming the structure of a composite odour, and as a result of these operations his sense of smell had acquired an almost infallible flair.

Just as a wine-merchant can recognize a vintage from the taste of a single drop; just as a hop-dealer, the moment he sniffs at a sack, can fix the precise value of the contents; just as a Chinese trader can tell at once the place of origin of the teas he has to examine, can say on what estate in the Bohea hills or in what Buddhist monastery each sample was grown and when the leaves were picked, can state precisely the degree of torrefaction involved and the effect produced on the tea by contact with plum blossom, with the Aglaia, with the Olea fragrans, indeed with any of the perfumes used to modify its flavour, to give it an unexpected piquancy, to improve its somewhat dry smell with a whiff of fresh and foreign flowers; so Des Esseintes, after one brief sniff at a scent, could promptly detail the amounts of its constituents, explain the psychology of its composition, perhaps even give the name of the artist who created it and marked it with the personal stamp of his style.

It goes without saying that he possessed a collection of all the products used by perfumers; he even had some of the genuine Balsam of Mecca, a balm so rare that it can be obtained only in certain regions of Arabia Petraea and remains a monopoly of the Grand Turk.

Sitting now at his dressing-room table, he was toying with the idea of creating a new *bouquet* when he was afflicted with that sudden hesitation so familiar to writers who, after months of idleness, make ready to embark on a new work.

Like Balzac, who was haunted by an absolute compulsion to blacken reams of paper in order to get his hand in, Des Esseintes felt that he ought to get back into practice with a few elementary exercises. He thought of making some heliotrope and picked up two bottles of almond and vanilla; then he changed his mind and decided to try sweet pea instead.

The relevant formula and working method escaped his memory, so that he had to proceed by trial and error. He knew, of course, that in the fragrance of this particular flower, orange-blossom was the dominant element; and after trying various combinations he finally hit on the right tone by mixing the orange-blossom with tuberose and rose, binding the three together with a drop of vanilla.

All his uncertainty vanished; a little fever of excitement took hold of him and he felt ready to set to work again. First he made some tea with a compound of cassia and iris; then, completely sure of himself, he resolved to go ahead, to strike a reverberating chord whose majestic thunder would drown the whisper of that artful frangipane which was still stealing stealthily into the room.

He handled, one after the other, amber, Tonquin musk, with its overpowering smell, and patchouli, the most pungent of all vegetable perfumes, whose flower, in its natural state, gives off an odour of mildew and mould. Do what he would, however, visions of the eighteenth century haunted him: gowns with panniers and flounces danced before his eyes; Boucher Venuses, all flesh and no bone, stuffed with pink cotton-wool, looked down at him from every wall; memories of the novel *Thémidore*, and especially of the exquisite Rosette with her skirts hoisted up in blushing despair, pursued him. He sprang to his feet in a fury, and to rid himself of these obsessions he filled his lungs with that unadulterated essence of spikenard which is so dear to Orientals and so abhorrent to Europeans on account of its excessive valerian content. He was stunned by the violence of the shock this gave him. The filigree of the delicate scent which had been troubling him vanished as if it had been pounded with a hammer; and he took advantage of this respite to escape from past epochs and antiquated odours in order to engage, as he had been used to do in other days, in less restricted and more up-to-date operations.

At one time he had enjoyed soothing his spirit with scented harmonies. He would use effects similar to those employed by the poets, following as closely as possible the admirable arrangement of certain poems by Baudelaire such as *L'Irréparable* and *Le Balcon*, in which the last of the five lines in each verse echoes the first, returning like a refrain to drown the soul in infinite depths of melancholy and languor. He used to roam haphazardly through the dreams conjured up for him by these aromatic stanzas, until he was suddenly brought back to his starting point, to the motif of his meditation, by the recurrence of the initial theme, reappearing at fixed intervals in the fragrant orchestration of the poem.

At present his ambition was to wander at will across a landscape full of changes and surprises, and he began with a simple phrase that was ample and sonorous, suddenly opening up an immense vista of countryside.

With his vaporizers he injected into the room an essence composed of ambrosia, Mitcham lavender, sweet pea, and other flowers – an extract which, when it is distilled by a true artist, well merits the name it has been given of 'extract of meadow blossoms'. Then into this meadow he introduced a carefully measured amalgam of tuberose, orange, and almond blossom; and immediately artificial lilacs came into being, while linden-trees swayed in the wind, shedding on the ground about them their pale emanations, counterfeited by the London extract of tilia.

Once he had roughed out this background in its main outlines, so that it stretched away into the distance behind his closed eyelids, he sprayed the room with a light rain of essences that were half-human, half-feline, smacking of the petticoat, indicating the presence of woman in her paint and powder – stephanotis, ayapana, opopanax, chypre, champaka, and schoenanthus – on which he superimposed a dash of syringa, to give the factitious, cosmetic, indoor life they evoked the natural appearance of laughing, sweating, rollicking pleasures out in the sun.

Next he let these fragrant odours escape through a ventilator, keeping only the country scent, which he renewed, increasing the dose so as to force it to return like a ritornel at the end of each stanza.

The women he had conjured up had gradually disappeared, and the countryside was once more uninhabited. Then, as if by magic, the horizon was filled with factories, whose fearsome chimneys belched fire and flame like so many bowls of punch.

A breath of industry, a whiff of chemical products now floated on the breeze he raised by fanning the air, though Nature still poured her sweet effluvia into this foul-smelling atmosphere.

Des Esseintes was rubbing a pellet of styrax between his fingers, warming it so that it filled the room with a most peculiar smell, an odour at once repugnant and delightful, blending the delicious scent of the jonquil with the filthy stench of gutta-percha and coal tar. He disinfected his hands, shut away his resin in a hermetically-sealed box, and the factories disappeared in their turn.

Now, in the midst of the revivified effluvia of linden-trees and meadow flowers, he sprinkled a few drops of the perfume 'New-mown Hay', and on the magic spot momentarily stripped of its lilacs there rose piles of hay, bringing a new season with them, spreading summer about them in these delicate emanations.

Finally, when he had sufficiently savoured this spectacle, he frantically scattered exotic perfumes around him, emptied his vaporizers, quickened all his concentrated essences and gave free rein to all his balms, with the result that the suffocating room was suddenly filled with an insanely sublimated vegetation, emitting powerful exhalations, impregnating an artificial breeze with raging alcoholates – an unnatural yet charming vegetation, paradoxically uniting tropical spices such as the pungent odours of Chinese sandalwood and Jamaican hediosmia with French scents such as jasmine, hawthorn, and vervain; defying climate and season to put forth trees of different smells and flowers of the most divergent colours and fragrances; creating out of the union or collision of all these tones one common perfume, unnamed, unexpected, unusual, in which there reappeared, like a persistent refrain, the decorative phrase he had started with, the smell of the great meadow and the swaying lilacs and linden-trees.

All of a sudden he felt a sharp stab of pain, as if a drill were boring into his temples. He opened his eyes, to find himself back in the middle of his dressing-room, sitting at his table; he got up and, still in a daze, stumbled across to the window, which he pushed ajar. A gust of air blew in and freshened up the stifling atmosphere that enveloped him. He walked up and down to steady his legs, and as he went to and fro he looked up at the ceiling, on which crabs and salt-encrusted seaweed stood out in relief against a grained background as yellow as the sand on a beach. A similar design adorned the plinths bordering the wall panels, which in their turn were covered with Japanese crape, a watery green in colour and slightly crumpled to imitate the surface of a river rippling in the wind, while down the gentle current floated a rose petal round which there twisted and turned a swarm of little fishes sketched in with a couple of strokes of the pen.

But his eyes were still heavy, and so he stopped pacing the short distance between font and bath and leaned his elbows on the window-sill. Soon his head cleared, and after carefully putting the stoppers back in all his scent-bottles, he took the opportunity to tidy up his cosmetic preparations. He had not touched these things since his arrival at Fontenay, and he was almost surprised to see once again this collection to which so many women had had recourse. Phials and jars were piled on top of each other in utter confusion. Here was a box of green porcelain containing schnouda, that marvellous white cream which, once it is spread on the cheeks, changes under the influence of the air to a delicate pink, then to a flesh colour so natural that it produces an entirely convincing illusion of a flushed complexion; there, lacquered jars inlaid with mother-of-pearl held Japanese gold and Athens green the colour of a blister-fly's wing, golds and greens that turn dark crimson as soon as they are moistened. And beside pots of filbert paste, of harem serkis, of Kashmir-lily emulsions, of strawberry and elder-berry lotions for the skin, next to little bottles full of China-ink and rose-water solutions for the eyes, lay an assortment of instruments fashioned out of ivory and mother-of-pearl, silver and steel, mixed up with lucern brushes for the gums – pincers, scissors, strigils, stumps, hair-pads, powder-puffs, back-scratchers, beauty-spots, and files.

He poked around among all this apparatus, bought long ago to please a mistress of his who used to go into raptures over certain aromatics and certain balms – an unbalanced, neurotic woman who loved to have her nipples macerated in scent, but who only really experienced complete and utter ecstasy when her scalp was scraped with a comb or when a lover's caresses were mingled with the smell of soot, of wet plaster from houses being built in rainy weather, or of dust thrown up by heavy rain-drops in a summer thunderstorm.

As he mused over these recollections, one memory in particular haunted him, stirring up a forgotten world of old thoughts and ancient perfumes – the memory of an afternoon he had spent with this woman at Pantin, partly for want of anything better to do and partly out of curiosity, at the house of one of her sisters. While the two women were chattering away and showing each other their frocks, he had gone to the window and, through the dusty panes, had seen the muddy street stretching into the distance and heard it echo with the incessant beat of galoshes tramping through the puddles.

This scene, though it belonged to a remote past, suddenly presented itself to him in astonishing detail. Pantin was there before him, bustling and alive in the dead green water of the moon-rimmed mirror into which his unthinking gaze was directed. An hallucination carried him away far from Fontenay; the looking-glass conjured up for him not only the Pantin street but also the thoughts that street had once evoked; and lost in a dream, he said over to himself the ingenious, melancholy, yet consoling anthem he had composed that day on getting back to Paris:

'Yes, the season of the great rains is upon us; hearken to the song of the gutter-pipes retching under the pavements; behold the horse-dung floating in the bowls of coffee hollowed out of the macadam; everywhere the foot-baths of the poor are overflowing.

'Under the lowering sky, in the humid atmosphere, the houses ooze black sweat and their ventilators breathe foul odours; the horror of life becomes more apparent and the grip of spleen more oppressive; the seeds of iniquity that lie in every man's heart begin to germinate; a craving for filthy pleasures takes hold of the puritanical, and the minds of respected citizens are visited by criminal desires.

'And yet here I am, warming myself in front of a blazing fire, while a basket of full-blown flowers on the table fills the room with the scent of benzoin, geranium, and vetiver. In mid-November it is still springtime at Pantin in the Rue de Paris, and I can enjoy a quiet laugh at the expense of those timorous families who, in order to avoid the approach of winter, scuttle away at full speed to Antibes or to Cannes.

'Inclement Nature has nothing to do with this extraordinary

phenomenon; let it be said at once that it is to industry, and industry alone, that Pantin owes this factitious spring.

'The truth is that these flowers are made of taffeta and mounted on binding wire, while this vernal fragrance has come filtering in through cracks in the window-frame from the neighbouring factories where the Pinaud and St James perfumes are made.

'For the artisan worn out by the hard labour of the workshops, for the little clerk blessed with too many offspring, the illusion of enjoying a little fresh air is a practical possibility – thanks to these manufacturers.

'Indeed, out of this fabulous counterfeit of the countryside a sensible form of medical treatment could be developed. At present, gay dogs suffering from consumption who are carted away to the south generally die down there, finished off by the change in their habits, by their nostalgic longing for the Parisian pleasures that have laid them low. Here, in an artificial climate maintained by open stoves, their lecherous memories would come back to them in a mild and harmless form, as they breathed in the languid feminine emanations given off by the scent factories. By means of this innocent deception, the physician could supply his patient platonically with the atmosphere of the boudoirs and brothels of Paris, in place of the deadly boredom of provincial life. More often than not, all that would be needed to complete the cure would be for the sick man to show a little imagination.

'Seeing that nowadays there is nothing wholesome left in this world of ours; seeing that the wine we drink and the freedom we enjoy are equally adulterate and derisory; and finally, seeing that it takes a considerable degree of goodwill to believe that the governing classes are worthy of respect and that the lower classes are worthy of help or pity, it seems to me,' concluded Des Esseintes, 'no more absurd or insane to ask of my fellow men a sum total of illusion barely equivalent to that which they expend every day on idiotic objects, to persuade themselves that the town of Pantin is an artificial Nice, a factitious Menton.'

*

'All that,' he muttered, interrupted in his reflections by a sudden feeling of faintness, 'doesn't alter the fact that I shall have to beware of these delicious, atrocious experiments, which are just wearing me out.'

He heaved a sigh.

'Ah, well, that means more pleasures to cut down on, more precautions to take!' – and he shut himself up in his study, hoping that there he would find it easier to escape from the obsessive influence of all these perfumes.

He threw the window wide open, delighted to take a bath of fresh air; but suddenly it struck him that the breeze was bringing with it a whiff of bergamot oil, mingled with a smell of jasmine, cassia, and rose-water. He gave a gasp of horror, and began to wonder whether he might not be in the grip of one of those evil spirits they used to exorcize in the Middle Ages. Meanwhile the odour, though just as persistent, underwent a change. A vague scent of tincture of Tolu, Peruvian balsam, and saffron, blended with a few drops of musk and amber, now floated up from the sleeping village at the foot of the hill; then all at once the metamorphosis took place, these scattered whiffs of perfume came together, and the familiar scent of frangipane, the elements of which his sense of smell had detected and recognized, spread from the valley of Fontenay all the way to the Fort, assailing his jaded nostrils, shaking anew his shattered nerves, and throwing him into such a state of prostration that he fell fainting, almost dying, across the window-sill.

XI

THE frightened servants immediately sent for the Fontenay doctor, who was completely baffled by Des Esseintes' condition. He muttered a few medical terms, felt the patient's pulse, examined his tongue, tried in vain to get him to talk, ordered sedatives and rest, and promised to come back the next day. But at this Des Esseintes summoned up enough strength to reprove his servants for their excessive zeal and to dismiss the intruder, who went off to tell the whole village about the house, the eccentric furnishings of which had left him dumbfounded and flabbergasted.

To the amazement of the two domestics, who now no longer dared to budge from the pantry, their master recovered in a day or two; and they came upon him drumming on the window-panes and casting anxious glances at the sky. And then, one afternoon, he rang for them and gave orders that his bags were to be packed for a long journey.

While the old man and his wife hunted out the things he said he would need, he paced feverishly up and down the cabin-style dining-room, consulted the timetables of the Channel steamers, and scrutinized the clouds from his study window with an impatient yet satisfied air.

For the past week, the weather had been atrocious. Sooty rivers flowing across the grey plains of the sky carried along an endless succession of clouds, like so many boulders torn out of the earth. Every now and then there would be a sudden downpour, and the valley would disappear under torrents of rain.

But that particular day, the sky had changed in appearance: the floods of ink had dried up, the clouds had lost their rugged outlines, and the heavens were now covered with a flat, opaque film. This film seemed to be falling ever lower, and at the same time the countryside was enveloped in a watery mist; the rain no longer cascaded down as it had done the day before, but fell in a fine, cold, unrelenting spray, swamping the lanes, submerging the roads, joining heaven and earth with its countless threads. Daylight in the village dimmed to a ghastly twilight, while the village itself looked like a lake of mud, speckled by the quicksilver needles of rain pricking the surface of the slimy puddles. From this desolate scene all colour had faded away, leaving only the roofs to glisten brightly above the supporting walls.

'What terrible weather!' sighed the old manservant, as he laid on a chair the clothes his master had asked for, a suit ordered some time before from London.

Des Esseintes made no reply except to rub his hands and sit down before a glass-fronted bookcase in which a collection of silk socks was displayed in the form of a fan. For a few moments he hesitated between the various shades; then, taking into account the cheerless day, his cheerless clothes, and his cheerless destination, he picked out a pair in a drab silk and quickly pulled them on. They were followed by the suit, a mottled check in mouse grey and lava grey, a pair of laced ankle-boots, a little bowler hat, and a flax-blue Inverness cape. In this attire, and accompanied by his manservant, who was bent under the burden of a trunk, an expanding valise, a carpet-bag, a hat-box, and a bundle of sticks and umbrellas rolled up in a travelling-rug, he made his way to the station. There, he told his man that he could not say definitely when he would be back – in a year perhaps, or a month, or a week, or even sooner; gave instructions that during his absence nothing in the house should be moved or changed; handed over enough money to cover household expenses; and got into the train, leaving the bewildered old man standing awkward and agape behind the barrier.

He was alone in his compartment. Through the rainswept windows the countryside flashing past looked blurred and dingy, as if he were seeing it through an aquarium full of murky water. Closing his eyes, Des Esseintes gave himself up to his thoughts.

Once again, he told himself, the solitude he had longed for so ardently and finally obtained had resulted in appalling unhappiness, while the silence which he had once regarded as well merited compensation for the nonsense he had listened to for years now weighed unbearably upon him. One morning, he had woken up feeling as desperate as a man who finds himself locked in a prison cell; his lips trembled when he tried to speak, his eyes filled with tears, and he choked and spluttered like someone who has been weeping for hours. Possessed by a sudden desire to move about, to look upon a human face, to talk to some other living creature, and to share a little in the life of ordinary folk, he actually summoned his servants on some pretext or other and asked them to stay with him. But conversation was impossible, for apart from the fact that years of silence and sick-room routine had practically deprived the two old people of the power of speech, their master's habit of keeping them at a distance was scarcely calculated to loosen their tongues. In any event, they were a dull-witted pair, and quite incapable of answering a question in anything but monosyllables.

Scarcely had Des Esseintes realized that they could offer him no solace or relief than he was disturbed by a new phenomenon. The works of Dickens, which he had recently read in the hope of soothing his nerves, but which had produced the opposite effect, slowly began to act upon him in an unexpected way, evoking visions of English life which he contemplated for hours on end. Then, little by little, an idea insinuated itself into his mind – the idea of turning dream into reality, of travelling to England in the flesh as well as in the spirit, of checking the accuracy of his visions; and this idea was allied with a longing to experience new sensations and thus afford some relief to a mind dizzy with hunger and drunk with fantasy.

The abominably foggy and rainy weather fostered these thoughts by reinforcing the memories of what he had read, by keeping before his eyes the picture of a land of mist and mud, and by preventing any deviation from the direction his desires had taken.

Finally he could stand it no longer, and he had suddenly decided to go. Indeed, he was in such a hurry to be off that he fled from home with hours to spare, eager to escape into the future and to plunge into the hurly-burly of the streets, the hubbub of crowded stations.

'Now at last I can breathe,' he said to himself, as the train waltzed to a stop under the dome of the Paris terminus, dancing its final pirouettes to the staccato accompaniment of the turn-tables.

Once out in the street, on the Boulevard d'Enfer, he hailed a cab, rather enjoying the sensation of being cluttered up with trunks and travelling-rugs. The cabby, resplendent in nut-brown trousers and scarlet waistcoat, was promised a generous tip, and this helped the two men to reach a speedy understanding.

'You'll be paid by the hour,' said Des Esseintes; and then, remembering that he wanted to buy a copy of Baedeker's or Murray's Guide to London, he added: 'When you get to the Rue de Rivoli, stop outside *Galignani's Messenger*.'

The cab lumbered off, its wheels throwing up showers of slush. The roadway was nothing but a swamp; the clouds hung so low that the sky seemed to be resting on the roof-tops; the walls were streaming with water from top to bottom; the gutters were full to overflowing; and the pave-ments were coated with a slippery layer of mud the colour of gingerbread. As the omnibuses swept by, groups of people on the pavement stood still, and women holding their um-brellas low and their skirts high flattened themselves against the shopwindows to avoid being splashed.

The rain was slanting in at the windows, so that Des Esseintes had to pull up the glass; this was quickly streaked with trickles of water, while clots of mud spurted up from all sides of the cab like sparks from a firework. Lulled by the monotonous sound of the rain beating down on his trunks and on the carriage roof, like sacks of peas being emptied out over his head, Des Esseintes began dreaming of his coming jour-ney. The appalling weather struck him as an instalment of English life paid to him on account in Paris; and his mind con-jured up a picture of London as an immense, sprawling, rain-drenched metropolis, stinking of soot and hot iron, and wrapped in a perpetual mantle of smoke and fog. He could see in imagination a line of dockyards stretching away into the distance, full of cranes, capstans, and bales of merchandise, and swarming with men – some perched on the masts and sitting astride the yards, while hundreds of others, their heads down and bottoms up, were trundling casks along the quays and into the cellars.

All this activity was going on in warehouses and on wharves washed by the dark, slimy waters of an imaginary Thames, in the midst of a forest of masts, a tangle of beams and girders piercing the pale, lowering clouds. Up above, trains raced by at full speed; and down in the underground sewers, others rumbled along, occasionally emitting ghastly screams or vomiting floods of smoke through the gaping mouths of air-shafts. And meanwhile, along every street, big or small, in an eternal twilight relieved only by the glaring infamies of modern advertising, there flowed an endless stream of traffic between two columns of earnest, silent Londoners, marching along with eyes fixed ahead and elbows glued to their sides.

Des Esseintes shuddered with delight at feeling himself lost in this terrifying world of commerce, immersed in this isolating fog, involved in this incessant activity, and caught up in this ruthless machine which ground to powder millions of poor wretches – outcasts of fortune whom philanthropists urged, by way of consolation, to sing psalms and recite verses of the Bible.

But then the vision vanished as the cab suddenly jolted him up and down on the seat. He looked out of the windows and saw that night had fallen; the gas lamps were flickering in the fog, each surrounded by its dirty yellow halo, while strings of lights seemed to be swimming in the puddles and circling the wheels of the carriages that jogged along through a sea of filthy liquid fire. Des Esseintes tried to see where he was and caught sight of the Arc du Carrousel; and at that very moment, for no reason except perhaps as a reaction from his recent imaginative flights, his mind fixed on the memory of an utterly trivial incident. He suddenly remembered that, when the servant had packed his bags under his supervision, the man had forgotten to put a toothbrush with his other toilet necessaries. He mentally reviewed the list of belongings which had been packed and found that everything else had been duly fitted into his portmanteau; but his annoyance at having left his toothbrush behind persisted until the cabby drew up and so broke the chain of his reminiscences and regrets.

He was now in the Rue de Rivoli, outside *Galignani's Messenger*. There, on either side of a frosted-glass door whose panels were covered with lettering and with newspaper-cuttings and blue telegram-forms framed in passe-partout, were two huge windows crammed with books and picture-albums. He went up to them, attracted by the sight of books bound in paper boards coloured butcher's-blue or cabbage-green and decorated along the seams with gold and silver flowers, as well as others covered in cloth dyed nut-brown, leek-green, lemon-yellow, or currant-red, and stamped with black lines on the back and sides. All this had an un-Parisian air about it, a mercantile flavour, coarser yet less contemptible than the impression produced by cheap French bindings. Here and there, among open albums showing comic scenes by Du Maurier or John Leech and chromos of wild cross-country gallops by Caldecott, a few French novels were in fact to be seen, tempering this riot of brilliant colours with the safe, stolid vulgarity of their covers.

Eventually, tearing himself away from this display, Des Esseintes pushed open the door and found himself in a vast bookshop crowded with people, where women sat unfolding maps and jabbering to each other in strange tongues. An assistant brought him an entire collection of guidebooks, and he in turn sat down to examine these volumes, whose flexible covers bent between his fingers. Glancing through them, he was suddenly struck by a page of Baedeker describing the London art-galleries. The precise, laconic details given by the guide aroused his interest, but before long his attention wandered from the older English paintings to the modern works, which appealed to him more strongly. He remembered certain examples he had seen at international exhibitions and thought that he might well come across them in London – pictures by Millais such as *The Eve of St Agnes*, with its moonlight effect of silvery-green tones; and weirdly coloured pictures by Watts, speckled with gamboge and indigo, and looking as if they had been sketched by an ailing Gustave Moreau, painted in by an anaemic Michael Angelo, and retouched by a romantic Raphael. Among other canvases he remembered a *Curse of Cain*, an *Ida*, and more than one *Eve*, in which the strange and mysterious amalgam of these three masters was informed by the personality, at once coarse and refined, of a dreamy, scholarly Englishman afflicted with a predilection for hideous hues.

All these paintings were crowding into his memory when the shop-assistant, surprised to see a customer sitting day-dreaming at a table, asked him which of the guidebooks he had chosen. For a moment Des Esseintes could not remember where he was, but then, with a word of apology for his absentmindedness, he bought a Baedeker and left the shop.

Outside, he found it bitterly cold and wet, for the wind was blowing across the street and lashing the arcades with rain.

'Drive over there,' he told the cabby, pointing to a shop at the very end of the gallery, on the corner of the Rue de Rivoli and the Rue Castiglione, which with its brightly lit windows looked like a gigantic night-light burning cheerfully in the pestilential fog.

This was the Bodega. The sight which greeted Des Esseintes as he went in was of a long, narrow hall, its roof supported by cast-iron pillars and its walls lined with great casks standing upright on barrel-horses. Hooped with iron, girdled with a sort of pipe-rack in which tulip-shaped glasses hung upside-down, and fitted at the bottom with an earthenware spigot, these barrels bore, besides a royal coat of arms, a coloured card giving details of the vintage they contained, the amount of wine they held, and the price of that wine by the hogshead, by the bottle, and by the glass.

In the passage which was left free between these rows of barrels, under the hissing gas-jets of an atrocious iron-grey chandelier, there stood a line of tables loaded with baskets of

Palmer's biscuits and stale, salty cakes, and plates heaped with mince-pies and sandwiches whose tasteless exteriors concealed burning mustard-plasters. These tables, with chairs arranged on both sides, stretched to the far end of this cellar-like room, where still more hogsheads could be seen stacked against the walls, with smaller branded casks lying on top of them.

The smell of alcohol assailed Des Esseintes' nostrils as he took a seat in this dormitory for strong wines. Looking around him, he saw on one side a row of great casks with labels listing the entire range of ports, light or heavy in body, mahogany or amaranthine in colour, and distinguished by laudatory titles such as 'Old Port', 'Light Delicate', 'Cock-burn's Very Fine', and 'Magnificent Old Regina'; and on the other side, standing shoulder to shoulder and rounding their formidable bellies, enormous barrels containing the martial wine of Spain in all its various forms, topaz-coloured sherries light and dark, sweet and dry – San Lucar, Vino de Pasto, Pale Dry, Oloroso, and Amontillado.

The cellar was packed to the doors. Leaning his elbow on the corner of a table, Des Esseintes sat waiting for the glass of port he had ordered of a barman busy opening explosive, eggshaped soda-bottles that looked like giant-sized capsules of gelatine or gluten such as chemists use to mask the taste of their more obnoxious medicines.

All around him were swarms of English people. There were pale, gangling clergymen with clean-shaven chins, round spectacles, and greasy hair, dressed in black from head to foot – soft hats at one extremity, laced shoes at the other, and in between, incredibly long coats with little buttons running down the front. There were laymen with bloated pork-butcher faces or bulldog muzzles, apoplectic necks, ears like tomatoes, winy cheeks, stupid bloodshot eyes, and whiskery collars as worn by some of the great apes. Further away, at the far end of the wine-shop, a tow-haired stick of a man with a chin sprouting white hairs like an artichoke, was using a microscope to decipher the minute print of an English newspaper. And facing him was a sort of American naval officer, stout and stocky, swarthy and bottle-nosed, a cigar stuck in the hairy orifice of his mouth, and his eyes sleepily contemplating the framed champagne advertisements on the walls – the trademarks of Perrier and Rœderer, Heidsieck and Mumm, and the hooded head of a monk identified in Gothic lettering as Dom Pérignon of Reims.

Des Esseintes began to feel somewhat stupefied in this heavy guard-room atmosphere. His senses dulled by the monotonous chatter of these English people talking to one another, he drifted into a daydream, calling to mind some of Dickens' characters, who were so partial to the rich red port he saw in glasses all about him, and peopling the cellar in fancy with a new set of customers – imagining here Mr Wickfield's white hair and ruddy complexion, there the sharp, expressionless features and unfeeling eyes of Mr Tulkinghorn, the grim lawyer of *Bleak House*. These characters stepped right out of his memory to take their places in the Bodega, complete with all their mannerisms and gestures, for his recollections, revived by a recent reading of the novels, were astonishingly precise and detailed. The Londoner's home as described by the novelist – well lighted, well heated, and well appointed, with bottles being slowly emptied by Little Dorrit, Dora Copperfield, or Tom Pinch's sister Ruth – appeared to him in the guise of a cosy ark sailing snugly through a deluge of soot and mire. He settled down comfortably in this London of the imagination, happy to be indoors, and believing for a moment that the dismal hootings of the tugs by the bridge behind the Tuileries were coming from boats on the Thames. But his glass was empty now; and despite the warm fug in the cellar and the added heat from the smoke of pipes and cigars, he shivered slightly as he came back to reality and the foul, dank weather.

He asked for a glass of Amontillado, but at the sight of this pale dry wine, the English author's soothing stories and gentle lenitives gave place to the harsh revulsives and painful irritants provided by Edgar Allan Poe. The spine-chilling nightmare of the cask of Amontillado, the story of the man walled up in an underground chamber, took hold of his imagination; and behind the kind, ordinary faces of the American and

English customers in the Bodega he fancied he could detect foul, uncontrollable desires, dark and odious schemes. But then he suddenly noticed that the place was emptying and that it was almost time for dinner; he paid his bill, got slowly to his feet, and in a slight daze made for the door.

The moment he set foot outside, he got a wet slap in the face from the weather. Swamped by the driving rain, the street lamps flickered feebly instead of shedding a steady light, while the sky seemed to have been taken down a few pegs, so that the clouds now hung below roof level. Des Esseintes looked along the arcades of the Rue de Rivoli, bathed in shadow and moisture, and imagined that he was standing in the dismal tunnel beneath the Thames. But sharp pangs of hunger recalled him to reality, and going back to the cab, he gave the driver the address of the tavern in the Rue d'Amsterdam, by the Gare Saint-Lazare.

It was now seven o'clock by his watch: he had just time enough to dine before catching his train, which was due to leave at eight-fifty. He worked out how long the crossing from Dieppe to Newhaven would take, added up the hours on his fingers, and finally told himself: 'If the times given in the guide are correct, I shall arrive in London dead on twelve-thirty tomorrow afternoon.'

The cab came to a stop in front of the tavern. Once again Des Esseintes got out, and made his way into a long hall, decorated with brown paint instead of the usual gilt mouldings, and divided by means of breast-high partitions into a number of compartments, rather like the loose-boxes in a stable. In this narrow room, which broadened out near the door, a line of beer-pulls stood at attention along a counter spread with hams as brown as old violins, lobsters the colour of red lead, and salted mackerel, as well as slices of onion, raw carrot, and lemon, bunches of bay-leaves and thyme, juniper berries and peppercorns swimming in a thick sauce.

One of the boxes was empty. He took possession of it and hailed a young man in a black coat, who treated him to a ceremonious bow and a flow of incomprehensible words. While the table was being laid, Des Esseintes inspected his neighbours. As at the Bodega, he saw a crowd of islanders with china-blue eyes, crimson complexions, and earnest or arrogant expressions, skimming through foreign newspapers; but here there were a few women dining in pairs without male escorts, robust Englishwomen with boyish faces, teeth as big as palette-knives, cheeks as red as apples, long hands and long feet. They were enthusiastically attacking helpings of rump-steak pie – meat served hot in mushroom sauce and covered with a crust like a fruit tart.

The voracity of these hearty trencherwomen brought back with a rush the appetite he had lost so long ago. First, he ordered and enjoyed some thick, greasy oxtail soup; next, he examined the list of fish and asked for a smoked haddock, which also came up to his expectations; and then, goaded on by the sight of other people guzzling, he ate a huge helping of roast beef and potatoes and downed a couple of pints of ale, savouring the musky cowshed flavour of this fine pale beer.

His hunger was now almost satisfied. He nibbled a bitter-sweet chunk of blue Stilton, pecked at a rhubarb tart, and then, to make a change, quenched his thirst with porter, that black beer which tastes of liquorice with the sugar extracted.

He drew a deep breath: not for years had he stuffed and swilled with such abandon. It was, he decided, the change in his habits together with the choice of strange and satisfying dishes which had roused his stomach from its stupor. He settled contentedly in his chair, lit a cigarette, and prepared to enjoy a cup of coffee laced with gin.

Outside, the rain was still falling steadily; he could hear it pattering on the glass skylight at the far end of the room and cascading into the water-spouts. Inside, no one stirred; all were dozing like himself over their liqueur glasses, pleasantly conscious that they were in the dry.

After a while, their tongues were loosened; and as most of them looked up in the air as they spoke, Des Esseintes concluded that these Englishmen were nearly all discussing the weather. Nobody laughed or smiled, and their suits matched their expressions: all of them were sombrely dressed in grey cheviot with nankin-yellow or blotting-paper-pink stripes. He cast a pleased look at his own clothes, which in colour and cut did not differ appreciably from those worn by the people around him, delighted to find that he was not out of keeping with these surroundings and that superficially at least he could claim to be a naturalized citizen of London. Then he gave a start: what of the time? He consulted his watch; it was ten minutes to eight. He still had nearly half-an-hour to stay where he was, he told himself; and once again he fell to thinking over his plans.

In the course of his sedentary life, only two countries had exerted any attraction upon him – Holland and England. He had surrendered to the first of these two temptations; unable to resist any longer, he had left Paris one fine day and visited the cities of the Low Countries, one by one. On the whole, this tour had proved a bitter disappointment to him. He had pictured to himself a Holland such as Teniers and Jan Steen, Rembrandt and Ostade had painted, imagining for his own private pleasure ghettoes swarming with splendid figures as suntanned as cordovan leather, looking forward to stupendous village fairs with never-ending junketings in the country, and expecting to find the patriarchal simplicity and riotous joviality which the old masters had depicted in their works.

There was no denying that Haarlem and Amsterdam had fascinated him; the common people, seen in their natural un-polished state and their normal rustic surroundings, were very much like Van Ostade's subjects, with their rowdy, untamed brats and their elephantine old gossips, big-bosomed and pot-bellied. But there was no sign of wild revelry or domestic drunkenness, and he had to admit that the paintings of the Dutch School exhibited in the Louvre had led him astray. They had in fact served as a spring-board from which he had soared into a dream world of false trails and impossible ambitions, for nowhere in this world had he found the fairyland of which he had dreamt; nowhere had he seen rustic youths and maidens dancing on a village green littered with wine casks, weeping with sheer happiness, jumping for joy, and laughing so up-roariously that they wet their petticoats and breeches.

No, there was certainly nothing of the sort to be seen at

present. Holland was just a country like any other, and what was more, a country entirely lacking in simplicity and geniality, for the Protestant faith was rampant there with all its stern hypocrisy and unbending solemnity.

Still thinking of this past disappointment, he once more consulted his watch: there were only ten minutes now before his train left.

'It's high time to ask for my bill and go,' he told himself. But the food he had eaten was lying heavy on his stomach, and his whole body felt incapable of movement.

'Come now,' he muttered, trying to screw up his courage. 'Drink the stirrup-cup, and then you must be off.'

He poured himself a brandy, and at the same time called for his bill. This was the signal for a black-coated individual to come up with a napkin over one arm and a pencil behind his ear – a sort of majordomo with a bald, eggshaped head, a rough beard shot with grey, and a clean-shaven upper lip. He took up a concert-singer's pose, one leg thrown forward, drew a note-book from his pocket, and fixing his gaze on a spot close to one of the hanging chandeliers, he made out the bill without even looking at what he was writing.

'There you are, sir,' he said, tearing a leaf from his pad and handing it to Des Esseintes, who was examining him with unconcealed curiosity, as if he were some rare animal. What an extraordinary creature, he thought, as he surveyed this phlegmatic Englishman, whose hairless lips reminded him, oddly enough, of an American sailor.

At that moment the street door opened and some people came in, bringing with them a wet doggy smell. The wind blew clouds of steam back into the kitchen and rattled the unlatched door. Des Esseintes felt incapable of stirring a finger; a soothing feeling of warmth and lassitude was seeping into every limb, so that he could not even lift his hand to light a cigar.

'Get up, man, and go,' he kept telling himself, but these orders were no sooner given than countermanded. After all, what was the good of moving, when a fellow could travel so magnificently sitting in a chair? Wasn't he already in London,

142

whose smells, weather, citizens, food, and even cutlery, were all about him? What could he expect to find over there, save fresh disappointments such as he had suffered in Holland?

Now he had only just time enough to run across to the station, but an immense aversion for the journey, an urgent longing to remain where he was, came over him with growing force and intensity. Lost in thought, he sat there letting the minutes slip by, thus cutting off his retreat.

'If I went now,' he said to himself, 'I should have to dash up to the barriers and hustle the porters along with my luggage. What a tiresome business it would be!'

And once again he told himself:

'When you come to think of it, I've seen and felt all that I wanted to see and feel. I've been steeped in English life ever since I left home, and it would be madness to risk spoiling such unforgettable experiences by a clumsy change of locality. As it is, I must have been suffering from some mental aberration to have thought of repudiating my old convictions, to have rejected the visions of my obedient imagination, and to have believed like any ninny that it was necessary, interesting, and useful to travel abroad.'

He looked at his watch.

'Time to go home,' he said. And this time he managed to get to his feet, left the tavern, and told the cabby to drive him back to the Gare de Sceaux. Thence he returned to Fontenay with his trunks, his packages, his portmanteaux, his rugs, his umbrellas, and his sticks, feeling all the physical weariness and moral fatigue of a man who has come home after a long and perilous journey.

XII

DURING the days that followed his return home, Des
Esseintes browsed through the books in his library, and
at the thought that he might have been parted from them
for a long time he was filled with the same heart-felt
satisfaction he would have enjoyed if he had come back to
them after a genuine separation. Under the impulse of this
feeling, he saw them in a new light, discovering beauties in
them he had forgotten ever since he had bought and read
them for the first time.

Everything indeed – books, bric-à-brac, and furniture –
acquired a peculiar charm in his eyes. His bed seemed softer in
comparison with the pallet he would have occupied in London; the discreet and silent service he got at home delighted
him, exhausted as he was by the very thought of the noisy
garrulity of hotel waiters; the methodical organization of his
daily life appeared more admirable than ever, now that the
hazard of travelling was a possibility.

He steeped himself once more in this refreshing bath of
settled habits, to which artificial regrets added a more bracing
and more tonic quality.

But it was his books that chiefly engaged his attention. He
took them all down from their shelves and examined them before putting them back, to see whether, since his coming to
Fontenay, the heat and damp had not damaged their bindings
or spotted their precious papers.

He began by going through the whole of his Latin library;
then he rearranged the specialist works by Archelaus, Albertus
Magnus, Raymond Lully, and Arnaud de Villanova dealing
with the cabbala and the occult sciences; and lastly he checked
all his modern books one by one. To his delight he discovered
that they had one and all kept dry and were in good condition.

This collection had cost him considerable sums of money,
for the truth was that he could not bear to have his favourite

authors printed on rag-paper, as they were in other people's libraries, with characters like hobnails in a peasant's boots.

In Paris in former days, he had had certain volumes set up just for himself and printed on hand-presses by specially hired workmen. Sometimes he would commission Perrin of Lyons, whose slim, clear types were well adapted for archaic reimpressions of old texts; sometimes he would send to England or America for new characters to print works of the present century; sometimes he would apply to a house at Lille which for hundreds of years had possessed a complete fount of Gothic letters; sometimes again he would commandeer the fine old Enschedé printing-works at Haarlem, whose foundry has preserved the stamps and matrices of the so-called *lettres de civilité*.

He had done the same with the paper for his books. Deciding one fine day that he was tired of the ordinary expensive papers – silver from China, pearly gold from Japan, white from Whatman's, greyish brown from Holland, buff from Turkey and the Seychal mills – and disgusted with the machine-made varieties, he had ordered special hand-made papers from the old mills at Vire where they still use pestles once employed to crush hempseed. To introduce a little variety into his collection, he had at various times imported certain dressed fabrics from London – flock papers and rep papers – while to help mark his contempt for other bibliophiles, a Lübeck manufacturer supplied him with a glorified candle-paper, bluish in colour, noisy and brittle to the touch, in which the straw fibres were replaced by flakes of gold such as you find floating in Danzig brandy.

In this way he had got together some unique volumes, always choosing unusual formats and having them clothed by Lortic, by Trautz-Bauzonnet, by Chambolle, by Capé's successors, in irreproachable bindings of old silk, of embossed ox-hide, of Cape goat-skin – all full bindings, patterned and inlaid, lined with tabby or watered silk, adorned in ecclesiastic fashion with metal clasps and corners, sometimes even decorated by Gruel-Engelmann in oxidized silver and shining enamel.

Thus he had had Baudelaire's works printed with the admirable episcopal type of the old house of Le Clere, in a large format similar to that of a mass-book, on a very light Japanese felt, a bibulous paper as soft as elder-pith, its milky whiteness faintly tinged with pink. This edition, limited to a single copy and printed in a velvety China-ink black, had been dressed outside and lined inside with a mirific and authentic flesh-coloured pigskin, one in a thousand, dotted all over where the bristles had been and blind-tooled in black with designs of marvellous aptness chosen by a great artist.

On this particular day, Des Esseintes took this incomparable volume down from his shelves and fondled it reverently, re-reading certain pieces which in this simple but priceless setting seemed to him deeper and subtler than ever.

His admiration for this author knew no bounds. In his opinion, writers had hitherto confined themselves to exploring the surface of the soul, or such underground passages as were easily accessible and well lit, measuring here and there the deposits of the seven deadly sins, studying the lie of the lodes and their development, recording for instance, as Balzac did, the stratification of a soul possessed by some monomaniacal passion – ambition or avarice, paternal love or senile lust.

Literature, in fact, had been concerned with virtues and vices of a perfectly healthy sort, the regular functioning of brains of a normal conformation, the practical reality of current ideas, with never a thought for morbid depravities and other-worldly aspirations; in short, the discoveries of these analysts of human nature stopped short at the speculations, good or bad, classified by the Church; their efforts amounted to no more than the humdrum researches of a botanist who watches closely the expected development of ordinary flora planted in common or garden soil.

Baudelaire had gone further; he had descended to the bottom of the inexhaustible mine, had picked his way along abandoned or unexplored galleries, and had finally reached those districts of the soul where the monstrous vegetations of the sick mind flourish.

There, near the breeding-ground of intellectual aberrations and diseases of the mind – the mystical tetanus, the burning fever of lust, the typhoids and yellow fevers of crime – he had found, hatching in the dismal forcing-house of *ennui*, the frightening climacteric of thoughts and emotions.

He had laid bare the morbid psychology of the mind that has reached the October of its sensations, and had listed the symptoms of souls visited by sorrow, singled out by spleen; he had shown how blight affects the emotions at a time when the enthusiasms and beliefs of youth have drained away, and nothing remains but the barren memory of hardships, tyrannies, and slights, suffered at the behest of a despotic and freakish fate.

He had followed every phase of this lamentable autumn, watching the human creature, skilled in self-torment and adept in self-deception, forcing its thoughts to cheat one another in order to suffer more acutely, and ruining in advance, thanks to its powers of analysis and observation, any chance of happiness it might have.

Then, out of this irritable sensitivity of soul, out of this bitterness of mind that savagely repulses the embarrassing attentions of friendship, the benevolent insults of charity, he witnessed the gradual and horrifying development of those middle-aged passions, those mature love-affairs where one partner goes on blowing hot when the other has already started blowing cold, where lassitude forces the amorous pair to indulge in filial caresses whose apparent juvenility seems something new, and in motherly embraces whose tenderness is not only restful but also gives rise, so to speak, to interesting feelings of remorse about a vague sort of incest.

In a succession of magnificent pages he had exposed these hybrid passions, exacerbated by the impossibility of obtaining complete satisfaction, as well as the dangerous subterfuges of narcotic and toxic drugs, taken in the hope of deadening pain and conquering boredom. In a period when literature attributed man's unhappiness almost exclusively to the misfortunes of unrequited love or the jealousies engendered by adulterous love, he had ignored these childish ailments and sounded instead those deeper, deadlier, longer-lasting wounds that are inflicted by satiety, disillusion, and contempt upon souls tortured by the present, disgusted by the past, terrified and dismayed by the future.

The more Des Esseintes re-read his Baudelaire, the more he appreciated the indescribable charm of this writer who, at a time when verse no longer served any purpose except to depict the external appearance of creatures and things, had succeeded in expressing the inexpressible – thanks to a solid, sinewy style which, more than any other, possessed that remarkable quality, the power to define in curiously healthy terms the most fugitive and ephemeral of the unhealthy conditions of weary spirits and melancholy souls.

After Baudelaire, the number of French books that had found their way on to his shelves was very limited. Without a doubt he was utterly insensible to the merits of those works it is good form to enthuse over. The 'side-splitting mirth' of Rabelais and the 'common-sense humour' of Molière had never brought so much as a smile to his lips; and the antipathy he felt to these buffooneries was so great that he did not hesitate to liken them, from the artistic point of view, to the knockabout turns given by the clowns at any country fair.

As regards the poetry of past ages, he read very little apart from Villon, whose melancholy ballades he found rather touching, and a few odd bits of D'Aubigné that stirred his blood by the incredible virulence of their apostrophes and their anathemas.

As for prose, he had little respect for Voltaire and Rousseau, or even Diderot, whose vaunted 'Salons' struck him as remarkable for the number of moralizing inanities and stupid aspirations they contained. Out of hatred of all this twaddle, he confined his reading almost entirely to the exponents of Christian oratory, to Bourdaloue and Bossuet, whose sonorous and ornate periods greatly impressed him; but he was even fonder of tasting the pith and marrow of stern, strong phrases such as Nicole fashioned in his meditations, and still more Pascal, whose austere pessimism and agonized attrition went straight to his heart.

Apart from these few books, French literature, so far as his library was concerned, started at the beginning of the nineteenth century.

It fell into two distinct categories, one comprising ordinary profane literature, the other the works of Catholic writers – a very special literature, almost unknown to the general reader, and yet disseminated by enormous, long-established firms to the far corners of the earth.

He had summoned up enough courage to explore these literary crypts, and as in the realm of secular literature, he had discovered, underneath a gigantic pile of insipidities, a few works written by true masters.

The distinctive characteristic of this literature was the absolute immutability of its ideas and its idiom; just as the Church had perpetuated the primordial form of its sacred objects, so also it had kept intact the relics of its dogmas and piously preserved the reliquary that contained them – the oratorical style of the seventeenth century. As one of its own writers – Ozanam – declared, the Christian idiom had nothing to learn from the language of Rousseau, and should employ exclusively the style used by Bourdaloue and Bossuet.

In spite of this declaration, the Church, showing a more tolerant spirit, winked at certain expressions, certain turns of phrase borrowed from the lay language of the same century; and as a result the Catholic idiom had to some extent purged itself of its massive periods, weighed down, especially in Bossuet's case, by the inordinate length of its parentheses, the painful redundancy of its pronouns. But there the concessions had stopped, and indeed any more would doubtless have been superfluous, for with its ballast gone, this prose was quite adequate for the narrow range of subjects to which the Church restricted itself.

Incapable of dealing with contemporary life, of making visible and palpable the simplest aspect of creatures and things, and ill fitted to explain the complicated ruses of a brain unconcerned about states of grace, this idiom was none the less excellent in the treatment of abstract subjects. Useful in the discussion of a controversy, in the qualification of a

149

commentary, it also possessed more than any other the necessary authority to state dogmatically the value of a doctrine.

Unfortunately, here as everywhere else, an immense army of pedants had invaded the sanctuary and by their ignorance and lack of talent debased its noble and uncompromising dignity. As a crowning disaster, several pious females had decided to try their hands at writing, and maladroit sacristies had joined with silly salons in extolling as works of genius the wretched prattlings of these women.

Des Esseintes had been curious enough to read a number of these works, among them those of Madame Swetchine, the Russian general's wife whose house in Paris attracted the most fervent of Catholics. Her writings had filled him with an infinite and overwhelming sense of boredom; they were worse than bad, they were banal; the abiding impression was of a lingering echo from a private chapel in which a clique of sanctimonious snobs could be heard muttering their prayers, asking in whispers for each other's news, and repeating with a portentous air a string of commonplaces on politics, the predictions of the barometer, and the present state of the weather.

But there was worse to come: there was Mrs Augustus Craven, an accredited laureate of the Institut, author of the *Récit d'une Sœur* as well as of an *Éliane* and a *Fleurange*, books which were all greeted with blaring trumpets and rolling organ by the entire apostolic press. Never, no never, had Des Esseintes imagined that it was possible to write such trivial trash. These books were based on such stupid concepts and were written in such a nauseating style that they almost acquired a rare and distinctive personality of their own.

In any case, it was not among the female writers that Des Esseintes, who was neither pure in mind nor sentimental by nature, could expect to find a literary niche adapted to his particular tastes. However, he persevered and, with a diligence unaffected by any feeling of impatience, tried his hardest to appreciate the work of the child of genius, the blue-stocking virgin of this group, Eugénie de Guérin. His efforts were in vain: he found it impossible to take to the famous *Journal* and

Letters in which she extols, without any sense of discretion or discrimination, the prodigious talent of a brother who rhymed with such marvellous ingenuity and grace that one must surely go back to the works of Monsieur de Jouy and Monsieur Écouchard Lebrun to find anything so bold or so original.

Try as he might, he could not see what attraction lay in books distinguished by remarks such as these: 'This morning I hung up by papa's bed a cross a little girl gave him yesterday' and 'We are invited tomorrow, Mimi and I, to attend the blessing of a bell at Monsieur Roquier's – a welcome diversion'; or by mention of such momentous events as this: 'I have just hung about my neck a chain bearing a medal of Our Lady which Louise sent me as a safeguard against cholera'; or by poetry of this calibre: 'Oh, what a lovely moonbeam has just fallen on the Gospel I was reading!' – or finally, by observations as subtle and perspicacious as this: 'Whenever I see a man cross himself or take his hat off on passing a crucifix, I say to myself: There goes a Christian.'

And so it went on for page after page, without pause, without respite, until Maurice de Guérin died and his sister could launch out into her lamentations, written in a wishy-washy prose dotted here and there with scraps of verse of such pathetic insipidity that Des Esseintes was finally moved to pity.

No, in all fairness there was no denying the fact that the Catholic party was not very particular in its choice of protégées, and not very perceptive either. These lymphs it had made so much of and for whom it had exhausted the good will of its press, all wrote like convent schoolgirls in a milk-and-water style, all suffered from a verbal diarrhoea no astringent could conceivably check.

As a result, Des Esseintes turned his back in horror on these books. Nor did he think it likely that the priestly writers of modern times could offer him sufficient compensation for all his disappointments. These preachers and polemists wrote impeccable French, but in their sermons and books the Christian idiom had ended up by becoming impersonal and stereotyped, a rhetoric in which every movement and pause was predetermined, a succession of periods copied from a single model. All these ecclesiastics, in fact, wrote alike, with a little more or a little less energy or emphasis, so that there was virtually no difference between the grisailles they turned out, whether they were signed by their Lordships Dupanloup or Landriot, La Bouillerie or Gaume, by Dom Guéranger or Father Ratisbonne, by Bishop Freppel or Bishop Perraud, by Father Ravignan or Father Gratry, by the Jesuit Olivain, the Carmelite Dosithée, the Dominican Didon, or the sometime Prior of Saint-Maximin, the Reverend Father Chocarne.

Time and again Des Esseintes had told himself that it would need a very genuine talent, a very profound originality, a very firm conviction to thaw this frozen idiom, to animate this communal style that stifled every unconventional idea, that suffocated every audacious opinion.

Yet there were one or two authors whose burning eloquence somehow succeeded in melting and moulding this petrified language, and the foremost of these was Lacordaire, one of the few genuine writers the Church had produced in a great many years.

Confined, like all his colleagues, within the narrow circle of orthodox speculation; obliged, as they were, to mark time and to consider only such ideas as had been conceived and consecrated by the Fathers of the Church and developed by the great preachers, he none the less managed to pull a bluff, to rejuvenate and almost modify these same ideas, simply by giving them a more personal and lively form. Here and there in his *Conférences de Notre-Dame*, happy phrases, startling expressions, accents of love, bursts of passion, cries of joy and demonstrations of delight occurred that made the time-honoured style sizzle and smoke under his pen. And then, over and above his oratorical gifts, this brilliant, gentle-hearted monk who had used up all his skill and all his energy in a hopeless attempt to reconcile the liberal doctrines of a modern society with the authoritarian dogmas of the Church, was also endowed with a capacity for fervent affection, for discreet tenderness. Accordingly, the letters he wrote to young men used to contain fond paternal exhortations, smiling reprimands, kindly words of advice, indulgent words of for-giveness. Some of these letters were charming, as when he admitted his greed for love, and others were quite impressive, as when he sustained his correspondents' courage and dis-sipated their doubts by stating the unshakeable certitude of his own beliefs. In short, this feeling of fatherhood, which under his pen acquired a dainty feminine quality, lent his prose an accent unique in clerical literature.

After him, few indeed were the ecclesiastics and monks who showed any signs of individuality. At the very most, there were half-a-dozen pages by his pupil the Abbé Peyreyve that were readable. This priest had left some touching biographical studies of his master, written one or two delightful letters, produced a few articles in a sonorous oratorical style, and pro-nounced a few panegyrics in which the declamatory note was sounded too often. Obviously the Abbé Peyreyve had neither the sensibility nor the fire of Lacordaire; there was too much of the priest in him and too little of the man; and yet now and then his pulpit rhetoric was lit up by striking analogies, by ample, weighty phrases, by well-nigh sublime flights of oratory.

But it was only among writers who had not been ordained, among secular authors who were devoted to the Catholic cause and had its interests at heart, that prosaists worthy of attention were to be found.

The episcopal style, so feebly handled by the prelates, had acquired new strength and regained some of its old masculine vigour in the hands of the Comte de Falloux. Despite his gentle appearance, this Academician positively oozed venom; the speeches he made in Parliament in 1848 were dull and diffuse, but the articles he contributed to the *Correspondant* and later published in book form were cruel and biting under their exaggerated surface politeness. Conceived as polemic tirades, they displayed a certain caustic wit and expressed opinions of surprising intolerance.

A dangerous controversialist by reason of the traps he laid for his adversaries, and a crafty logician forever outflanking the enemy and taking him by surprise, the Comte de Falloux had also written some penetrating pages on the death of Madame Swetchine, whose correspondence he had edited and whom he revered as a saint. But where the man's temperament really showed itself was in two pamphlets which appeared in 1846 and 1880, the later work bearing the title *L'Unité nationale*.

Here, filled with a cold fury, the implacable Legitimist delivered a frontal assault for once, contrary to his usual custom, and by way of peroration fired off this round of abuse at the sceptics:

'As for you, you doctrinaire Utopians who shut your eyes to human nature, you ardent atheists who feed on hatred and delusion, you emancipators of woman, you destroyers of family life, you genealogists of the simian race, you whose name was once an insult in itself, be well content: you will have been the prophets and your disciples will be the pontiffs of an abominable future!'

The other pamphlet was entitled *Le Parti catholique* and was directed against the despotism of the *Univers* and its editor Veuillot, whom it took care not to mention by name. Here the flank attacks were resumed, with poison concealed in every line of this brochure in which the bruised and battered gentleman answered the kicks of the professional wrestler with scornful sneers.

Between them they represented to perfection the two parties in the Church whose differences have always turned to uncompromising hatred. Falloux, the more arrogant and cunning of the two, belonged to that liberal sect which already included both Montalembert and Cochin, both Lacordaire and Broglie; he subscribed whole-heartedly to the principles upheld by the *Correspondant*, a review which did its best to cover the imperious doctrines of the Church with a varnish of tolerance. Veuillot, a more honest, outspoken man, spurned these subterfuges, unhesitatingly admitted the tyranny of ultramontane dictates, openly acknowledged and invoked the merciless discipline of ecclesiastical dogma.

The latter writer had fashioned for the fight a special language which owed something to La Bruyère and something to the working-man living out in the Gros-Caillou. This style, half solemn, half vulgar, and wielded by such a brutal character, had the crushing weight of a life-preserver. An extraordinarily brave and stubborn fighter, Veuillot had used this dreadful weapon to fell free-thinkers and bishops alike, laying about him with all his might, lashing out savagely at his foes whether they belonged to one party or the other. Held in suspicion by the Church, which disapproved of both his contraband idiom and his cut-throat conduct, this religious blackguard had none the less compelled recognition by sheer force of talent, goading the Press on till he had the whole pack at his heels, pummelling them till he drew blood in his *Odeurs de Paris*, standing up to every attack, kicking himself free of the vile pen-pushers that came snapping and snarling after him.

Unfortunately, his undeniable brilliance showed only in a fight; in cold blood, he was just a run-of-the-mill writer. His poems and novels were pitiful; his pungent language lost all its flavour in a peaceful atmosphere; between bouts, the Catholic wrestler was transformed into a dyspeptic old man, wheezing out banal litanies and stammering childish canticles.

Stiffer, starchier, and statelier was the Church's favourite apologist, the Grand Inquisitor of the Christian idiom, Ozanam. Though he was not easily surprised, Des Esseintes never failed to wonder at the aplomb with which this author spoke of the inscrutable purposes of the Almighty, when he should have been producing evidence for the impossible assertions he was making; with marvellous sangfroid the man would twist events about, contradict, with even greater impudence than the panegyrists of the other parties, the acknowledged facts of history, declare that the Church had never made any secret of the great regard it had for science, describe heresies as foul miasmas, and treat Buddhism and all other religions with such contempt that he apologized for sullying Catholic prose by so much as attacking their doctrines.

From time to time religious enthusiasm breathed a certain ardour into his oratorical style, under whose icy surface there seethed a current of suppressed violence; in his copious writings on Dante, on St Francis, on the author of the *Stabat*, on the Franciscan poets, on Socialism, on commercial law, on everything under the sun, he invariably undertook the defence of the Vatican, which he considered incapable of doing wrong, judging every case alike according to the greater or lesser distance separating it from his own.

This practice of looking at every question from a single point of view was also followed by that paltry scribbler some people held up as his rival – Nettement. The latter was not quite so strait-laced, and what pretensions he had were social rather than spiritual. Now and again he had actually ventured outside the literary cloister in which Ozanam had shut himself up, and had dipped into various profane works with a view to passing judgement on them. He had groped his way into this unfamiliar realm like a child in a cellar, seeing nothing around him but darkness, perceiving nothing in the gloom but the flame of the taper lighting his way ahead for a little distance.

In this total ignorance of the locality, in this absolute obscurity, he had tripped up time and time again. Thus he had spoken of Murger's style as 'carefully chiselled and meticulously polished'; he had said that Hugo sought after what was foul and filthy, and had dared to make comparisons between him and Monsieur de Laprade; he had criticized Delacroix because he broke the rules, and praised Paul Delaroche and the poet Reboul because they seemed to him to have the faith. Des Esseintes could not help shrugging his shoulders over these unfortunate opinions, wrapped up in a dowdy prose-style, the well-worn material of which caught and tore on the corner of every sentence.

In another domain, the works of Poujoulat and Genoude, of Montalembert, Nicolas, and Carné failed to awaken any livelier feelings of interest in him; nor was he conscious of any pronounced predilection for the historical problems treated with painstaking scholarship and in a worthy style by the Duc de Broglie, or for the social and religious questions tackled by Henry Cochin – who had, however, given his measure in a letter describing a moving ceremony at the Sacré-Cœur, a taking of the veil. It was years since he had opened any of these books, and even longer since he had thrown away the puerile lucubrations of the sepulchral Pontmartin and the pitiable Féval, and had handed over to the servants for some sordid purpose the little tales of such as Aubineau and Lasserre, those contemptible hagiographers of the miracles performed by Monsieur Dupont of Tours and the Blessed Virgin.

In a word, Des Esseintes failed to find in this literature even a passing distraction from his boredom; and so he tucked away in the darkest corners of his library all these books that he had read long ago after leaving the Jesuit college.

'I'd have done better to leave these behind in Paris,' he muttered, as he pulled out from behind the rest two sets of books he found particularly insufferable: the works of the Abbé Lamennais and those of that fanatical bigot, that pompous bore, that conceited ass, Comte Joseph de Maistre.

On one shelf, a solitary volume was left standing within his reach, and that was *L'Homme*, by Ernest Hello.

This man was the absolute antithesis of his colleagues in religion. Virtually isolated in the group of devotional writers, who were shocked by the attitudes he adopted, he had ended up by leaving the main road that leads from earth to heaven. Sickened no doubt by the banality of this highway, and by the mob of literary pilgrims who for centuries had been filing along the same road, following in each other's footsteps, stopping in the same spots to exchange the same commonplaces about religion and the Fathers of the Church, about the same beliefs and the same masters, he had turned off into the by-paths, had come out in the bleak forest clearing of Pascal, where he had stopped for quite a time to get his second wind; then he had gone on his way, penetrating deeper than the Jansenist, whom he happened to despise, into the regions of human thought.

Full of subtle complexity and pompous affectation, Hello with his brilliant, hair-splitting analyses reminded Des Esseintes of the exhaustive and meticulous studies of some of the atheistic psychologists of the eighteenth and nineteenth centuries. There was something of a Catholic Duranty in him, but more dogmatic and perceptive, a practised master of the magnifying-glass, an able engineer of the soul, a skilful watchmaker of the brain, who liked nothing better than to examine the mechanism of a passion and show just how the wheels went round.

In this oddly constituted mind of his were to be found the most unexpected associations of thought, the most surprising analogies and contrasts; there was also a curious trick he had of using etymological definitions as a springboard from which to leap in pursuit of fresh ideas, joined together by links that were sometimes rather tenuous but almost invariably original and ingenious.

In this way, and in spite of the faulty balance of his constructions, he had taken to pieces, so to speak, with remarkable perspicacity, the miser and the common man, had analysed the liking for company and the passion for suffering, and had revealed the interesting comparisons that can be established between the processes of photography and memory.

But this skill in the use of the delicate analytical instrument he had stolen from the Church's enemies represented only one aspect of the man's temperament. There was another person in him, another side to his dual nature – and this was the religious fanatic, the Biblical prophet.

Like Hugo, whom he recalled at times by the twist he gave to an idea or a phrase, Ernest Hello had loved posing as a little St John on Patmos, only in his case he pontificated and vaticinated from the top of a rock manufactured in the ecclesiastical knick-knack shops of the Rue Saint-Sulpice, haranguing the reader in an apocalyptic style salted here and there with the bitter gall of an Isaiah.

On these occasions he displayed exaggerated pretensions to profundity, and there were a few flatterers who hailed him as a genius, pretending to regard him as the great man of his day, the fount of knowledge of his time. And a fount of knowledge he may have been – but one whose waters were often far from clear.

In his volume *Paroles de Dieu*, in which he paraphrased the

Scriptures and did his best to complicate their fairly simple message, in his other book *L'Homme*, and in his pamphlet *Le Jour du Seigneur*, which was written in an obscure, uneven Biblical style, he appeared in the guise of a vindictive apostle, full of pride and bitterness, a mad deacon suffering from mystical epilepsy, a Joseph de Maistre blessed with talent, a cantankerous and ferocious bigot.

On the other hand, reflected Des Esseintes, these morbid excesses frequently obstructed ingenious flights of casuistry, for with even greater intolerance than Ozanam, Hello resolutely rejected everything that lay outside his little world, propounded the most astonishing axioms, maintained with disconcerting dogmatism that 'geology had gone back to Moses', that natural history, chemistry, indeed all modern science furnished proof of the scientific accuracy of the Bible; every page spoke of the Church as the sole repository of truth and the source of superhuman wisdom, all this enlivened with startling aphorisms and with furious imprecations spewed out in torrents over the art and literature of the eighteenth century.

To this strange mixture was added a love of sugary piety revealed in translations of the *Visions* of Angela da Foligno, a book of unparalleled stupidity and fluidity, and selections from Jan van Ruysbroeck, a thirteenth-century mystic whose prose presented an incomprehensible but attractive amalgam of gloomy ecstasies, tender raptures, and violent rages.

All the affectation there was in Hello the bumptious pontiff had come out in a preface he wrote for this book. As he said himself, 'extraordinary things can only be stammered out' – and stammer he did, declaring that 'the sacred obscurity in which Ruysbroeck spreads his eagle's wings is his ocean, his prey, his glory, and for him the four horizons would be too close-fitting a garment'.

Be that as it may, Des Esseintes felt drawn to this unbalanced but subtle mind; the fusion of the skilled psychologist with the pious pedant had proved impossible, and these jolts, these incoherences even, constituted the personality of the man.

The recruits who joined his standard made up the little group of writers who operated on the colour-line of the clerical camp. They did not belong to the main body of the army; strictly speaking, they were rather the scouts of a religion that distrusted men of talent like Veuillot and Hello, for the simple reason that they were neither servile enough nor insipid enough. What it really wanted was soldiers who never reasoned why, regiments of those purblind mediocrities Hello used to attack with all the ferocity of one who had suffered their tyranny. Accordingly Catholicism had made haste to close the columns of its papers to one of its partisans, Léon Bloy, a savage pamphleteer who wrote in a style at once precious and furious, tender and terrifying, and to expel from its bookshops, as one plague-stricken and unclean, another author who had bawled himself hoarse singing its praises: Barbey d'Aurevilly.

Admittedly this latter writer was far too compromising, far too independent a son of the Church. In the long run, the others would always eat humble pie and fall back into line, but he was the *enfant terrible* the party refused to own, who went whoring through literature and brought his women half-naked into the sanctuary. It was only because of the boundless contempt Catholicism has for all creative talent that an excommunication in due and proper form had not outlawed this strange servant who, under the pretext of doing honour to his masters, broke the chapel windows, juggled with the sacred vessels, and performed step-dances round the tabernacle.

Two of Barbey d'Aurevilly's works Des Esseintes found particularly enthralling: *Un Prêtre marié* and *Les Diaboliques*. Others, such as *L'Ensorcelée*, *Le Chevalier des Touches* and *Une Vieille Maîtresse*, were doubtless better balanced and more complete works, but they did not appeal so strongly to Des Esseintes who was really interested only in sickly books, undermined and inflamed by fever.

In these comparatively healthy volumes Barbey d'Aurevilly was constantly tacking to and fro between those two channels of Catholic belief which eventually run into one: mysticism and sadism. But in the two books which Des Esseintes was now glancing through, Barbey had thrown caution to the winds, had given rein to his steed, and had ridden full tilt down one road after another, as far as he could go.

All the horrific mystery of the Middle Ages brooded over that improbable book *Un Prêtre marié*; magic was mixed up with religion, sorcery with prayer; while the God of original sin, more pitiless, more cruel than the Devil, submitted his innocent victim Calixte to uninterrupted torments, branding her with a red cross on the forehead, just as in olden times he had one of his angels mark the houses of the unbelievers he meant to kill.

These scenes, like the fantasies of a fasting monk affected with delirium, were unfolded in the disjointed language of a fever patient. But unfortunately, among all the characters galvanized into an unbalanced life like so many Hoffmann Coppelias, there were some, the Néel de Néhou for instance, who seemed to have been imagined in one of those periods of prostration that always follow crises; and they were out of keeping in this atmosphere of melancholy madness, into which they introduced the same note of unintentional humour as is sounded by the little zinc lordling in hunting-boots who stands blowing his horn on the pedestal of so many mantel-piece clocks.

After these mystical divagations, Barbey had enjoyed a period of comparative calm, but then a frightening relapse had occurred.

The belief that man is an irresolute creature pulled this way and that by two forces of equal strength, alternately winning and losing the battle for his soul; the conviction that human life is nothing more than an uncertain struggle between heaven and hell; the faith in two opposed entities, Satan and Christ – all this was bound to engender those internal discords in which the soul, excited by the incessant fighting, stimulated as it were by the constant promises and threats, ends up by giving in and prostitutes itself to whichever of the two combatants has been the more obstinate in its pursuit.

In *Un Prêtre marié*, it was Christ whose temptations had been successful and whose praises were sung by Barbey d'Aurevilly;

but in *Les Diaboliques*, the author had surrendered to the Devil, and it was Satan he extolled. At this point there appeared on the scene that bastard child of Catholicism which for centuries the Church has pursued with its exorcisms and its *autos-da-fé* – sadism.

This strange and ill-defined condition cannot in fact arise in the mind of an unbeliever. It does not consist simply in riotous indulgence of the flesh, stimulated by bloody acts of cruelty, for in that case it would be nothing more than a deviation of the genetic instincts, a case of satyriasis developed to its fullest extent; it consists first and foremost in a sacrilegious manifestation, in a moral rebellion, in a spiritual debauch, in a wholly idealistic, wholly Christian aberration. There is also something in it of joy tempered by fear, a joy analogous to the wicked delight of disobedient children playing with forbidden things for no other reason than that their parents have expressly forbidden them to go near them.

The truth of the matter is that if it did not involve sacrilege, sadism would have no *raison d'être*; on the other hand, since sacrilege depends on the existence of a religion, it cannot be deliberately and effectively committed except by a believer, for a man would derive no satisfaction whatever from profaning a faith that was unimportant or unknown to him.

The strength of sadism then, the attraction it offers, lies entirely in the forbidden pleasure of transferring to Satan the homage and the prayers that should go to God; it lies in the flouting of the precepts of Catholicism, which the sadist actually observes in topsy-turvy fashion when, in order to offend Christ the more grievously, he commits the sins Christ most expressly proscribed – profanation of holy things and carnal debauch.

In point of fact, this vice to which the Marquis de Sade had given his name was as old as the Church itself; the eighteenth century, when it was particularly rife, had simply revived, by an ordinary atavistic process, the impious practices of the witches' sabbath of medieval times – to go no further back in history.

Des Esseintes had done no more than dip into the *Malleus*

Maleficorum, that terrible code of procedure of Jacob Sprenger's which permitted the Church to send thousands of necromancers and sorcerers to the stake; but that was enough to enable him to recognize in the witches' sabbath all the obscenities and blasphemies of sadism. Besides the filthy orgies dear to the Evil One – nights devoted alternately to lawful and unnatural copulation, nights befouled by the bestialities of bloody debauch – he found the same parodies of religious processions, the same ritual threats and insults hurled at God, the same devotion to his Rival – as when the Black Mass was celebrated over a woman on all fours whose naked rump, repeatedly soiled, served as the altar, with the priest cursing the bread and wine, and the congregation derisively taking communion in the shape of a black host stamped with a picture of a he-goat.

This same outpouring of foul-mouthed jests and degrading insults was to be seen in the works of the Marquis de Sade, who spiced his frightful sensualities with sacrilegious profanities. He would rail at Heaven, invoke Lucifer, call God an abject scoundrel, a crazy idiot, spit on the sacrament of communion, do his best in fact to besmirch with vile obscenities a Divinity he hoped would damn him, at the same time declaring, as a further act of defiance, that that Divinity did not exist.

This psychic condition Barbey d'Aurevilly came close to sharing. If he did not go as far as Sade in shouting atrocious curses at the Saviour; if, out of greater caution or greater fear, he always professed to honour the Church, he none the less addressed his prayers to the Devil in true medieval fashion, and in his desire to defy the Deity, likewise slipped into demonic erotomania, coining new sensual monstrosities, or even borrowing from *La Philosophie dans le boudoir* a certain episode which he seasoned with fresh condiments to make the story *Le Dîner d'un athée*.

The extraordinary book that contained this tale was Des Esseintes' delight; he had therefore had printed for him in bishop's-purple ink, within a border of cardinal red, on a genuine parchment blessed by the Auditors of the Rota, a copy of *Les Diaboliques* set up in those *lettres de civilité* whose peculiar hooks and flourishes, curling up or down, assume a satanic appearance.

Not counting certain poems of Baudelaire's which, in imitation of the prayers chanted on the nights of the witches' sabbath, took the form of infernal litanies, this book, among all the works of contemporary apostolic literature, was the only one to reveal that state of mind, at once devout and impious, towards which nostalgic memories of Catholicism, stimulated by fits of neurosis, had often impelled Des Esseintes.

With Barbey d'Aurevilly, the series of religious writers came to an end. To tell the truth, this pariah belonged more, from every point of view, to secular literature than to that other literature in which he claimed a place that was denied him. His wild romantic style, for instance, full of twisted expressions, outlandish turns of phrase, and far-fetched similes, whipped up his sentences as they galloped across the page, farting and jangling their bells. In short, Barbey looked like a stallion among the geldings that filled the ultramontane stables.

Such were Des Esseintes' reflections as he dipped into the book, re-reading a passage here and there; and then, comparing the author's vigorous and varied style with the lymphatic, stereotyped style of his fellow writers, he was led to consider that evolution of language so accurately described by Darwin.

Closely associated with the secular writers of his time, brought up in the Romantic school, familiar with the latest books and accustomed to reading modern publications, Barbey inevitably found himself in possession of an idiom which had undergone many profound modifications, and which had been largely renovated since the seventeenth century.

The very opposite had been the case with the ecclesiastical writers; confined to their own territory, imprisoned within an identical, traditional range of reading, knowing nothing of the literary evolution of more recent times and absolutely determined, if need be, to pluck their eyes out rather than recognize it, they necessarily employed an unaltered and unalterable language, like that eighteenth-century language which the

164

descendants of the French settlers in Canada normally speak and write to this day, no variation in vocabulary or phraseology having ever been possible in their idiom, cut off as it is from the old country and surrounded on all sides by the English tongue.

Des Esseintes' musings had reached this point when the silvery sound of a bell tinkling a little angelus told him that breakfast was ready. He left his books where they were, wiped his forehead and made for the dining-room, telling himself that of all the volumes he had been rearranging, the works of Barbey d'Aurevilly were still the only ones whose thought and style offered those gamy flavours and unhealthy spots, that bruised skin and sleepy taste which he so loved to savour in the decadent writers, both Latin and monastic, of olden times.

XIII

THE weather had begun behaving in the most peculiar fashion. That year the seasons all overlapped, so that after a period of squalls and mists, blazing skies, like sheets of white-hot metal, suddenly appeared from over the horizon. In a couple of days, without any transition whatever, the cold, dank fogs and pouring rain were followed by a wave of torrid heat, an appallingly sultry atmosphere. As if it were being energetically poked with gigantic fire-irons, the sun glowed like an open furnace, sending out an almost white light that burnt the eyes; fiery particles of dust rose from the scorched roads, grilling the parched trees, browning the dry grass. The glare reflected by whitewashed walls and the flames kindled in window-panes and zinc roofs were absolutely blinding; the temperature of a foundry in full blast weighed down on Des Esseintes' house.

Wearing next to nothing, he threw open a window, to be hit full in the face by a fiery blast from outside; the dining-room, where he next sought refuge, was like an oven, and the rarefied air seemed to have reached boiling-point. He sat down feeling utter despair, for the excitement that had kept his mind busy with day-dreams while he was sorting out his books had died away. Like every other victim of neurosis, he found heat overpowering; his anaemia, held in check by the cold weather, got the better of him again, taking the strength out of a body already debilitated by copious perspiration.

With his shirt clinging to his moist back, his perineum sodden, his arms and legs wet, and his forehead streaming with sweat that ran down his cheeks like salty tears, Des Esseintes lay back exhausted in his chair. Just then he became aware of the meat on the table before him and the sight of it sickened him; he ordered it to be taken away and boiled eggs brought instead. When these arrived, he tried to swallow some sippets dipped in the yolk, but they stuck in his throat.

Waves of nausea rose to his lips, and when he drank a few drops of wine they pricked his stomach like arrows of fire. He mopped his face, where the sweat, which had been warm a few minutes before, was now running down his temples in cold trickles; and he tried sucking bits of ice to stave off the feeling of nausea – but all in vain.

Overcome with infinite fatigue, he slumped helplessly against the table. After a while he got to his feet, gasping for breath, but the sippets had swollen and were slowly rising in his throat, choking him. Never had he felt so upset, so weak, so ill at ease; on top of it all, his eyes were affected and he started seeing double, with things spinning round in pairs; soon he lost his sense of distance, so that his glass seemed miles away. He told himself he was the victim of optical illusions, but even so he was unable to shake them off. Finally he went and lay down on the sofa in the sitting-room; but it promptly began pitching and rolling like a ship at sea, and his nausea grew worse. He got up again, this time deciding to take a digestive to help down the eggs, which were still troubling him.

Returning to the dining-room, he wryly likened himself, there in his ship's cabin, to a traveller suffering from sea-sickness. He staggered over to the cupboard and looked at the mouth organ, but refrained from opening it; instead, he reached up to the shelf above for a bottle of Benedictine – a bottle he kept in the house on account of its shape, which he considered suggestive of ideas at once pleasantly wanton and vaguely mystical.

But for the moment he remained unmoved, and just stared dully at the squat, dark-green bottle, which normally conjured up visions of medieval priories for him, with its antique monkish paunch, its head and neck wrapped in a parchment cowl, its red seal quartered with three silver mitres on a field azure and fastened to the neck with lead like a Papal bull, its label inscribed in sonorous Latin, on paper apparently yellowed and faded with age: *Liquor Monachorum Benedictinorum Abbatiæ Fiscanensis.*

Under this truly monastic habit, certified by a cross and the ecclesiastical initials D. O. M., and enclosed in parchment and ligatures like an authentic charter, there slumbered a saffron-coloured liqueur of exquisite delicacy. It gave off a subtle aroma of angelica and hyssop mixed with seaweed whose iodine and bromine content was masked with sugar; it stimulated the palate with a spirituous fire hidden under an altogether virginal sweetness; and it flattered the nostrils with a hint of corruption wrapped up in a caress that was at once childlike and devout.

This hypocrisy resulting from the extraordinary discrepancy between container and contents, between the liturgical form of the bottle and the utterly feminine, utterly modern soul inside it, had set him dreaming before now. Sitting with the bottle in front of him, he had spent hours thinking about the monks who sold it, the Benedictines of the Abbey of Fécamp who, belonging as they did to the congregation of Saint-Maur, famous for its historical researches, were subject to the Rule of St Benedict, yet did not follow the observances of either the white monks of Cîteaux or the black monks of Cluny. They forced themselves upon his imagination, looking just as if they had come straight out of the Middle Ages, growing medicinal herbs, heating retorts, distilling in alembics sovereign cordials, infallible panaceas.

He took a sip of the liqueur and felt a little better for a minute or two; but soon the fire a drop of wine had kindled in his innards blazed up again. He threw down his napkin and went back into his study, where he began pacing up and down; he felt as if he were under the receiver of an air-pump in which a vacuum was being gradually created, and a dangerously pleasant lethargy spread from his brain into every limb. Unable to stand any more of this, he pulled himself together and, for perhaps the first time since his coming to Fontenay, sought refuge in the garden, where he took shelter in the patch of shadow cast by a tree. Sitting on the grass, he gazed vacantly at the rows of vegetables the servants had planted. But it was only after an hour's gazing that he realized what they were, for a greenish mist floated before his eyes, preventing him from seeing anything more than blurred, watery images which kept changing colour and appearance.

In the end, however, he recovered his balance and was able to distinguish clearly onions and cabbages in front, further off a huge patch of lettuce, and at the back, all along the hedge, a row of white lilies standing motionless in the sultry air.

A smile puckered his lips, for he suddenly remembered the quaint comparison old Nicander once made, from the point of view of shape, between the pistil of a lily and the genitals of an ass, and also the passage in Albertus Magnus where that miracle-worker expounds a most peculiar method of discovering, with the aid of a lettuce, whether a girl is still a virgin.

These recollections cheered him up somewhat, and he began looking round the garden, examining the plants that had been withered by the heat and noticing how the baked earth was smoking under the scorching, dusty rays of the sun. Then, over the hedge separating the low-lying garden from the raised roadway going up to the Fort, he caught sight of a bunch of boys rolling about on the ground in the blazing sunshine.

He was fixing his attention on them when another lad appeared on the scene. He was smaller than the rest, and a really squalid specimen; his hair looked like sandy seaweed, two green bubbles hung from his nose, and his lips were coated with the disgusting white mess he was eating – skim-milk cheese spread on a hunk of bread and sprinkled with chopped garlic.

Des Esseintes sniffed the air, and a depraved longing, a perverse craving took hold of him; the nauseating snack positively made his mouth water. He felt sure that his stomach, which rebelled against all normal food, would digest this frightful titbit and his palate enjoy it as much as a banquet.

He sprang to his feet, ran to the kitchen, and ordered his servants to send to the village for a round loaf, some white cheese, and a little garlic, explaining that he wanted a snack exactly like the one the child was having. This done, he went back to where he had been sitting under the tree.

The lads were fighting now, snatching bits of bread from each other's hands, ramming them into their mouths and licking their fingers afterwards. Kicks and blows fell thick and fast, and the weaker boys were knocked to the ground, where they lay thrashing about and crying as the broken stones dug into their bottoms.

The sight put new life into Des Esseintes; the interest this fight aroused in him took his mind off his own sickly condition. Faced with the savage fury of these vicious brats, he reflected on the cruel and abominable law of the struggle for life, and contemptible though these children were, he could not help feeling sorry for them and thinking it would have been better for them if their mothers had never borne them.

After all, what did their lives amount to but impetigo, colic, fevers, measles, smacks, and slaps in childhood; degrading jobs with plenty of kicks and curses at thirteen or so; deceiving mistresses, foul diseases, and unfaithful wives in manhood; and then, in old age, infirmities and death-agonies in workhouses or hospitals?

And the future, when you came to think of it, was the same for all, and nobody with any sense would dream of envying anybody else. For the rich, though the setting was different, it was a case of the same passions, the same worries, the same sorrows, the same diseases – and also the same paltry pleasures, whether these were alcoholic, literary, or carnal. There was even a vague compensation for every sort of suffering, a kind of rough justice that restored the balance of unhappiness between the classes, granting the poor greater resistance to physical ills that wreaked worse havoc on the feebler and thinner bodies of the rich.

What madness it was to beget children, reflected Des Esseintes. And to think that the priestery, who had taken a vow of sterility, had carried inconsistency to the point of canonizing St Vincent de Paul because he saved innocent babes for useless torments!

Thanks to his odious precautions, the man had postponed for years to come the deaths of creatures devoid of thought or feeling, so that later, having acquired a little understanding and a far greater capacity for suffering, they could look into the future, could expect and dread that death whose very name had hitherto been unknown to them, could even, in some cases, call upon it to release them from the hateful life-sentence to which he had condemned them in virtue of an absurd theological code.

And since the old man's death, his ideas had won universal acceptance; for instance, children abandoned by their mothers were given homes instead of being left to die quietly without knowing what was happening; and yet the life that was kept for them would grow harder and bleaker day by day. Similarly, under the pretext of encouraging liberty and progress, society had discovered yet another means of aggravating man's wretched lot, by dragging him from his home, rigging him out in a ridiculous costume, putting specially designed weapons into his hands, and reducing him to the same degrading slavery from which the negroes were released out of pity – and all this to put him in a position to kill his neighbour without risking the scaffold, as ordinary murderers do who operate single-handed, without uniforms, and with quieter, poorer weapons.

What a peculiar age this was, Des Esseintes thought to himself, which, ostensibly in the interests of humanity, strove to perfect anaesthetics in order to do away with physical suffering, and at the same time concocted stimulants such as this to aggravate moral suffering!

Ah! if in the name of pity the futile business of procreation was ever to be abolished, the time had surely come to do it. But here again, the laws enacted by men like Portalis and Homais stood in the way, ferocious and unreasonable.

Justice regarded as perfectly legitimate the tricks that were used to prevent conception; it was a recognized, acknowledged fact; there was never a couple in the land, no matter how well-to-do, that did not send its children to the wash or use devices that could be bought openly in the shops – devices nobody would ever dream of condemning. And yet, if these natural or mechanical subterfuges proved ineffectual, if the trickery failed, and if to make good the failure recourse was had to more reliable methods, why then there were not prisons, jails, or penitentiaries enough to accommodate the people convicted out of hand, and in all good faith, by other individuals who the same night, in the conjugal bed, used every trick they knew to avoid begetting brats of their own.

It followed that the fraud itself was not a crime, but that the attempt to make good its failure was.

In short, society regarded as a crime the act of killing a creature endowed with life; and yet expelling a foetus simply meant destroying an animal that was less developed, less alive, certainly less intelligent and less prepossessing, than a dog or a cat, which could be strangled at birth with impunity.

It should also be remarked, thought Des Esseintes, that to add to the justice of it all, it was not the unskilful operator – who generally beat a speedy retreat – but the woman in the case, the victim of his clumsiness, who paid the penalty for saving an innocent creature from the misery of life.

All the same, it was a fantastically prejudiced world that tried to outlaw operations so natural that the most primitive of men, the South Sea islander, was led to perform them by instinct alone.

Just then Des Esseintes' manservant interrupted these charitable reflections of his by bringing him the snack he had asked for on a silver-gilt salver. His gorge rose at the sight; he had not the courage to take even a bite at the bread, for his morbid appetite had deserted him. A dreadful feeling of debility came over him again, but he was forced to get to his feet; the sun was moving round and gradually encroaching on his patch of shadow, the heat becoming fiercer and more oppressive.

'You see those children fighting in the road?' he said to the man. 'Well, throw the thing to them. And let's hope that the weaklings are badly mauled about, that they don't get so much as a crumb of bread, and that on top of it all they're soundly thrashed when they get home with their breeches torn and a couple of black eyes to boot. That'll give them a foretaste of the sort of life they can expect!' And he went back into the house, where he sank limply into an armchair.

'Still, I really must see if there isn't something I can eat,' he muttered – and he tried soaking a biscuit in a glass of old

J. P. Cloete Constantia, of which he still had a few bottles in his cellar.

This wine, the colour of singed onion skins, and tasting of old malaga and port, but with a sugary bouquet all its own and an after-taste of grapes whose juices have been condensed and sublimated by burning suns, had often braced him up and even given new vigour to a stomach weakened by the fasting he was forced to practise; but this time the cordial, usually so helpful, failed to have any effect.

Next, in the hope that an emollient might cool the hot irons that were burning his innards, he resorted to Nalifka, a Russian liqueur contained in a bottle covered with a dull gold glaze; but this unctuous, raspberry-flavoured syrup was just as ineffective. Alas, the time was long past when Des Esseintes, then enjoying comparatively good health, would get into a sledge he kept at home – this in the hottest period of the year – and sit there wrapped in furs that he pulled tightly round him, shivering to the best of his ability and saying through deliberately chattering teeth: 'What an icy wind! Why, it's freezing here, it's freezing!' – until he almost convinced himself that it really was cold.

Unfortunately, now that his sufferings were real, these remedies were no longer of any avail.

Nor was it any use his having recourse to laudanum; instead of acting as a sedative, it irritated his nerves and thus robbed him of his sleep. At one time he had also resorted to opium and hashish in the hope of seeing visions, but these two drugs had only brought on vomiting and violent nervous disorders; he had been obliged to stop using them at once and, without the help of these crude stimulants, to ask his brain, alone and unaided, to carry him far away from everyday life into the land of dreams.

'What a day!' he groaned as he mopped his neck, feeling what little strength was left in him melting away in fresh floods of perspiration. A feverish restlessness again prevented him from sitting still, so that once more he wandered from room to room, trying one chair after another. Finally, tired of walking round the house, he sank into his desk-chair, and resting his elbows on the desk, started idly and unconsciously playing with an astrolabe that was being used as a paper-weight on top of a pile of books and notes.

He had bought this instrument, which was made of engraved and gilded copper, of German workmanship and dating from the seventeenth century, in a second-hand dealer's in Paris, after a visit he had paid to the Cluny Museum, where he had stood for hours enraptured by a wonderful astrolabe of carved ivory, whose cabbalistic appearance had captivated him.

The paper-weight stirred up in him a whole swarm of memories. Set in motion by the sight of this little curio, his thoughts went from Fontenay to Paris, to the old curiosity shop where he had bought it, then back to the Thermes Museum; and he conjured up a mental picture of the ivory astrolabe while his eyes continued to dwell, though now unseeingly, on the copper astrolabe on his desk.

Then, still in memory, he left the Museum and went for a stroll through the city streets, wandering along the Rue de Sommerard and the Boulevard Saint-Michel, turning off into the adjoining streets, and stopping outside certain establishments whose multiplicity and peculiar appearance had often struck him.

Beginning with an astrolabe, this mental excursion ended up in the low taverns of the Latin Quarter.

He remembered what a tremendous number of these places there were all along the Rue Monsieur-le-Prince and down the Odéon end of the Rue de Vaugirard; sometimes they stood cheek by jowl like the old *riddecks* of the Rue du Canal-aux-Harengs at Antwerp, lined up along the pavement one after the other, all looking very much alike.

Through half-open doors and windows only partially obscured by coloured panes or curtains, he could recall catching glimpses of women walking up and down, dragging their feet and sticking their necks out like so many geese; others sitting dejectedly on benches were wearing their elbows out on marble-topped tables, lost in their thoughts and singing softly to themselves, with their heads in their hands; yet others

174

would be swaying about in front of looking-glasses, patting with their fingertips the switches of hair they had just dressed; others again would be emptying purses with broken clasps of piles of silver and copper, and methodically arranging the money in little heaps.

Most of them had heavy features, hoarse voices, pendulous breasts, and painted eyes, and all of them, like automata wound up at the same time with the same key, threw out the same invitations in the same tone of voice, flashed the same smiles, made the same odd remarks, the same peculiar comments.

Ideas began to link up in Des Esseintes' mind, and he found himself coming to a definite conclusion, now that his memory had provided him, so to speak, with a bird's-eye view of these crowded taverns and streets.

He grasped the true significance of all these cafés, realized that they corresponded to the state of mind of an entire generation, and saw that they offered him a synthesis of the age.

The symptoms were indeed plain and undeniable; the licensed brothels were disappearing, and every time one of them closed its doors, a tavern opened in its place.

This diminution of official prostitution in favour of unofficial promiscuity was obviously to be accounted for by the incomprehensible illusions to which men are subject in affairs of the flesh.

Monstrous as this might appear, the tavern satisfied an ideal.

The fact was that although the utilitarian tendencies handed down by heredity, and encouraged by the precocious discourtesies and constant incivilities of school life, had made the younger generation singularly boorish and also singularly cold and materialistic, it had none the less kept, deep down in its heart, a little old-fashioned sentimentality, a vague, stale, old-fashioned ideal of love.

The result was that nowadays, when its blood caught fire, it could not stomach just walking in, taking its pleasure, paying the bill, and walking out again. This, in its eyes, was sheer bestiality, like a dog covering a bitch without any preamble;

besides, a man's vanity obtained no sort of satisfaction in these houses of ill fame where there was no show of resistance, no semblance of victory, no hope of preferential treatment, no possibility even of obtaining liberal favours from a tradeswoman who measured out her caresses in proportion to the price paid. On the other hand, to court a girl in a tavern was to avoid wounding all these amorous susceptibilities, all these sentimental feelings. There were always several men after a girl like that, and those to whom she agreed, at a price, to grant a rendezvous, honestly imagined that they were the object of an honorary distinction, a rare favour.

Yet the staff of a tavern were every bit as stupid and mercenary, as base and depraved, as the staff of a brothel. Like the latter, they drank without being thirsty, laughed without being amused, drooled over the caresses of the filthiest workman, and went for each other hammer and tongs at the slightest provocation. But in spite of everything, the young men of Paris had still not learnt that from the point of view of looks, dress, and technique, the waitresses in these taverns were vastly inferior to the women cooped up in the luxurious sitting-rooms of licensed houses.

Lord, what fools they must be, Des Esseintes used to think to himself, these young chaps who hang around the beer-houses, because quite apart from their ridiculous illusions, they actually come to forget the risks involved in sampling shop-soiled goods of dubious quality, and to take no account of the money spent on a fixed number of drinks priced beforehand by the landlady, the time wasted in waiting for delivery of the goods, which are held back to raise the price, and the perpetual shillyshallying intended to start the money flowing and keep it flowing.

This idiotic sentimentality combined with ruthless commercialism clearly represented the dominant spirit of the age; these same men who would have gouged anybody's eyes out to make a few coppers, lost all their flair and shrewdness when it came to dealing with the shifty tavern girls who harried them without pity and fleeced them without mercy. The wheels of industry turned, and families cheated one another in the name of trade, only to let themselves be robbed of money by their sons, who in turn allowed themselves to be swindled by these women, who in the last resort were bled white by their own fancy men.

Over the whole of Paris, from east to west and north to south, there stretched an unbroken network of confidence tricks, a chain of organized thefts acting one upon the other – and all because, instead of being served straight away, customers were kept waiting and left to cool their heels.

The fact was that human wisdom was essentially a matter of spinning things out, of saying no first and yes later; for the best way of handling men has always been to keep putting them off.

'Ah, if only the same were true of my stomach!' sighed Des Esseintes, as he was suddenly doubled up with a spasm of pain that jolted his thoughts back to Fontenay from the distant regions they had been roaming.

XIV

THE next few days went by without too much trouble, thanks to various devices that were used to trick the stomach into acquiescence; but one morning the sauces which disguised the smell of fat and the aroma of blood rising from Des Esseintes' meat proved unacceptable in themselves, and he anxiously asked himself whether his already alarming weakness was not going to get worse and force him to keep to his bed. Then, all of a sudden, a gleam of light shone through his distress: he remembered that one of his friends who had been very ill some time before had succeeded, by using a patent digester, in checking his anaemia, halting the wasting process, and keeping what little strength remained in him.

He sent his manservant off to Paris to buy one of these precious instruments, and with the help of the manufacturer's directions, he was able to instruct his cook how to chop some roast beef up into little pieces, put it dry into the digester, add a slice of leek and one of carrot, then screw down the lid and leave the whole thing to boil in a double saucepan for four hours.

At the end of that time you pressed the juice out of the threads of meat, and you drank a spoonful of this muddy, salty liquid that was left at the bottom of the digester. Then you felt something slipping down like warm marrow-fat, with a soothing, velvety caress.

This meat extract put a stop to the pains and nausea caused by hunger, and even stimulated the stomach so that it no longer refused to take in a few spoonfuls of soup.

Thanks to the digester, Des Esseintes' nervous trouble got no worse, and he told himself:

'At any rate, that's so much gained; now perhaps the temperature will drop and the heavens scatter a little ash over that abominably enervating sun. If that happens I'll be able to hang on till the first fogs and frosts without too much difficulty.'

In his present state of apathy and bored inactivity, his library, which he had been unable to finish rearranging, got on his nerves. Tied as he was to his chair, he was confronted all the time with his profane books, stacked higgledy-piggledy on their shelves, leaning against each other, propping each other up, or lying flat on their sides like a pack of cards. This disorder shocked him all the more in that it formed such a contrast to the perfect order of his religious works, carefully lined up on parade along the walls.

He tried to remedy this confusion, but after ten minutes' work he was bathed in sweat. The effort was obviously too much for him; utterly exhausted, he lay down on a couch and rang for his servant.

Following his instructions, the old man set to work, bringing him the books one by one so that he could examine each and say where it was to go.

This job did not take long, for Des Esseintes' library contained only a very limited number of contemporary lay works.

By dint of passing them through the critical apparatus of his mind, just as a metal worker passes strips of metal through a steel drawing-machine, from which they emerge thin and light, reduced to almost invisible threads, he had found in the end that none of his books could stand up to this sort of treatment, that none was sufficiently hardened to go through the next process, the reading-mill. Trying to eliminate the inferior works, he had in fact curtailed and practically sterilized his pleasure in reading, emphasizing more than ever the irremediable conflict between his ideas and those of the world into which chance had ordained that he should be born. Things had now got to the point where he found it impossible to discover a book that satisfied his secret longings; indeed, he even began to lose his admiration for the very works that had undoubtedly helped to sharpen his mind and make it so subtle and critical.

Yet his literary opinions had started from a very simple point of view. For him, there were no such things as schools; the only thing that mattered to him was the writer's personality, and the only thing that interested him was the working of the writer's brain, no matter what subject he was tackling. Unfortunately this criterion of appreciation, so obviously just, was practically impossible to apply, for the simple reason that, however much a reader wants to rid himself of prejudice and refrain from passion, he naturally prefers those works which correspond most intimately with his own personality, and ends by relegating all the rest to limbo.

This process of selection had taken place slowly in his case. At one time he had worshipped the great Balzac, but as his constitution had become unbalanced and his nerves had gained the upper hand, so his tastes had been modified and his preferences changed.

Soon indeed, and this although he realized how unjust he was being to the prodigious author of the *Comédie humaine*, he had given up so much as opening his books, put off by their robust health; other aspirations stirred him now, that were in a way almost indefinable.

By diligent self-examination, however, he realized first of all that to attract him a book had to have that quality of strangeness that Edgar Allan Poe called for; but he was inclined to venture further along this road, and to insist on Byzantine flowers of thought and deliquescent complexities of style; he demanded a disquieting vagueness that would give him scope for dreaming until he decided to make it still vaguer or more definite, according to the way he felt at the time. He wanted, in short, a work of art both for what it was in itself and for what it allowed him to bestow on it; he wanted to go along with it and on it, as if supported by a friend or carried by a vehicle, into a sphere where sublimated sensations would arouse within him an unexpected commotion, the causes of which he would strive patiently and even vainly to analyse.

Lastly, since leaving Paris, he had withdrawn further and further from reality and above all from the society of his day, which he regarded with ever-growing horror; this hatred he felt had inevitably affected his literary and artistic tastes, so that he shunned as far as possible pictures and books whose subjects were confined to modern life.

The result was that, losing the faculty of admiring beauty in whatever guise it appeared, he now preferred, among Flaubert's works, *La Tentation de Saint Antoine* to *L'Éducation sentimentale*; among Goncourt's works, *La Faustin* to *Germinie Lacerteux*; among Zola's works, *La Faute de l'Abbé Mouret* to *L'Assommoir*.

This seemed to him a logical point of view; these books, not as topical of course but just as stirring and human as the others, let him penetrate further and deeper into the personalities of their authors, who revealed with greater frankness their most mysterious impulses, while they lifted him, too, higher than the rest, out of the trivial existence of which he was so heartily sick.

And then, reading these works, he could enter into complete intellectual fellowship with the writers who had conceived them, because at the moment of conception those writers had been in a state of mind analogous to his own.

The fact is that when the period in which a man of talent is condemned to live is dull and stupid, the artist is haunted, perhaps unknown to himself, by a nostalgic yearning for another age.

Unable to attune himself, except at rare intervals, to his environment, and no longer finding in the examination of that environment and the creatures who endure it sufficient pleasures of observation and analysis to divert him, he is aware of the birth and development in himself of unusual phenomena. Vague migratory longings spring up which find fulfilment in reflection and study. Instincts, sensations, inclinations bequeathed to him by heredity awake, take shape, and assert themselves with imperious authority. He recalls memories of people and things he has never known personally, and there comes a time when he bursts out of the prison of his century and roams about at liberty in another period, with which, as a crowning illusion, he imagines he would have been more in accord.

In some cases there is a return to past ages, to vanished civilizations, to dead centuries; in others there is a pursuit of dream and fantasy, a more or less vivid vision of a future whose image reproduces, unconsciously and as a result of atavism, that of past epochs.

In Flaubert's case, there was a series of vast, imposing scenes, grandiose pageantries of barbaric splendour in which there participated creatures delicate and sensitive, mysterious and proud, women cursed, in all the perfection of their beauty, with suffering souls, in the depths of which he discerned atrocious delusions, insane aspirations, born of the disgust they already felt for the dreadful mediocrity of the pleasures awaiting them.

The personality of the great writer was revealed in all its splendour in those incomparable pages of *La Tentation de Saint Antoine* and *Salammbô* in which, leaving our petty modern civilization far behind, he conjured up the Asiatic glories of distant epochs, their mystic ardours and doldrums, the aberrations resulting from their idleness, the brutalities arising from their boredom – that oppressive boredom which emanates from opulence and prayer even before their pleasures have been fully enjoyed.

With Goncourt, it was a case of nostalgia for the eighteenth century, a longing to return to the elegant graces of a society that had vanished for ever. The gigantic backcloth of seas dashing against great backwaters, of deserts stretching away to infinity under blazing skies, found no place in his nostalgic masterpiece, which confined itself, within the precincts of an aristocratic park, to a boudoir warm with the voluptuous effluvia of a woman with a weary smile, a pouting expression, and pensive, brooding eyes. Nor was the spirit with which he animated his characters the same spirit Flaubert breathed into his creations, a spirit revolted in advance by the inexorable certainty that no new happiness was possible; it was rather a spirit revolted after the event, by bitter experience, at the thought of all the fruitless efforts it had made to invent new spiritual relationships and to introduce a little variety into the immemorial pleasure that is repeated down the ages in the satisfaction, more or less ingeniously obtained, of lusting couples.

Although she lived in the late nineteenth century and was physically and effectively a modern, by virtue of ancestral influences La Faustin was a creature of the eighteenth century, sharing to the full its spiritual perversity, its cerebral lassitude, its sensual satiety.

This book of Edmond de Goncourt's was one of Des Esseintes' favourites, for the dream-inducing suggestiveness he wanted abounded in this work, where beneath the printed line lurked another line visible only to the soul, indicated by an epithet that opened up vast vistas of passion, by a reticence that hinted at spiritual infinities no ordinary idiom could compass. The idiom used in this book was quite different from the language of Flaubert, inimitable in its magnificence; this style was penetrating and sickly, tense and subtle, careful to record the intangible impression that affects the senses and produces feeling, and skilled in modulating the complicated nuances of an epoch that was itself extraordinarily complex. It was, in fact, the sort of style that is indispensable to decrepit civilizations which, in order to express their needs, and to whatever age they may belong, require new acceptations, new uses, new forms both of word and phrase.

In Rome, expiring paganism had modified its prosody and transmuted its language through Ausonius, through Claudian, above all through Rutilius, whose style, careful and scrupulous, sensuous and sonorous, presented an obvious analogy with the Goncourt brothers' style, especially when describing light and shade and colour.

In Paris, a phenomenon unique in literary history had come about; the moribund society of the eighteenth century, though it had been well provided with painters, sculptors, musicians, and architects, all familiar with its tastes and imbued with its beliefs, had failed to produce a genuine writer capable of rendering its dying graces or manifesting the essence of its feverish pleasures, that were soon to be so cruelly expiated. It had had to wait for Goncourt, whose personality was made up of memories and regrets made still more poignant by the distressing spectacle of the intellectual poverty and base aspirations of his time, to resuscitate, not only in his historical studies but also in a nostalgic work like *La Faustin*, the very soul of the period, and to embody its neurotic charms in this actress, so painfully eager to torment her heart and torture her brain in order to savour to the point of exhaustion the cruel revulsives of love and art.

In Zola the longing for some other existence took a different form. In him there was no desire to migrate to vanished civilizations, to worlds lost in the darkness of time; his sturdy, powerful temperament, enamoured of the luxuriance of life, of full-blooded vigour, of moral stamina, alienated him from the artificial graces and the painted pallors of the eighteenth century, as also from the hieratic pomp, the brutal ferocity, and the effeminate, ambiguous dreams of the ancient East. On the day when he too had been afflicted with this longing, this craving which in fact is poetry itself, to fly far away from the contemporary society he was studying, he had fled to an idyllic region where the sap boiled in the sunshine; he had dreamt of fantastic heavenly copulations, of long earthly ecstasies, of fertilizing showers of pollen falling into the palpitating genitals of flowers; he had arrived at a gigantic pantheism, and with the Garden of Eden in which he placed his Adam and Eve he had created, perhaps unconsciously, a prodigious Hindu poem, singing the glories of the flesh, extolling, in a style whose broad patches of crude colour had something of the weird brilliance of Indian paintings, living animate matter, which by its own frenzied procreation revealed to man and woman the forbidden fruit of love, its suffocating spasms, its instinctive caresses, its natural postures.

With Baudelaire, these three masters had captured and moulded Des Esseintes' imagination more than any others; but through re-reading them until he was saturated with their works and knew them completely by heart, he had eventually been obliged, to make it possible to absorb them again, to try and forget them, to leave them for a while undisturbed on his shelves.

Accordingly, he scarcely looked at them when his man handed them to him. He confined himself to pointing out where they should go, taking care to see that they were arranged in an orderly fashion and given plenty of elbow-room.

Next the man brought him another series of books which

caused him rather more trouble. These were works of which he had gradually grown fonder, works which by their very defects provided a welcome change from the perfect productions of greater writers. Here again, the process of elimination had led Des Esseintes to search through pages of uninspiring matter for odd sentences which would give him a shock as they discharged their electricity in a medium that seemed at first to be non-conducting.

Imperfection itself pleased him, provided it was neither base nor parasitic, and it may be that there was a certain amount of truth in his theory that the minor writer of the decadence, the writer who is incomplete but none the less individual, distils a balm more irritant, more sudorific, more acid than the author of the same period who is truly great and truly perfect. In his opinion, it was in their confused efforts that you could find the most exalted flights of sensibility, the most morbid caprices of psychology, the most extravagant aberrations of language called upon in vain to control and repress the effervescent salts of ideas and feelings.

It was therefore inevitable that, after the masters, he should turn to certain minor writers whom he found all the more attractive and endearing by reason of the contempt in which they were held by a public incapable of understanding them.

One of these writers, Paul Verlaine, had made his début a good many years before with a volume of verse, *Poèmes saturniens*, a work which might almost be described as feeble, in which pastiches of Leconte de Lisle rubbed shoulders with exercises in romantic rhetoric, but which already revealed in certain pieces, such as the sonnet *Mon Rêve familier*, the real personality of the poet.

Looking for his antecedents, Des Esseintes discovered underlying the unsureness of these early efforts a talent already profoundly marked by Baudelaire, whose influence had since become more obvious, though the borrowings Verlaine had made from his generous master had never amounted to flagrant thefts.

Moreover, some of his later books, *La Bonne Chanson*, *Fêtes galantes*, *Romances sans paroles*, and finally his last volume,

Sagesse, contained poems in which a writer of originality was revealed, standing out against the mass of his fellow authors.

Furnished with rhymes provided by the tenses of verbs, and sometimes even by lengthy adverbs preceded by a monosyllable, from which they fell like a heavy cascade of water dropping from a stone ledge, his lines, divided by unlikely caesuras, were often singularly obscure, with their daring ellipses and curious solecisms that were yet not without a certain grace.

Handling metre better than anyone, he had tried to rejuvenate the stereotyped forms of poetry, the sonnet for example, which he turned upside down, like those Japanese fish in coloured earthenware that are stood gills down on their pedestals, or which he perverted by coupling only masculine rhymes, for which he seemed to have a special affection. Similarly and not infrequently he had adopted a weird form such as a stanza of three lines with the middle one left unrhymed, or a monorhyme tercet followed by a single line serving as a refrain and echoing itself, like the line 'Dansons la gigue' in the poem *Streets*. He had used other rhythms too whose faint beat could be only half-heard behind the stanzas, like the muffled sound of a bell.

But his originality lay above all in his ability to communicate deliciously vague confidences in a whisper in the twilight. He alone had possessed the secret of hinting at certain strange spiritual aspirations, of whispering certain thoughts, of murmuring certain confessions, so softly, so quietly, so haltingly that the ear that caught them was left hesitating, and passed on to the soul a languor made more pronounced by the vagueness of these words that were guessed at rather than heard. The essence of Verlaine's poetry could be found in those wonderful lines from his *Fêtes galantes*:

> *Le soir tombait, un soir équivoque d'automne:*
> *Les belles se pendant rêveuses à nos bras,*
> *Dirent alors des mots si spécieux, tout bas,*
> *Que notre âme depuis ce temps tremble et s'étonne.**

* Night was falling, an equivocal autumn night: the fair ones hanging dreamily on to our arms whispered words so specious that ever since our soul has been trembling and amazed.

This was not the vast horizon revealed through the portals of Baudelaire's unforgettable poetry, but rather a glimpse of a moonlit scene, a more limited, intimate view peculiar to the author who, incidentally, had formulated his poetic method in a few lines of which Des Esseintes was particularly fond:

> *Car nous voulons la nuance encore,*
> *Pas la couleur, rien que la nuance*
> *. . . . .*
> *Et tout le reste est littérature.**

Des Esseintes had gladly followed him through all his varied works. After the publication of his *Romances sans paroles*, distributed by the printing-office of a newspaper at Sens, Verlaine had written nothing for quite a time; then, in charming verses that echoed the gentle, naïve accents of Villon, he had reappeared, singing the Virgin's praises, 'far from our days of carnal spirit and weary flesh'. Often Des Esseintes would re-read this book, *Sagesse*, allowing the poems it contained to inspire in him secret reveries, impossible dreams of an occult passion for a Byzantine Madonna able to change at a given moment into a Cydalisa who had strayed by accident into the nineteenth century; she was so mysterious and so alluring that it was impossible to tell whether she was longing to indulge in depravities so monstrous that, once accomplished they would become irresistible, or whether she herself was soaring heavenwards in an immaculate dream, in which the adoration of the soul would float about her in a love for ever unconfessed, for ever pure.

There were other poets, too, who could still excite his interest and admiration. One of these was Tristan Corbière, who in 1873, amid general indifference, had published a fantastically eccentric book of verse entitled *Les Amours jaunes*. Des Esseintes, who, in his hatred of all that was trite and vulgar, would have welcomed the most outrageous follies, the most bizarre extravagances, spent many happy hours with this book in which droll humour was combined with turbulent

* For we still want light and shade, not colour, nothing but light and shade . . . and all the rest is *literature*.

energy, and in which lines of disconcerting brilliance occurred in poems of wonderful obscurity. There were the litanies in his *Sommeil*, for instance, where he described sleep at one point as the

*Obscène confesseur des dévotes mort-nées.**

It was scarcely French; the poet was talking 'pidgin', using a telegram idiom, suppressing far too many verbs, trying to be waggish, and indulging in cheap commercial-traveller jokes; but then, out of this jungle of comical conceits and smirking witticisms there would suddenly rise a sharp cry of pain, like the sound of a violoncello string breaking. What is more, in this rugged, arid, utterly fleshless style, bristling with unusual terms and unexpected neologisms, there sparkled and flashed many a felicitous expression, many a stray line that had lost its rhyme but was none the less superb. Finally, to say nothing of his *Poèmes parisiens*, from which Des Esseintes used to quote this profound definition of woman:

Éternel féminin de l'éternel jocrisse,†

Tristan Corbière had, in a style of almost incredible concision, sung of the seas of Brittany, the sailors' seraglios, the Pardon of St Anne, and had even attained the eloquence of passionate hatred in the insults he heaped, when speaking of the camp at Conlie, on the individuals whom he described as 'mountebanks of the Fourth of September'.

The gamy flavour which Des Esseintes loved, and which was offered him by this poet of the condensed epithet and the perpetually suspect charm, he found also in another poet, Théodore Hannon, a disciple of Baudelaire and Gautier who was actuated by a very special understanding of studied elegances and factitious pleasures.

Unlike Verlaine, who was directly descended from Baudelaire, without any cross-breeding, especially in his psychology, in the sophistical slant of his thought, in the skilled distillation of his feeling, Théodore Hannon's kinship with the master

* Obscene confessor of fair bigots still-born.
† Eternal feminine of the eternal fool.

could be seen chiefly in the plastic side of his poetry, in his external view of people and things.

His delightful corruptness corresponded with Des Esseintes' tastes, and when it was foggy or raining the latter would often shut himself up in the retreat imagined by this poet and intoxicate his eyes with the shimmer of his fabrics, with the sparkle of his jewels, with all his exclusively material luxuries, which helped to excite his brain and rose like cantharides in a cloud of warm incense towards a Brussels idol with a painted face and a belly tanned with perfumes.

With the exception of these authors and of Stéphane Mallarmé, whom he instructed his man to put on one side, to be set in a class apart, Des Esseintes was only very moderately drawn to the poets.

In spite of his magnificent formal qualities, in spite of the imposing majesty of his verse, which had such a splendid air that even Hugo's hexameters seemed dull and drab in comparison, Leconte de Lisle could now no longer satisfy him. The ancient world which Flaubert had resuscitated with such marvellous success remained cold and lifeless in his hands. Nothing stirred in his poetry; it was all a façade with, most of the time, not a single idea to prop it up. There was no life in these empty poems, and their frigid mythologies ended up by repelling him.

Similarly, after cherishing him for many years, Des Esseintes was beginning to lose interest in Gautier's work; his admiration for the incomparable painter of word-pictures that Gautier was had recently been diminishing day by day, so that now he was more astonished than delighted by his almost apathetic descriptions. Outside objects had made a lasting impression on his remarkably perceptive eye, but that impression had become localized, had failed to penetrate any further into brain or body; like a marvellous reflector, he had always confined himself to sending back the image of his surroundings with impersonal precision.

Of course, Des Esseintes still appreciated the works of these two poets, in the same way that he appreciated rare jewels or precious substances; but none of the variations of these brilliant instrumentalists could now enrapture any more, for none possessed the makings of a dream, none opened up, at least for him, one of those lively vistas that enabled him to speed the weary flight of the hours.

He used to put their books down feeling hungry and unsatisfied, and the same was true of Hugo's. The Oriental, patriarchal aspect was too trite and hollow to retain his interest, while the nursery-maidish, grandfatherly pose annoyed him intensely. It was not until he came to the *Chansons des rues et des bois* that he could unreservedly enjoy the impeccable jugglery of Hugo's prosody; and even then, he would gladly have given all these *tours de force* for a new work of Baudelaire's of the same quality as the old, for the latter was without a doubt almost the only author whose verses, underneath their splendid shell, contained a balsamic and nutritious kernel.

Jumping from one extreme to the other, from form bereft of ideas to ideas bereft of form, left Des Esseintes just as circumspect and critical. The psychological labyrinths of Stendhal and the analytical amplifications of Duranty aroused his interest, but their arid, colourless, bureaucratic style, their utterly commonplace prose, fit for nothing better than the ignoble industry of the stage, repelled him. Besides, the most interesting of their delicate analytical operations were performed, when all was said and done, on brains fired by passions that no longer moved him. Little he cared about ordinary emotions or common associations of ideas, now that his mind had grown so overstocked and had no room for anything but superfine sensations, religious doubts, and sensual anxieties.

In order to enjoy a literature that united, just as he wished, an incisive style and a subtle, feline skill in analysis, he had to wait till he reached that master of induction, the wise and wonderful Edgar Allan Poe, for whom his admiration had not suffered in the least from re-reading his work.

Better perhaps than anyone else, Poe possessed those intimate affinities that could satisfy the requirements of Des Esseintes' mind.

If Baudelaire had made out among the hieroglyphics of the soul the critical age of thought and feeling, it was Poe who, in the sphere of morbid psychology, had carried out the closest scrutiny of the will.

In literature he had been the first, under the emblematic title *The Imp of the Perverse*, to study those irresistible impulses which the will submits to without fully understanding them, and which cerebral pathology can now explain with a fair degree of certainty; he had been the first again, if not to point out, at least to make known the depressing influence fear has on the will, which it affects in the same way as anaesthetics which paralyse the senses and curare which cripples the motory nerves. It was on this last subject, this lethargy of the will, that he had concentrated his studies, analysing the effects of this moral poison and indicating the symptoms of its progress – mental disturbances beginning with anxiety, developing into anguish, and finally culminating in a terror that stupefies the faculties of volition, yet without the intellect, however badly shaken it may be, giving way.

As for death, which the dramatists had so grossly abused, he had in a way given it a sharper edge, a new look, by introducing into it an algebraic and superhuman element; though to tell the truth, it was not so much the physical agony of the dying he described as the moral agony of the survivor, haunted beside the death-bed by the monstrous hallucinations engendered by grief and fatigue. With awful fascination he dwelt on the effects of terror, on the failures of will-power, and discussed them with clinical objectivity, making the reader's flesh creep, his throat contract, his mouth go dry at the recital of these mechanically devised nightmares of a fevered brain.

Convulsed by hereditary neuroses, maddened by moral choreas, his characters lived on their nerves; his women, his Morellas and Ligeias, possessed vast learning steeped in the mists of German philosophy and in the cabbalistic mysteries of the ancient East, and all of them had the inert, boyish breasts of angels, all were, so to speak, unsexed.

Baudelaire and Poe, whose two minds had often been

compared on account of their common poetic inspiration and the penchant they shared for the examination of mental diseases, differed radically in the emotional concepts which played a large part in their works – Baudelaire with his thirsty, ruthless passion, whose disgusted cruelty recalled the tortures of the Inquisition, and Poe with his chaste, ethereal amours, in which the senses had no share and only the brain was roused, followed by none of the lower organs, which, if they existed at all, remained forever frozen and virgin.

This cerebral clinic where, vivisecting in a stifling atmosphere, this spiritual surgeon became, as soon as his attention wandered, the prey of his imagination, which sprayed about him, like delicious miasmas, angelic, dream-like apparitions, was for Des Esseintes a source of indefatigable conjectures; but now that his neurosis had grown worse, there were days when reading these works exhausted him, when it left him with his hands trembling and his ears cocked, overcome, like the unfortunate Usher, by an unreasoning fear, an unspoken terror.

He therefore had to hold himself in check and only rarely indulge in these formidable elixirs, just as he could no longer visit with impunity his red entrance-hall and feast his eyes on the horrors of Odilon Redon and the tortures of Jan Luyken.

And yet, when he was in this frame of mind, almost anything he read seemed insipid after these terrible philtres imported from America. He would therefore turn to Villiers de l'Isle-Adam, in whose scattered writings he discovered observations just as unorthodox, vibrations just as spasmodic, but which, except perhaps in *Claire Lenoir*, did not convey such an overwhelming sense of horror.

Published in 1867 in the *Revue des lettres et des arts*, this *Claire Lenoir* was the first of a series of stories linked together by the generic title of *Histoires moroses*. Against a background of abstruse speculations borrowed from old Hegel, there moved two deranged individuals, a Doctor Tribulat Bonhomet who was pompous and puerile, and a Claire Lenoir who was droll and sinister, with blue spectacles as big and round as five-franc pieces covering her almost lifeless eyes.

This story concerned a commonplace case of adultery, but ended on a note of indescribable terror when Bonhomet, uncovering the pupils of Claire's eyes as she lay on her death-bed, and probing them with monstrous instruments, saw clearly reflected on the retina a picture of the husband brandishing at arm's length the severed head of the lover and, like a Kanaka, howling a triumphant war-chant.

Based on the more or less valid observation that, until decomposition sets in, the eyes of certain animals, oxen for instance, preserve like photographic plates the image of the people and things lying at the moment of death within the range of their last look, the tale obviously owed a great deal to those of Edgar Allan Poe, from which it derived its wealth of punctilious detail and its horrific atmosphere.

The same was true of *L'Intersigne*, which had later been incorporated in the *Contes cruels*, a collection of stories of indisputable talent which also included *Véra*, a tale Des Esseintes regarded as a little masterpiece.

Here the hallucination was endowed with an exquisite tenderness; there was nothing here of the American author's gloomy mirages, but a well-nigh heavenly vision of sweetness and warmth, which in an identical style formed the antithesis of Poe's Beatrices and Ligeias, those pale, unhappy phantoms engendered by the inexorable nightmare of black opium.

This story too brought into play the operations of the will, but it no longer showed it undermined and brought low by fear; on the contrary, it studied its intoxication under the influence of a conviction which had become an obsession, and it also demonstrated its power, which was so great that it could saturate the atmosphere and impose its beliefs on surrounding objects.

Another book of Villiers', *Isis*, he considered remarkable for different reasons. The philosophical lumber that littered *Claire Lenoir* also cluttered up this book, which contained an incredible hotch-potch of vague, verbose observations on the one hand and reminiscences of hoary melodramas on the other – oubliettes, daggers, rope-ladders, in fact all the romantic bric-à-brac that would reappear, looking just as old-fashioned, in Villiers' *Elën* and *Morgane*, long-forgotten works published by a Monsieur Francisque Guyon, an obscure little printer in Saint-Brieuc.

The heroine of this book, a Marquise Tullia Fabriana, who was supposed to have assimilated the Chaldean learning of Poe's women and the diplomatic sagacity of Stendhal's San-severina-Taxis, not content with all this, had also assumed the enigmatic expression of a Bradamante crossed with an antique Circe. These incompatible mixtures gave rise to a smoky vapour in which philosophical and literary influences jostled each other around, without managing to sort themselves out in the author's mind by the time he began writing the pro-legomena to this work, which was intended to fill no less than seven volumes.

But there was another side to Villiers' personality, alto-gether clearer and sharper, marked by grim humour and ferocious banter; when this side was uppermost, the result was not one of Poe's paradoxical mystifications, but a lugubriously comic jeering similar to Swift's bitter raillery. A whole series of tales, *Les Demoiselles de Bienfilâtre*, *L'Affichage céleste*, *La Machine à gloire* and *Le plus beau dîner du monde*, revealed a singu-larly inventive and satirical sense of humour. All the filthiness of contemporary utilitarian ideas, all the money-grubbing ignominy of the age were glorified in stories whose pungent irony sent Des Esseintes into raptures of delight.

In this realm of biting, poker-faced satire, no other book existed in France. The next best thing was a story by Charles Cros, *La Science de l'amour*, originally published in the *Revue du Monde Nouveau*, which was calculated to astonish the reader with its chemical extravagances, its tight-lipped humour, its icily comic observations; but the pleasure it gave was only relative, for in execution it was fatally defective. Villiers' style, solid, colourful, often original, had disappeared, to be supplanted by a sort of sausage-meat scraped from the table of some literary pork-butcher.

'Lord, how few books there are that are worth reading again!' sighed Des Esseintes, watching his man as he climbed down the step-ladder he had been perched on and stood to one side to let his master have a clear view of all the bookshelves.

Des Esseintes gave a nod of approval. There were now only two thin booklets left on the table. Dismissing the old man with a wave of his hand, he began looking through one of these, comprised of a few pages bound in onager-skin that had been glazed under a hydraulic press, dappled in water-colour with silver clouds, and provided with end-papers of old lampas, the floral pattern of which, now rather dim with age, had that faded charm which Mallarmé extolled in a truly delightful poem.

These pages, nine in all, had been taken out of unique copies of the first two *Parnasses*, printed on parchment, and preceded by a title-page bearing the words: *Quelques vers de Mallarmé*, executed by a remarkable calligrapher in uncial letters, coloured and picked out, like those in ancient manuscripts, with specks of gold.

Among the eleven pieces brought together between these covers, a few, *Les Fenêtres*, *L'Épilogue*, and *Azur*, he found extremely attractive, but there was one in particular, a fragment of *Hérodiade*, that seemed to lay a magic spell on him at certain times.

Often of an evening, sitting in the dim light his lamp shed over the silent room, he had imagined he felt her brush past him – that same Herodias who in Gustave Moreau's picture had withdrawn into the advancing shadows, so that nothing could be seen but the vague shape of a white statue in the midst of a feebly glowing brazier of jewels.

The darkness hid the blood, dimmed the bright colours and gleaming gold, enveloped the far corners of the temple in gloom, concealed the minor actors in the criminal drama where they stood wrapped in their dark garments, and, sparing only the white patches in the water-colour, drew the woman from the scabbard of her jewels and emphasized her nakedness.

His eyes were irresistibly drawn towards her, following the familiar outlines of her body until she came to life again

before him, bringing to his lips those sweet, strange words
that Mallarmé puts into her mouth:

> . . . . *O miroir!*
> *Eau froide par l'ennui dans ton cadre gelée*
> *Que de fois et pendant les heures, désolée*
> *Des songes et cherchant mes souvenirs qui sont*
> *Comme des feuilles sous ta glace au trou profond,*
> *Je m'apparus en toi comme une ombre lointaine,*
> *Mais, horreur! des soirs, dans ta sévère fontaine,*
> *J'ai de mon rêve épars connu la nudité!**

He loved these verses as he loved all the works of this poet
who, in an age of universal suffrage and a time of commercial
greed, lived outside the world of letters, sheltered from the
raging folly all around him by his lofty scorn; taking pleasure,
far from society, in the caprices of the mind and the visions of
his brain; refining upon thoughts that were already subtle
enough, grafting Byzantine niceties on them, perpetuating
them in deductions that were barely hinted at and loosely
linked by an imperceptible thread.

These precious, interwoven ideas he knotted together with
an adhesive style, a unique, hermetic language, full of con-
tracted phrases, elliptical constructions, audacious tropes.

Sensitive to the remotest affinities, he would often use a
term that by analogy suggested at once form, scent, colour,
quality, and brilliance, to indicate a creature or thing to which
he would have had to attach a host of different epithets in
order to bring out all its various aspects and qualities, if it had
merely been referred to by its technical name. By this means
he managed to do away with the formal statement of a comparison that the reader's mind made by itself as soon as it had
understood the symbol, and he avoided dispersing the reader's
attention over all the several qualities that a row of adjectives

* Oh mirror! cold water frozen by boredom within your frame, how
many times, for hours on end, saddened by dreams and searching for my
memories, which are like dead leaves in the deep hole beneath your glassy
surface, have I seen myself in you as a distant ghost! But, oh horror! on
certain evenings, in your cruel pool, I have recognized the bareness of my
disordered dream!

would have presented one by one, concentrating it instead on a single word, a single entity, producing, as in the case of a picture, a unique and comprehensive impression, an overall view.

The result was a wonderfully condensed style, an essence of literature, a sublimate of art. It was a style that Mallarmé had first employed only sparingly in his earliest works, and then used openly and audaciously in a piece he wrote on Théophile Gautier and in *L'Après-midi d'un faune*, an eclogue in which the subtleties of sensual pleasure were unfolded in mysterious, tender verse, suddenly interrupted by this bestial, frenzied cry of the faun:

> *Alors m'éveillerai-je à la ferveur première,*
> *Droit et seul sous un flot antique de lumière,*
> *Lys! et l'un de vous tous pour l'ingénuité.**

This last line, which with the monosyllable *Lys!* carried over from the previous line, conjured up a picture of something tall, white, and rigid, and the meaning of which was made even clearer by the choice of the noun *ingénuité* to provide the rhyme, expressed in an allegorical manner and in a single word the passion, the effervescence, the momentary excitement of the virgin faun, maddened with desire by the sight of the nymphs.

In this extraordinary poem, new and surprising images occurred in almost every line when the poet came to describe the longings and regrets of the goat-footed god, standing on the edge of the swamp and looking at the clumps of rushes that still retained an ephemeral impression of the rounded forms of the naiads who had rested there.

Des Esseintes also derived a certain perverse pleasure from handling this minute volume, whose covers, made of Japanese felt as white as curdled milk, were fastened with two silk cords, one China pink, the other black.

Concealed behind the covers, the black ribbon met the pink ribbon, which was busy adding a note of silken luxury, a

* Then shall I awake to the original fervour, upright and alone in an ancient flood of light, lilies! and one of you for innocence.

suggestion of modern Japanese rouge, a hint of eroticism, to the antique whiteness, the virginal pallor of the book, and embraced it, joining together in a dainty bow its own sombre hue and the other's lighter colour, and thereby giving a discreet intimation, a vague warning, of the melancholy regrets that follow the appeasement of sexual desire, the abatement of sensual frenzy.

Des Esseintes put *L'Après-midi d'un faune* back on the table and began glancing through another slim volume which he had had printed for his personal pleasure – an anthology of prose poetry, a little chapel dedicated to Baudelaire and opening on to the cathedral square of his poems.

This anthology included selected passages from the *Gaspard de la nuit* of that whimsical author Aloysius Bertrand, who applied Leonardo da Vinci's methods to prose and painted with his metal oxides a series of little pictures whose brilliant colours shine like bright enamels. To these Des Esseintes had added Villiers' *Vox populi*, a superb piece struck in a style of gold with the effigies of Flaubert and Leconte de Lisle, and a few extracts from that dainty *Livre de jade* whose exotic perfume of ginseng and tea is mingled with the fresh fragrance of the moonlit waters that ripple through the book from cover to cover.

But this was not all. The collection also contained sundry pieces rescued from extinct reviews: *Le Démon de l'analogie*, *La Pipe*, *Le Pauvre Enfant pâle*, *Le Spectacle interrompu*, *Le Phénomène futur*, and above all *Plainte d'automne* and *Frisson d'hiver*. These were Mallarmé's masterpieces and also ranked among the masterpieces of prose poetry, for they combined a style so magnificently contrived than in itself it was as soothing as a melancholy incantation, an intoxicating melody, with irresistibly suggestive thoughts, the soul-throbs of a sensitive artist whose quivering nerves vibrate with an intensity that fills you with painful ecstasy.

Of all forms of literature, the prose poem was Des Esseintes' favourite. Handled by an alchemist of genius it should, he maintained, contain within its small compass and in concentrated form the substance of a novel, while dispensing with the latter's long-winded analyses and superfluous descriptions. Many were the times that Des Esseintes had pondered over the fascinating problem of writing a novel concentrated in a few sentences and yet comprising the cohobated juice of the hundreds of pages always taken up in describing the setting, drawing the characters, and piling up useful observations and incidental details. The words chosen for a work of this sort would be so unalterable that they would take the place of all the others; every adjective would be sited with such ingenuity and finality that it could never be legally evicted, and would open up such wide vistas that the reader could muse on its meaning, at once precise and multiple, for weeks on end, and also ascertain the present, reconstruct the past, and divine the future of the characters in the light of this one epithet.

The novel, thus conceived, thus condensed in a page or two, would become an intellectual communion between a hieratic writer and an ideal reader, a spiritual collaboration between a dozen persons of superior intelligence scattered across the world, an aesthetic treat available to none but the most discerning.

In short, the prose poem represented in Des Esseintes' eyes the dry juice, the osmazome of literature, the essential oil of art.

This succulent extract concentrated in a single drop could already be found in Baudelaire, and also in those poems of Mallarmé's that he savoured with such rare delight.

When he had closed his anthology, the last book in his library, Des Esseintes told himself that in all probability he would never add another to his collection.

The truth of the matter was that the decadence of French literature, a literature attacked by organic diseases, weakened by intellectual senility, exhausted by syntactical excesses, sensitive only to the curious whims that excite the sick, and yet eager to express itself completely in its last hours, determined to make up for all the pleasures it had missed, afflicted on its death-bed with a desire to leave behind the subtlest memories of suffering, had been embodied in Mallarmé in the most consummate and exquisite fashion.

Here, carried to the further limits of expression, was the quintessence of Baudelaire and Poe; here their refined and potent substances had been distilled yet again to give off new savours, new intoxications.

This was the death-agony of the old tongue which, after going a little greener every century, had now reached the point of dissolution, the same stage of deliquescence as the Latin language when it breathed its last in the mysterious concepts and enigmatic phrases of St Boniface and St Adhelm.

The only difference was that the decomposition of the French language had occurred suddenly and speedily. In Latin, there had been a lengthy period of transition, a gap of four hundred years, between the superbly variegated idiom of Claudian and Rutilius and the gamy idiom of the eighth century. In French, on the contrary, there had been no lapse of time, no intervening sequence of centuries; the superbly variegated style of the Goncourts and the gamy style of Verlaine and Mallarmé rubbed shoulders in Paris, where they existed at the same time, in the same period, in the same century.

And Des Esseintes smiled to himself as he glanced at one of the folios lying open on his church lectern, thinking that the time would come when a learned professor would compile for the decadence of the French language a glossary like the one in which the erudite Du Cange had recorded the last stammerings, the last paroxysms, the last brilliant sallies of the Latin language as it perished of old age in the depths of the medieval monasteries.

XV

AFTER blazing up like a flash in the pan, Des Esseintes' enthusiasm for his digester died down just as suddenly. His dyspepsia, banished for a little while, began plaguing him again, while all this concentrated food was so binding and brought on such an irritation of the bowels that he had to stop using the apparatus straight away.

His illness promptly resumed its course, accompanied by hitherto unknown symptoms. The nightmares, the eye troubles, the hacking cough that came on at fixed intervals as regular as clockwork, the throbbing of the arteries and heart, and the cold sweats were now followed by aural illusions, the sort of derangement that occurs only when the complaint has entered its final phase.

Consumed with a burning fever, Des Esseintes suddenly heard the sounds of running water, of buzzing wasps; then these noises merged into one which resembled the humming of a lathe, and this humming grew shriller and clearer until it eventually changed into the silvery note of a bell.

At this point he felt his disordered brain being carried away on waves of music and plunged into the religious atmosphere of his adolescence. The chants he had learnt from the Jesuit Fathers came back to him, recalling the college chapel where they had been sung, and passing the hallucinations on to the senses of sight and smell, which they enveloped in clouds of incense and the gloomy light filtering through stained-glass windows under lofty vaults.

With the Fathers, the rites of religion were performed with great pomp; an excellent organist and a remarkable choir made sure that these pious exercises provided both spiritual edification and aesthetic pleasure. The organist loved the old masters, and on feast-days he would make his choice from Palestrina's or Orlando Lasso's masses, Marcello's psalms, Handel's oratorios, and Bach's motets, rejecting the sensuous, facile compilations of Father Lambillotte, so popular with the clergy, in favour of certain *Laudi spirituali* of the sixteenth century whose hieratic beauty had many a time captivated Des Esseintes.

But above all else he had derived ineffable pleasure from listening to plainsong, to which the organist had remained faithful in defiance of current fashion.

This type of music, at present considered an effete and barbarous form of the Christian liturgy, as an archaeological curiosity, as a relic of the distant past, was the idiom of the ancient Church, the very soul of the Middle Ages; it was the sempiternal prayer, sung and modulated to accord with the movements of the soul, the diuturnal hymn which had risen for centuries past towards the Most High.

This traditional melody was the only one which, with its powerful unison, its harmonies as massive and imposing as blocks of freestone, could tone in with the old basilicas and fill their Romanesque vaults, of which it seemed to be the emanation, the very voice.

Time and again an awe-struck Des Esseintes had bowed his head in response to an irresistible impulse when the *Christus factus est* of the Gregorian chant had soared up in the nave, whose pillars trembled amid the floating clouds of incense, or when the faux-bourdon of the *De Profundis* groaned forth, mournful as a stifled sob, poignant as a despairing appeal by mankind bewailing its mortal destiny and imploring the tender mercy of its Saviour.

Compared with this magnificent chant, created by the genius of the Church, as impersonal and anonymous as the organ itself, whose inventor is unknown, all other religious music struck him as profane. At bottom, in all the works of Jomelli and Porpora, of Carissimi and Durante, in the finest compositions of Handel and Bach, there was no real renunciation of popular success, no real sacrifice of artistic effect, no real abdication of human pride listening to itself at prayer; only in the imposing masses by Lesueur he had heard at Saint-Roch did the true religious style come into its own again, solemn and august, approaching the austere majesty of plainsong in its stark nudity.

Since then, utterly revolted by the pretexts a Rossini and a Pergolese had thought up for composing a *Stabat Mater*, by the general invasion of liturgical art by fashionable artists, Des Esseintes had held aloof from all these equivocal compositions tolerated by the over-indulgent Church.

The fact was that this indulgent attitude, ostensibly intended to attract the faithful and really intended to attract their money, had promptly resulted in a crop of arias borrowed from Italian operas, contemptible cavatinas and objectionable quadrilles, sung with full orchestra accompaniment, in churches converted into boudoirs, by barnstormers bellowing away up in the roof, while down below the ladies waged a war of fashions and went into raptures over the shrieks of the mountebanks whose impure voices were defiling the sacred notes of the organ.

For years now he had steadfastly refused to take part in these pious entertainments, preferring to recall his memories of childhood, even regretting having heard certain of the great masters' *Te Deums* when he remembered that admirable *Te Deum* of plainsong, that simple, awe-inspiring hymn composed by some saint or other, a St Ambrose or a St Hilary, who, without the complicated resources of an orchestra, without the musical contrivances of modern science, displayed a burning faith, a delirious joy, the faith and joy of all humanity, expressed in ardent, confident, well-nigh celestial accents.

The odd thing was that Des Esseintes' ideas on music were in flagrant contradiction with the theories he professed about the other arts. The only religious music he really approved of was the monastic music of the Middle Ages, that emaciated music which provoked an instinctive nervous reaction in him, like certain pages of the old Christian Latinists; besides, as he himself admitted, he was incapable of understanding whatever new devices the present-day masters might have introduced into Catholic art.

In the first place, he had not studied music with the same passionate enthusiasm that had drawn him to painting and literature. He could play the piano as well as the next man, and after long practice had learnt how to read a score more or less inefficiently; but he knew nothing of the harmony and the technique that were necessary to be able really to appreciate every nuance, to understand every subtlety, to derive the maximum pleasure from every refinement.

Then again, secular music is a promiscuous art in that you cannot enjoy it at home, by yourself, as you can a book; to savour it he would have had to join the mob of inveterate theatre-goers that fills the Cirque d'Hiver, where under a broiling sun and in a stifling atmosphere you can see a hulking brute of a man waving his arms about and massacring disconnected snatches of Wagner to the huge delight of an ignorant crowd.

He had never had the courage to plunge into this mob-bath to listen to Berlioz, even though he admired some fragments of his work for their passionate ardour and fiery spirit; and he was well aware that there was not a single scene, not even a single phrase, in any of the mighty Wagner's operas that could be divorced from its context with impunity.

Slices cut off and served up at a concert lost all sense and meaning, for like chapters in a book that are complementary to one another and combine to reach the same goal, the same conclusion, Wagner's melodies were used to define the characters of his dramatis personae, to represent their thoughts, to express their visible or secret motives, and their ingenious and persistent repetitions could only be understood by an audience that followed the subject from the start and watched the characters gradually taking shape and developing in a setting from which they could not be removed without dying like branches cut from a tree.

Des Esseintes was therefore convinced that of the mob of melomaniacs who went into ecstasies every Sunday on the benches of the Cirque d'Hiver, barely twenty could tell what the orchestra was murdering, even when the attendants were kind enough to stop chattering and give it a chance of being heard.

Considering also that the intelligent patriotism of the French made it impossible for any theatre in the country to put on a Wagner opera, there was nothing left for the keen amateur who was ignorant of the arcana of music and could not or would not travel to Bayreuth but to stay at home, and this was the reasonable course Des Esseintes had adopted.

On a different level, cheaper, more popular music and isolated extracts from the old operas scarcely appealed to him; the trivial little tunes of Auber and Boïeldieu, of Adam and Flotow, and the rhetorical commonplaces turned out by such men as Ambroise Thomas and Bazin were just as repugnant to him as the antiquated sentimentalities and vulgar graces of the Italians. He had therefore resolutely abstained from all musical indulgence, and the only pleasant memories he retained from these years of abstinence were of certain chamber concerts at which he had heard some Beethoven and above all some Schumann and Schubert which had stimulated his nerves in the same way as Poe's most intimate and anguished poems.

Certain settings for the violoncello by Schumann had left him positively panting with emotion, choking with hysteria; but it was chiefly Schubert's *Lieder* that had excited him, carried him away, then prostrated him as if he had been squandering his nervous energy, indulging in a mystical debauch.

This music thrilled him to the very marrow, reawakening a host of forgotten sorrows, of old grievances, in a heart surprised at containing so many confused regrets and vague mortifications. This desolate music, surging up from the uttermost depths of the soul, terrified and fascinated him at the same time. He had never been able to hum *Des Mädchens Klage* without nervous tears rising to his eyes, for in this *lamento* there was something more than sadness, a note of despair that tore at his heartstrings, something reminiscent of a dying love-affair in a melancholy landscape.

Every time they came back to his lips, these exquisite, funereal laments called to mind a suburban scene, a shabby, silent piece of waste land, and in the distance, lines of men and women, harassed by the cares of life, shuffling away, bent double, into the twilight, while he himself, steeped in bitterness and filled with disgust, felt alone in the midst of tearful Nature, all alone, overcome by an unspeakable melancholy, by an obstinate distress, the mysterious intensity of which precluded any prospect of consolation, of pity, of repose. Like the sound of a passing-bell, these mournful melodies haunted him now that he lay in bed, exhausted by fever and tormented by an anxiety that was all the more irresistible in that he could no longer discover its cause. He finally abandoned himself to the current of his emotions, swept away by the torrent of anguish let loose by this music – a torrent that was suddenly stemmed for a moment by the sound of the psalms echoing slowly and softly in his head, whose aching temples felt as though they were being beaten by the clappers of tolling bells.

One morning, however, these noises died away; he felt in fuller possession of his faculties and asked his man to hand him a mirror. After a single glance it slipped from his hands. He scarcely knew himself; his face was an earthen colour, the lips dry and swollen, the tongue all furrowed, the skin wrinkled; his untidy hair and beard, which his servant had not trimmed since the beginning of his illness, added to the horrific impression created by the hollow cheeks and the big, watery eyes burning with a feverish brightness in this hairy death's-head.

This change in his facial appearance alarmed him more than his weakness, more than the uncontrollable fits of vomiting that thwarted his every attempt at taking food, more than the depression into which he was gradually sinking. He thought he was done for; but then, in spite of his overwhelming despondency, the energy of a man in desperate straits brought him to a sitting position in bed and gave him the strength to write a letter to his Paris doctor and order his servant to go to him immediately and bring him back with him, whatever the cost, the same day.

His mood promptly changed from the darkest despair to the brightest hope. This doctor he had sent for was a famous specialist, a physician renowned for his successes in treating nervous disorders, and Des Esseintes told himself:

'He must have cured plenty of cases that were more difficult and dangerous than mine. No, there's no doubt about it – I shall be on my feet again in a few days' time.'

But soon this spirit of confidence was followed by a feeling of blank pessimism. He was convinced that no matter how learned or perspicacious they might be, doctors really knew nothing about nervous diseases, not even their causes. Like all the rest, this man would prescribe the inevitable zinc oxide and quinine, potassium bromide and valerian.

'Who knows?' he went on, clinging to a last, slender hope. 'If these remedies have done me no good so far, it's probably because I haven't taken the proper doses.'

In spite of everything, the prospect of obtaining some relief put new heart into him, but then fresh anxieties assailed him: perhaps the doctor was not in Paris, perhaps he would refuse to come and see him, perhaps his servant had not even succeeded in finding him. He began to lose heart again, jumping, from one minute to the next, from the most unreasonable hopefulness to the most illogical apprehension, exaggerating both his chances of sudden recovery and his fears of immediate danger. The hours slipped by and eventually, exhausted and in despair, convinced that the doctor would never come, he angrily told himself over and over again that if only he had been seen to in time he would undoubtedly have been saved. Then his anger at his servant's inefficiency and his doctor's callousness in apparently letting him die abated, and he finally took to blaming himself for having waited so long before sending for help, persuading himself that by now he would have been completely fit if, even the day before, he had insisted on having potent medicines and skilled attention.

Little by little these alternating hopes and fears jostling around in his otherwise empty mind subsided, though not before the succession of swift changes had worn him out. He fell into a sleep of exhaustion broken by incoherent dreams, a sort of swoon interrupted by periods of barely conscious wakefulness. He had finally forgotten what he wanted and what he feared so completely that he was simply bewildered, and felt neither surprise nor pleasure, when the doctor suddenly came into the room.

The manservant had doubtless told him what kind of life Des Esseintes had been leading, and described the various symptoms he himself had been in a position to observe since the day he had found his master lying by the window, overcome by the potency of his perfumes, for he put hardly any questions to his patient, whose medical history over the past few years was in any case well known to him. But he examined him, sounded him, and carefully scrutinized his urine, in which certain white streaks told him what one of the chief determining causes of his nervous trouble was. He wrote out a prescription, and after saying he would come again soon, took his leave without another word.

His visit revived Des Esseintes' spirits, but he was somewhat alarmed at the doctor's silence and told his servant not to keep the truth from him any longer. The man assured him that the doctor had shown no signs of anxiety, and, suspicious as he was, Des Esseintes could detect no trace of prevarication in the old man's expressionless face.

His thoughts now became more cheerful; besides, his pains had gone and the weakness he felt in every limb had taken on a certain sweet languorous quality, at once vague and insinuating. What is more, he was both astounded and delighted at not being encumbered with drugs and medicine bottles, and a faint smile hovered over his lips when his servant eventually brought him a nourishing peptone enema and informed him that he was to repeat this injection three times every twenty-four hours.

The operation was successfully carried out, and Des Esseintes could not help secretly congratulating himself on this experience which was, so to speak, the crowning achievement of the life he had planned for himself; his taste for the artificial had now, without even the slightest effort on his part, attained its supreme fulfilment. No one, he thought, would ever go any further; taking nourishment in this way was undoubtedly the ultimate deviation from the norm.

'How delightful it would be,' he said to himself, 'to go on with this simple diet after getting well again. What a saving of time, what a radical deliverance from the repugnance meat inspires in people without any appetite. What an absolute release from the boredom that invariably results from the necessarily limited choice of dishes! What a vigorous protest against the vile sin of gluttony! And last but not least, what a slap in the face for old Mother Nature, whose monotonous demands would be permanently silenced!'

And talking to himself under his breath, he went on: 'It would be easy enough to get up an appetite by swallowing a strong aperient. Then, when you felt you might reasonably say: "Isn't it time for dinner? – I'm as hungry as a hunter," all you'd have to do to lay the table would be to deposit the noble instrument on the cloth. And before you had time to say grace you'd have finished the meal – without any of the vulgar, bothersome business of eating.'

A few days later, the servant brought him an enema altogether different in colour and smell from the peptone preparations.

'But it's not the same!' exclaimed Des Esseintes, anxiously inspecting the liquid that had been poured into the apparatus. He asked for the menu as he might have done in a restaurant, and unfolding the doctor's prescription, he read out:

Cod-liver oil	29 grammes
Beef-tea	200 grammes
Burgundy	200 grammes
Yolk of one egg	

This set him thinking. On account of the ruinous condition of his stomach, he had never been able to take a serious interest in the art of cooking, but now he found himself working out recipes of a perverse epicurism. Then an intriguing idea crossed his mind. Perhaps the doctor had supposed that his patient's unusual palate was already tired of the taste of peptone; perhaps, like a skilled chef, he had decided to vary the flavour of his concoctions, to prevent the monotony of the dishes leading to a complete loss of appetite. Once started on this line of thought, Des Esseintes began composing novel recipes and even planning meatless dinners for Fridays, increasing the doses of cod-liver oil and wine and crossing out the beef-tea because being meat it was expressly forbidden by the Church. But soon he had no need to deliberate any longer over these nourishing liquids, for the doctor gradually managed to stop his vomiting and to make him swallow through the ordinary channels a punch syrup containing powdered meat and giving off a vague aroma of cocoa that lingered pleasantly in his real mouth.

Weeks went by and at last the stomach decided to function properly; from time to time fits of nausea would still recur, but these were effectively overcome with potions of ginger-beer and Rivière's antemetic.

Eventually, little by little, the organs recovered, and with the help of pepsins ordinary food was digested. Des Esseintes' strength returned and he was able to get up and hobble around his bedroom, leaning on a stick and holding on to the furniture. But instead of being pleased with his progress, he forgot all his past sufferings, fretted over the time his convalescence was taking, and accused the doctor of spinning it out. It was true that a few unsuccessful experiments had slowed things down; iron proved no more acceptable than quinquina, even when it was mixed with laudanum, and these drugs had to be replaced by arseniates – this after a fortnight had been wasted in useless efforts, as Des Esseintes angrily pointed out.

At last the time came when he could stay up all afternoon and walk about the house unaided. Now his study began to get on his nerves; faults he had overlooked by force of habit struck him at once on coming back to the room after a long absence. The colours he had chosen to be seen by lamplight seemed at variance with one another in daylight; wondering how best to change them, he spent hours planning heterogeneous harmonies of hues, hybrid combinations of cloths and leathers.

'I'm on the road to recovery, and no mistake,' he told himself, noting the return of his former preoccupations, his old predilections.

One morning, as he was looking at his blue and orange walls, dreaming of ideal hangings made of stoles designed for the Greek Church, of gold-fringed Russian dalmatics, of brocaded copes inscribed with Slavonic lettering in pearls or in precious stones from the Urals, the doctor came in and, following the direction of his patient's gaze, asked him what he was thinking.

Des Esseintes told him of his unrealizable ideals and was beginning to outline new experiments in colour, to talk about new combinations and contrasts that he meant to organize, when the doctor threw cold water on his enthusiasm by declaring in peremptory fashion that wherever he put his ideas into effect it would certainly not be in that house.

Then, without giving him time to breathe, he stated that he had attended to the most urgent problem first by putting right the digestive functions, and that now he must tackle the general nervous trouble, which had not cleared up at all and to do so would require years of strict dieting and careful nursing. He concluded by saying that before trying any particular remedy, before embarking on any sort of hydropathic treatment – which in any case was impracticable at Fontenay – he would have to abandon this solitary existence, to go back to Paris, to lead a normal life again, above all to try and enjoy the same pleasures as other people.

'But I just don't enjoy the pleasures other people enjoy!' retorted Des Esseintes indignantly.

Ignoring this objection, the doctor simply assured him that this radical change of life he prescribed was in his opinion a matter of life and death – that it meant the difference between a good recovery on the one hand and insanity speedily followed by tuberculosis on the other.

'So I have to choose between death and deportation!' cried Des Esseintes in exasperation.

The doctor, who was imbued with all the prejudices of a man of the world, smiled and made for the door without answering.

XVI

Des Esseintes shut himself up in his bedroom and stopped his ears against the sound of hammering outside, where the removal men were nailing up the packing-cases his servants had got ready; every blow seemed to strike at his heart and send a stab of pain deep into his flesh. The sentence pronounced by the doctor was being executed; the dread of enduring all over again the sufferings he had recently undergone, together with the fear of an agonizing death, had had a more powerful effect on him than his hatred of the detestable existence to which medical jurisdiction condemned him.

'And yet,' he kept telling himself, 'there are people who live on their own with no one to talk to, who spend their lives in quiet contemplation apart from human society, people like Trappists and prisoners in solitary confinement, and there's nothing to show that those wise men and those poor wretches go either mad or consumptive.'

These examples he had quoted to the doctor, but in vain; the latter had simply repeated, in a curt manner that excluded any further argument, that his verdict, which incidentally was in line with the opinions of every specialist in nervous disorders, was that only relaxation, amusement, and enjoyment could have any effect on this complaint, which on the mental side remained entirely unaffected by chemical remedies. Finally, infuriated by his patient's recriminations, he had stated once for all that he refused to go on treating him unless he agreed to a change of air and a move to more hygienic conditions.

Des Esseintes had promptly gone to Paris to consult other specialists, to whom he had submitted his case with scrupulous impartiality; they had all unhesitatingly approved their colleague's advice. Thereupon he had taken a flat that was still vacant in a new apartment-house, had come back to Fontenay and, white with rage, had ordered his servants to start packing.

Buried deep in his armchair, he was now brooding over this unambiguous prescription which upset all his plans, broke all the ties binding him to his present life, and buried all his future projects in oblivion. So his beatific happiness was over! So he must leave the shelter of this haven of his and put out to sea again in the teeth of that gale of human folly that had battered and buffeted him of old!

The doctors spoke of amusement and relaxation, but with whom, with what, did they expect him to have fun and enjoy himself?

Had he not outlawed himself from society? Had he heard of anybody else who was trying to organize a life like this, a life of dreamy contemplation? Did he know a single individual who was capable of appreciating the delicacy of a phrase, the subtlety of a painting, the quintessence of an idea, or whose soul was sensitive enough to understand Mallarmé and love Verlaine?

Where and when should he look, into what social waters should he heave the lead, to discover a twin soul, a mind free of commonplace ideas, welcoming silence as a boon, ingratitude as a relief, suspicion as a haven and a harbour?

In the society he had frequented before his departure for Fontenay? – But most of the squireens he had known in those days must since have reached new depths of boredom in the drawing-room, of stupidity at the gaming table, and of depravity in the brothel. Most of them, too, must have got married; after treating themselves all their lives to the leavings of street-arabs, they now treated their wives to the leavings of street-walkers, for like a master of the first-fruits, the working class was the only one that did not feed on left-overs!

'What a pretty change of partners, what a glorious game of general post this prudish society of ours is enjoying!' muttered Des Esseintes.

But then, the decayed nobility was done for; the aristocracy had sunk into imbecility or depravity. It was dying from the degeneracy of its scions, whose faculties had deteriorated with each succeeding generation till they now consisted of the instincts of gorillas at work in the skulls of grooms and jockeys; or else, like the Choiseul-Praslins, the Polignacs, and the Chevreuses, it was wallowing in the mud of law-suits that brought it down to the same level of ignominy as the other classes.

The very mansions, age-old escutcheons, heraldic pomp, and stately ceremonial of this ancient caste had disappeared. As its estates had stopped yielding revenue, they and the great country houses had been put up for auction, for there was never enough money to pay for all the dark venereal pleasures of the besotted descendants of the old families.

The least scrupulous and the least obtuse among them threw all shame to the winds; they joined in shady deals, splashed about in the financial gutter, and finished up like common criminals in the Assize Court, serving at least to add a little lustre to human justice, which, finding it impossible to maintain absolute impartiality, solved the problem by making them prison librarians.

This passion for profits, this love of lucre, had also taken hold of another class, a class that had always leant upon the nobility – the clergy. At present, on the back page of every newspaper, you could see a corn-cure advertisement inserted by a priest. The monasteries had been turned into factories or distilleries, with every order manufacturing its specialities or selling the recipes. Thus the Cistercians derived their income from chocolate, Trappistine, semolina, and tincture of arnica; the Marists from biphosphate of chalk for medicinal purposes and arquebus water; the Dominicans from antapoplectic elixir; the disciples of St Benedict from Benedictine; the monks of St Bruno from Chartreuse.

Commercialism had invaded the cloisters, where, in lieu of antiphonaries, fat account-books lay on the lecterns. Like a foul leprosy, the present-day greed for gain was playing havoc with the Church, making the monks pore over inventories and invoices, turning the Superiors into confectioners and medicasters, the lay-brothers into common packers and base bottle-washers.

And yet, in spite of everything, it was still only among the ecclesiastics that Des Esseintes could hope to enjoy relations in some degree of accordance with his tastes. In the company of canons, who were generally men of learning and good breeding, he might have spent some affable and agreeable evenings; but then he would have had to share their beliefs and not oscillate between sceptical ideas and sudden fits of faith which recurred from time to time under the impulse of his childhood memories.

He would have had to hold identical views and refuse to acknowledge, as he readily did in his moments of enthusiasm, a Catholicism that was seaoned with a touch of magic, as in the reign of Henri III, and a touch of sadism, as in the closing years of the eighteenth century. This special brand of clericalism, this subtly depraved and perverse type of mysticism, to which he occasionally felt drawn, could not so much as be discussed with a priest, who would either have failed to understand him or would have instantly ordered him out of his sight in sheer horror.

For the twentieth time this insoluble problem tormented him. He would have dearly loved to escape from the state of doubt and suspicion against which he had struggled in vain at Fontenay; now that he was forced to turn over a new leaf, he would have liked to force himself to possess the faith, to glue it down as soon as he had it, to fasten it with clamps to his soul, in short to protect it against all those reflections that tend to shake and dislodge it. But the more he longed for it, the less the void in his mind was filled and the longer the visitation of Christ was delayed. Indeed, in proportion as his hunger for religion increased and he passionately craved, as a ransom for the future and a help in his new life, this faith that now showed itself to him, though the distance separating him from it appalled him, doubts crowded into his fevered mind, upsetting his unsteady will, rejecting on grounds of common sense and by mathematical demonstration the mysteries and dogmas of the Church.

'It ought to be possible to stop arguing with yourself,' he told himself miserably; 'it ought to be possible to shut your eyes, let yourself drift along with the stream, and forget all those damnable discoveries that have blasted religion from top to bottom in the last two hundred years.

'And yet,' he sighed, 'it isn't really the physiologists or the sceptics who are demolishing Catholicism; it's the priests themselves, whose clumsy writings would shake the firmest convictions.'

Among the Dominicans, for instance, there was a Doctor of Theology, the Reverend Father Rouard de Card, a preaching friar who, in a booklet entitled *The Adulteration of the Sacramental Substances*, had proved beyond all doubt that the majority of Masses were null and void, simply because the materials used by the priest were sophisticated by certain dealers.

For years now, the holy oil had been adulterated with poultry-fat; the taper wax with burnt bones; the incense with common resin and old benzoin. But what was worse was that the two substances that were indispensable for the holy sacrifice, the two substances without which no oblation was possible, had also been adulterated: the wine by repeated diluting and the illicit addition of Pernambuco bark, elderberries, alcohol, alum, salicylate, and litharge; the bread, that bread of the Eucharist which should be made from the finest of wheats, with bean-flour, potash, and pipe-clay!

And now they had gone even further; they had had the effrontery to leave out the wheat altogether, and most hosts were made by shameless dealers out of potato-flour!

Now God refused to come down to earth in the form of potato-flour; that was an undeniable, indisputable fact. In the second volume of his Moral Theology, His Eminence Cardinal Gousset had also dealt at length with this question of fraud from the divine point of view; according to this unimpeachable authority it was quite impossible to consecrate bread made of oatmeal, buckwheat, or barley, and if there was at least some doubt in the case of rye bread, there could be no doubt or argument about potato-flour, which, to use the ecclesiastic phrase, was in no sense a competent substance for the Blessed Sacrament.

Because of the easy manipulation of this flour and the

attractive appearance of the wafers made with it, this outrageous swindle had become so common that the mystery of
transubstantiation scarcely existed any longer and both priests
and faithful communicated, all unwittingly, with neutral
species.

Ah, the days were far distant when Radegonde, Queen of
France, used to make the altar-bread with her own hands; the
days when, according to the custom at Cluny, three fasting
priests or deacons, clad in alb and amice, after washing face
and fingers, sorted out the wheat grain by grain, crushed it
under a millstone, kneaded the dough with pure, cold water,
and baked it themselves over a bright fire, singing psalms all
the while.

'Still, there's no denying,' Des Esseintes told himself, 'that
the prospect of being constantly hoodwinked at the communion table itself isn't calculated to consolidate beliefs that
are already far from steady. Besides, how can you accept the
idea of an omnipotent deity balked by a pinch of potato-
flour and a drop of alcohol?'

These thoughts made his future look gloomier than ever,
his horizon darker and more threatening.

It was clear that no haven of refuge or sheltering shore was
left to him. What was to become of him in this city of Paris
where he had neither relatives nor friends? He no longer had
any connexion with the Faubourg Saint-Germain, which was
now quavering with old age, crumbling away into the dust of
desuetude, lying in the midst of a new society like a rotten,
empty husk. And what point of contact could there possibly
be between him and that bourgeois class which had gradually
climbed to the top, taking advantage of every disaster to fill
its pockets, stirring up every sort of trouble to command
respect for its countless crimes and thefts?

After the aristocracy of birth, it was now the turn of the
aristocracy of wealth, the caliphate of the counting-house, the
despotism of the Rue du Sentier, the tyranny of commerce
with its narrow-minded, venal ideas, its selfish, rascally
instincts.

More cunning and contemptible than the impoverished

aristocracy and the discredited clergy, the bourgeoisie borrowed their frivolous love of show and their old-world arro-
gance, which it cheapened through its own lack of taste, and
stole their natural defects, which it turned into hypocritical
vices. Overbearing and underhand in behaviour, base and
cowardly in character, it ruthlessly shot down its perennial and
essential dupe, the mob, which it had previously unmuzzled
and sent flying at the throats of the old castes.

Now it was all over. Once it had done its job, the plebs had
been bled white in the interests of public hygiene, while the
jovial bourgeois lorded it over the country, putting his trust
in the power of his money and the contagiousness of his
stupidity. The result of his rise to power had been the sup-
pression of all intelligence, the negation of all honesty, the
destruction of all art; in fact, artists and writers in their degradation had fallen on their knees and were covering with ardent
kisses the stinking feet of the high-placed jobbers and low-
bred satraps on whose charity they depended for a living.

In painting, the result was a deluge of lifeless inanities; in
literature, a torrent of hackneyed phrases and conventional
ideas – honesty to flatter the shady speculator, integrity to
please the swindler who hunted for a dowry for his son while
refusing to pay his daughter's, and chastity to satisfy the anticlerical who accused the clergy of rape and lechery when he
himself was forever haunting the local brothel, a stupid hypo-
crite without even the excuse of deliberate depravity, sniffing
at the greasy water in the wash-basins and the hot, spicy smell
of dirty petticoats.

This was the vast bagnio of America transported to the
continent of Europe; this was the limitless, unfathomable,
immeasurable scurviness of the financier and the self-made
man, beaming down like a shameful sun on the idolatrous
city, which grovelled on its belly, chanting vile songs of
praise before the impious tabernacle of the Bank.

'Well, crumble then, society! perish, old world!' cried Des
Esseintes, roused to indignation by the ignominious spectacle
he had conjured up – and the sound of his voice broke the
oppressive spell the nightmare had laid on him.

'Ah!' he groaned, 'To think that all this isn't just a bad dream! To think that I'm about to rejoin the base and servile riff-raff of the age!'

To soothe his wounded spirit he called upon the consoling maxims of Schopenhauer, and repeated to himself Pascal's sorrowful maxim: 'The soul sees nothing that does not distress it on reflection'; but the words echoed in his mind like meaningless noises, his weariness of spirit breaking them up, stripping them of all significance, all sedative virtue, all effective and soothing force.

He realized at last that the arguments of pessimism were powerless to comfort him, that only the impossible belief in a future life could bring him peace of mind.

A fit of rage swept away like a hurricane all his would-be resignation, all his attempted indifference. He could no longer shut his eyes to the fact that there was nothing to be done, nothing whatever, that it was all over; the bourgeois were guzzling like picnickers from paper bags among the imposing ruins of the Church – ruins which had become a place of assignation, a pile of debris defiled by unspeakable jokes and scandalous jests. Could it be that the terrible God of Genesis and the pale martyr of Golgotha would not prove their existence once for all by renewing the cataclysms of old, by rekindling the rain of fire that once consumed those accursed towns, the cities of the plain? Could it be that this slime would go on spreading until it covered with its pestilential filth this old world where now only seeds of iniquity sprang up and only harvests of shame were gathered?

The door suddenly flew open. In the distance, framed in the opening, some men in cocked hats appeared with clean-shaven cheeks and tufts of hair on their chins, trundling packing-cases along and moving furniture; then the door closed again behind the manservant, who disappeared carrying a bundle of books.

Des Esseintes collapsed into a chair.

'In two days' time I shall be in Paris,' he told himself. 'Well, it is all over now. Like a tide-race, the waves of human mediocrity are rising to the heavens and will engulf this refuge, for I am opening the flood-gates myself, against my will. Ah! but my courage fails me, and my heart is sick within me! – Lord, take pity on the Christian who doubts, on the unbeliever who would fain believe, on the galley-slave of life who puts out to sea alone, in the night, beneath a firmament no longer lit by the consoling beacon-fires of the ancient hope!'

ZOLA

TRANSLATED BY L. W. TANCOCK

GERMINAL

Germinal was written by Zola (1840–1902) to draw attention once again to the misery prevailing among the poor in France during the Second Empire. The novel, which has now become a sociological document, depicts the grim struggle between capital and labour in a coalfield in northern France. Yet through the blackness of this picture, humanity is constantly apparent, and the final impression is one of compassion and hope for the future, not only of organized labour, but also of man.

L'ASSOMMOIR

'I wanted to depict the inevitable downfall of a working-cla family in the polluted atmosphere of our urban areas', wr Zola of *L'Assommoir* (1877), which some critics rate the gr est of his Rougon-Macquart novels. In the result the bo triumphantly surmounts the author's moral and social intentio to become, perhaps, the first 'classical tragedy' of working-cl people living in the slums of a city – Paris. Vividly, with romantic illusion, Zola uses the coarse *argot* of the back-s to plot the descent of the easy-going Gervaise through id drunkenness, promiscuity, filth, and starvation to the The effect is at once humorous and pathetic.

THÉRÈSE RAQUIN

Thérèse Raquin is another intense and powerful great nineteenth-century French novelist. Zol here with sex, violence, and guilt, which he han realism.

Also available

NANA
THE DEBACL

THE PENGUIN CLASSICS

Some recent and forthcoming volumes

ZOLA

TRANSLATED BY L. W. TANCOCK

GERMINAL

Germinal was written by Zola (1840–1902) to draw attention once again to the misery prevailing among the poor in France during the Second Empire. The novel, which has now become a sociological document, depicts the grim struggle between capital and labour in a coalfield in northern France. Yet through the blackness of this picture, humanity is constantly apparent, and the final impression is one of compassion and hope for the future, not only of organized labour, but also of man.

L'ASSOMMOIR

'I wanted to depict the inevitable downfall of a working-class family in the polluted atmosphere of our urban areas', wrote Zola of *L'Assommoir* (1877), which some critics rate the great-est of his Rougon-Macquart novels. In the result the book triumphantly surmounts the author's moral and social intentions to become, perhaps, the first 'classical tragedy' of working-class people living in the slums of a city – Paris. Vividly, without romantic illusion, Zola uses the coarse *argot* of the back-streets to plot the descent of the easy-going Gervaise through idleness, drunkenness, promiscuity, filth, and starvation to the grave. The effect is at once humorous and pathetic.

THÉRÈSE RAQUIN

Thérèse Raquin is another intense and powerful novel by the great nineteenth-century French novelist. Zola is concerned here with sex, violence, and guilt, which he handles with forceful realism.

Also available

NANA
THE DEBACLE

MORE ABOUT PENGUINS
AND PELICANS

Penguinews, which appears every month, contains details of all the new books issued by Penguins as they are published. From time to time it is supplemented by *Penguins in Print*, which is a complete list of all titles available. (There are some five thousand of these.)

A specimen copy of *Penguinews* will be sent to you free on request. For a year's issues (including the complete lists) please send £1.00 if you live in the British Isles, or elsewhere. Just write to Dept EP, Penguin Books Ltd, Harmondsworth, Middlesex, enclosing a cheque or postal order, and your name will be added to the mailing list.

In the U.S.A.: For a complete list of books available from Penguin in the United States write to Dept CS, Penguin Books Inc., 7110 Ambassador Road, Baltimore, Maryland 21207.

In Canada: For a complete list of books available from Penguin in Canada write to Penguin Books Canada Ltd, 41 Steelcase Road West, Markham, Ontario.

*Alack, alas, and well-a-day!
Tonight I have a guest;
I wonder what to serve him,
And still have time to rest!*

APPLE FRITTERS

1 3/4 cups sifted flour
1 1/4 teaspoons baking powder
3/4 cup milk
1 teaspoon butter
3 tablespoons sugar
3 eggs, separated
1/4 teaspoon salt
2 cups apple, diced

Sift flour and baking powder. Then add milk and blend until smooth. Cream butter with sugar and add egg yolks. Add to flour and milk. Stir in diced apple. Beat white of eggs to frothy consistency. Then

5

add to batter, mixing thoroughly. Heat chafing dish pan over direct heat until piece of white paper turns brown as it touches the bottom of the pan. Melt butter in pan. Spoon out batter size of a walnut, and drop into hot pan. Brown on both sides until fluffy and thoroughly done in the center. Dust with cinnamon-sugar and serve with tiny hot sausages.

APPETIZING WELSH RAREBIT WITH PINEAPPLE

1 pound Old English or sharp cheese,
  cut into 1-inch chunks
½ cup milk
Salt and pepper
¼ teaspoon paprika
½ teaspoon dry mustard
2 eggs
4 slices buttered toast
1 cup drained pineapple chunks, if desired

First rinse ingredient pan of chafing dish with cold water to avoid milk sticking. Put in cheese chunks and milk and cook over boiling water about 20 minutes, or until cheese is melted. Be sure to stir often. Stir in seasoning. Remove from heat. Whip eggs until frothy. Stir 1 cup of the hot milk and cheese mixture into beaten eggs in bowl. Then return the egg mixture into the hot melted cheese sauce, stirring constantly.

Again heat cheese sauce, cooking over boiling water for 5 to 10 minutes, or until rarebit reaches the desired consistency. Serve at once on buttered toast squares. Add pineapple chunks if desired. Serves 4.

ASPARAGUS, CREAMED WITH CHEESE

2 tablespoons melted butter
½ cup soft bread crumbs
1 pound asparagus (cooked)
1 cup medium white sauce
1 cup cheese, grated

Heat ingredient pan of chafing dish over direct heat. Brown butter and bread crumbs slightly. Remove from direct heat and place pan over boiling water. In it place the cooked asparagus and medium white sauce to which cheese has been added — blending carefully with wooden fork. Cover and allow mixture to cook slowly 15 to 20 minutes. Serve piping hot. Serves 4.

7

Blinis with sour cream,
Or black caviar,
Make an elegant supper,
Fit for a Czar!

BROWN BETTY
WITH PISTACHIOS

2 tablespoons butter
2 cups dried bread crumbs
1/4 cup white sugar
1/4 cup brown sugar
1/8 teaspoon salt
1/2 teaspoon cinnamon
Dash of nutmeg
1 teaspoon orange peel, grated
1 cup home-made applesauce (unsweetened)

Heat chafing dish pan over direct heat. Melt butter in pan and add bread crumbs, turning until crumbs are slightly browned. Mix sugar, salt, cinnamon, nutmeg and grated orange peel together. Add this mixture to browned bread crumbs in chafing dish. Add applesauce and mix well. Fill dessert cups with this tangy pudding and top with sweetened cinnamon-whipped cream, with salted pistachio nutmeat for accent. Serves 4.

BACON OMELET WITH RED-CURRANT JELLY

4 egg yolks
1/2 teaspoon salt
Dash of pepper
Few grains cayenne
4 tablespoons hot water
4 egg whites
1 tablespoon butter
12 strips bacon

Beat egg yolks until thick and add salt, pepper, cayenne, and hot water. Mix well. Fold in the stiffly beaten egg whites lightly and blend thoroughly. Melt butter in chafing dish pan over direct heat. Pour egg mixture evenly in pan. When the bottom begins to brown and edges set, add cooked crisp bacon strips cut in half. Either roll quickly or fold the omelet and serve at once while the omelet is still puffy. Spread with red currant jelly or any tart preserve. Cheese is also a tasty variation with the omelet. Serves 4.

BARBECUED FRANKFURTERS WITH BEANS

2 tablespoons butter
2 onions, chopped fine
½ cup diced celery (half cooked)
1 cup sliced mushrooms
6 to 8 frankfurters
Salt and pepper
¼ cup catsup
1 cup canned tomatoes
1 cup water
Baked beans
Toasted rolls

Cook onions, celery, mushrooms in butter in chafing dish pan over direct heat until browned. Slit frankfurters lengthwise and lay face down in chafing dish pan and fry until lightly browned. Add catsup, tomatoes, and water. Season with salt and pepper. Cover closely, and simmer for 15 to 20 minutes. Serve over hot toasted frankfurter rolls with your favorite baked beans. Serves 6.

BEIGNETS

Batter:

1 cup sifted flour
1/8 teaspoon salt
1 cup milk
2 egg yolks
2 egg whites, beaten stiff

6 tart apples
1 tablespoon white sugar
1 tablespoon brown sugar
1/2 teaspoon cinnamon
Dash of nutmeg
1/4 cup Rum
1/4 cup margarine or butter
1/2 cup powdered sugar

Sift flour and salt together. Add egg yolks to milk gradually and stir well. Sift flour mixture into milk slowly and blend well. Cut in stiffly beaten egg whites.

Peel and core apples. Slice into 1/2-inch pieces. Place in a dish and sprinkle with sugar, cinnamon and nutmeg. Pour Rum over apples and let stand for 2 hours. Melt butter or margarine in chafing dish and add apples drained and dipped in batter. Fry until golden brown. Dust with powdered sugar. Serves 6.

Chicken à la Newburg,
Chicken à la King
No matter how you slice it,
The chicken is the thing!

CHICKEN CROQUETTES
WITH TOASTED ALMONDS

2 cups cooked chicken
Salt and pepper
2 tablespoons celery, finely chopped
Few grains nutmeg
1 cup thick white sauce
¾ cup fine bread crumbs
1 egg
2 tablespoons water
½ cup almonds, chopped

Dice cold cooked chicken, add salt, pepper, celery and nutmeg then the thick white sauce, and mix well. Chill in refrig-

PREFACE

CHAFING DISH COOKERY is once again very much in vogue — as it was in early Colonial America in the 1720's. Only today there are various sizes and shapes of chafing dishes, with all sorts of heating devices, including candles, alcohol lamps and electric units. And all can be used for spontaneous cooking — morning, noon, or night!

Some of the recipes selected in this book are complete meals in themselves. Others need additional trimmings. But the editor has endeavored to select those recipes with ingredients which every hostess keeps on hand so as not to send her off to the store for last-minute fill-ins.

The fun in owning a chafing dish is in using it often! The more you use it the more you will want to use it, and you will find that cooking can continue right in front of your television set and you won't miss a thing!

The suggestion of placing your chafing dish on a rolling tea wagon has been made. Then your patio or garden can become your kitchen indeed, and you will be the rare hostess who can spend all her time with her guests — while they watch and even help with the cooking!

THE

ABC

OF
CHAFING DISH
COOKERY

DECORATIONS BY RUTH McCREA

THE PETER PAUPER PRESS
MOUNT VERNON · NEW YORK

EGG DUMPLINGS WITH LAMB STEW

Lamb stew, previously cooked
1 egg
¾ cup milk
2 cups sifted flour
3 teaspoons baking powder
½ teaspoon salt
1 tablespoon melted butter

Place the prepared lamb stew in chafing dish pan. Cover and heat over boiling water 15 to 20 minutes, or until stew is thoroughly heated through. While stew is heating, break egg into bowl. Beat well. Add milk and sifted dry ingredients. Stir thoroughly until smooth. Add melted butter and drop from tablespoon on top of stew. Cover and cook 10 minutes over boiling water, or until dumplings are fluffy and light. Serves 4 to 6, depending on amount of stew being served, and the size of your guests' appetites!

Complete dinner in your chafing dish! The stew may be cooked ahead of time if you wish, or you may use canned beef stew if you must cut corners and want a meal in a hurry.

*Flirt while you bubble
and simmer the stew;
His mind's on the dinner
But his heart is with you!*

FRIED SCALLOPS

1 quart scallops
Salt, pepper, flour
1 egg
2 tablespoons water
¾ cup fine bread or cracker crumbs
3 tablespoons butter or margarine

Wash scallops and dry between towels. Sprinkle with salt, pepper and flour. Dip in slightly beaten egg, diluted with water, and roll in crumbs. Place chafing dish pan over direct heat. Melt butter or margarine. Add scallops. Fry about 5 minutes — turn often. Drain and serve with slices of lemon or tartar sauce. Serves 6.

EUROPEAN VEAL CUTLETS

1½ pounds boned veal
¼ cup milk
½ teaspoon salt
⅛ teaspoon pepper
1 cup dry bread crumbs
1 egg, beaten with
  2 tablespoons water

Grind veal finely, or have butcher grind veal for you. Add milk and seasoning. Shape into flat patties or cutlets. Roll in dry bread crumbs, then egg mixture, then crumbs again. Fry in butter or margarine in chafing dish pan over direct heat until cutlets are delicately brown on both sides. Cover and cook slowly over boiling water for 10 to 15 minutes. Serve on hot platter with paprika sauce. Serves 6.

Paprika Sauce:

To drippings left in chafing dish pan stir in 3 tablespoons flour. Slowly add 1 cup milk. Season with salt, pepper and 1 teaspoon paprika. Cook sauce until thick. Pour over cutlets.

A good, nourishing meal with the minimum of effort if prepared in advance.

Earthenware, copper, silver or brass; chafing dish glamor will always surpass!

EGGS SCRAMBLED WITH VIRGINIA HAM

2 tablespoons butter
½ cup milk
6 eggs, slightly beaten
Salt and pepper
1½ cups Virginia ham, chopped

Place chafing dish over boiling water. Melt butter. Add milk. Stir thoroughly. Add eggs and cook slowly. Add Virginia ham to eggs and continue to cook slowly until eggs are scrambled soft or firm as desired. Season. Serve with English muffins and marmalade. Serves 6.

17

*ear Cook, I beg you,
Keep up the good food;
Let not the minutiae
of living intrude!*

DUCK À L'ORANGE

2 cups cooked duck, 4 tablespoons butter
  cut in pieces Salt and pepper

Melt butter and add duck, salt, and pepper. Brown slightly. Remove from direct heat and cook over boiling water 20 minutes. Serve with orange sauce. Serves 4.

Orange Sauce:

1 cup orange juice 2 Tbs. cornstarch
¾ cup sugar ½ tsp. butter

Heat juice. Add sugar well blended with cornstarch. Cook until thickened, stirring constantly. Add butter after removing from heat. Stir well.

CRABMEAT NEWBURGH

2 tablespoons butter
  or vegetable shortening
1½ tablespoons flour
¾ teaspoon salt
Few grains cayenne
½ cup cream
¼ cup milk
2 cups cooked crabmeat
2 egg yolks
1 tablespoon Sherry
4 patty shells, or slices of toast

Melt butter or shortening in chafing dish over boiling water. Add flour, salt and cayenne and mix well. Add cream and milk gradually, and bring to the boiling point, stirring constantly. Add cooked and cleaned crabmeat. Just before serving add beaten egg yolks and Sherry wine for flavor. Serve on patty shells or squares of toast. Grated Parmesan cheese may be added instead of Sherry, if preferred, to make crabmeat au gratin. Serves 4 generously.

Truly a connoisseur's delight! A wonderful after-theater dish for your sophisticated friends.

15

CALF'S LIVER, FRENCH FRIED WITH ONIONS

1 pound calf's liver
  (slices cut ½ inch in thickness)
French dressing
4 tablespoons vegetable shortening
3 onions, sliced thin
Salt and pepper to taste

Soak 1 pound calf's liver in salted water for ½ hour. Scald with boiling water. Drain and cut into 3-inch strips. Marinate in French dressing for approximately 1 hour. Drain and dry with clean damp cloth. Heat chafing dish pan to very hot temperature. Fry liver in hot shortening until lightly brown, about 5 minutes. Add onions and season with salt and pepper. Cook until the onions are clear. Cover the chafing dish pan and cook until onions and liver are tender. Stir now and then. Do not over-cook liver. Serve with crisp bacon strips and steaming hot Idaho baked potatoes. Serves 3 to 4.

Hearty and satisfying supper! Or, with the addition of a mixed green salad, a simple dessert and good black coffee, a company dinner!

14

erator until mixture can be formed into croquettes. Roll in bread crumbs and dip into slightly beaten egg diluted with water. Then roll again in crumbs. Heat chafing dish pan to very hot. Roll croquettes in chopped almonds and fry in a little vegetable shortening or butter about 5 minutes. Drain, and serve at once with spiced peach half and a mixed green salad. Serves 4.

CREAMED CODFISH WITH PIMIENTO

1 cup medium white sauce
1½ cups cooked cod fish, flaked
1 tablespoon parsley
½ tablespoon pimiento, chopped
Salt and pepper to taste

Prepare white sauce in chafing dish over boiling water. Add cooked codfish pieces to white sauce. Add parsley and pimiento, and season to taste. Serve on hot buttered toast or on creamy mashed potatoes. Enough for 4.

Delicious with lively salad of mixed greens!

13

*Jambalaya in the dish
Is festive, yet hearty;
Easy to make,
Yet fit for a party!*

JAM-OVER-PORK CHOPS

1 tablespoon butter
1 large lean pork chop per serving
Salt and pepper to taste
1 teaspoon apricot jam per serving

Heat chafing dish pan over direct heat. Melt butter in pan and arrange pork chops in butter. Brown slightly, season and turn. Continue cooking slowly, turning chops now and then until well done when tested with fork. Arrange teaspoon of jam over chop on serving plate with boiled or baked potato.

Father will like this quick meal!

JELLY-GARNISHED ROAST LAMB SANDWICH

1½ cups lamb gravy, strained
2 cups sliced roast lamb
Salt and pepper to taste
1 teaspoon mint jelly per serving
2 slices bread per serving

Heat chafing dish over direct heat. Place gravy in hot pan over boiling water and heat for 10 to 15 minutes, stirring to dissolve any fatty particles in the gravy. When gravy is warmed thoroughly, add lamb slices. Cover pan and continue to heat over boiling water. Add more salt and pepper if needed. Arrange 2 slices of bread open-faced on each plate. Place mint jelly beside bread for flavor and color accent. Then carefully spoon the lamb slices in gravy on to the bread and serve at once as open-faced sandwiches.

JUBILEE CHERRIES

2 cups black Bing cherries
¼ cup Brandy
Vanilla ice cream

Heat the cherries in a small amount of

30

juice. Pour half of the Brandy in while the cherries are heating. Do not let them boil. When they are steaming hot, dash them with the rest of the Brandy, put a lighted match to it and serve on vanilla ice cream. Serves 4 to 6.

A Hollywood spectacular!

JOHNNY'S FAVORITE

1 tablespoon shortening
1 small onion, chopped
3/4 pound ground beef
8 ounces wide noodles
1/2 can cream-style corn
1/2 can condensed tomato soup
1 can tomato sauce
Salt and pepper

Melt shortening in chafing dish; add onion and cook until golden brown. Add meat and cook, stirring, until browned. Cook noodles in boiling, salted water until tender. Drain, rinse, and mix with the corn, tomato soup and tomato sauce. Combine with the meat mixture in chafing dish and season to taste with salt and pepper. Serves 4 or 5.

Kedgeree's a Scottish dish,
For brunch it can't be beat;
We like it best with kippers
For a Sunday morning treat!

KNOCKWURST WITH SAUERKRAUT

1 pound knockwurst
2 cups cooked sauerkraut

Pour enough boiling water in chafing dish pan to cover knockwurst. Allow to boil freely over direct heat for approximately half an hour. Serves 3-4.

Serve with cold or heated sauerkraut, with mashed potatoes and butter, and fresh hot rolls.

For hungry teen-agers in a hurry to get to the movies after an afternoon of skating!

32

*Lobster in the chafing dish,
Lobster in the pot;
Serve it many fancy ways,
Serve it cold or hot!*

LOBSTER ON PATTY SHELL

2 cups medium white sauce
  (using 1 cup light cream instead of
  1 cup milk in white sauce)
2 cups fresh, or canned, lobster meat
½ teaspoon salt
⅛ teaspoon pepper
1 tablespoon parsley, chopped
1 egg, well-beaten

Prepare medium white sauce in chafing dish over boiling water. Place lobster meat in white sauce and heat thoroughly. Add salt, pepper, parsley and well-beaten egg. Cook 2 minutes longer. Serve in flaky patty shell with slices of hard-boiled egg as garnish. Nice with fresh asparagus, new peas and potato chips. Serves 4.

Perfect summer luncheon for the ladies' bridge club!

LEMON-MOLASSES PUDDING

½ cup sugar
1 tablespoon cornstarch
⅛ teaspoon salt
1 cup boiling water
2 tablespoons margarine or butter
2 tablespoons lemon juice
1 egg yolk
4 servings moist spiced molasses cake

Mix sugar, cornstarch and salt in chafing dish pan. Place over boiling water and add 1 cup boiling water slowly, stirring constantly. Boil 5 minutes until thin. Remove from fire and add margarine or butter, lemon juice and beaten yolk. Return to fire and cook 1 minute longer. Serve at once over molasses cake sponge. To top, add sweetened whipped cream, vanilla ice cream or lemon sherbet. Serves 4.

A filling dessert with loads of flavor!

LUSCIOUS SUGARLESS MARSHMALLOW ICING

2 egg whites
1 cup light corn syrup
8 to 10 marshmallows
Pinch of salt
Fruit coloring, if desired

Beat 2 egg whites with corn syrup and a pinch of salt in chafing dish pan over boiling water until thick and fluffy. Stir in marshmallows. Remove from heat, and continue beating until icing forms peaks. Add pink or yellow fruit coloring if color effect is desired. Recipe makes enough to cover top and sides of a 3-layer cake, or toppings for 1 dozen cup cakes. Dainty candles may be added for birthday celebration.

A good prepared cake mix may be used instead of home-baked cake, if desired. Be sure to choose a mix that requires the addition of fresh eggs, as it is usually far superior to other brands. The dried egg for some reason seems to detract from the flavor of the cake.

A Birthday Party treat!

acaroni comes from Italy,
Oh, let us sing its praise;
We like it with tomatoes
And we like it Milanese!

MEXICAN CHILI

1 pound onions
Garlic
1 pound chuck beef, cut into 1½-inch cubes
1 can tomatoes
1 can red kidney beans
½ cup celery, diced
Salt, chili powder and cayenne pepper

Slice onions and fry with a little crushed garlic in chafing dish. When partly done, add beef and brown well. Add tomatoes, kidney beans and chopped celery. Season with salt, chili powder and cayenne pepper. Cook slowly for 1½ hours. Serves 4 generously.

Nobody loves me;
My, I feel low!
I'll learn how to cook
And catch me a beau!

NEW ENGLAND CLAM CHOWDER

1 dozen clams
2 tablespoons margarine or butter
4 tablespoons onions, chopped
3 cups cooked potatoes, diced
1½ teaspoons salt
⅛ teaspoon pepper
4 cups hot milk
2 tablespoons flour

Clean and carefully inspect clams, removing all particles of shell. Mince and return to liquor which has also been strained and freed of shell particles. Pour into chafing

37

dish pan and cook 10 minutes over direct heat. In separate pan cook margarine or butter with onion until delicate brown. Pour into clam mixture. Add cooked diced potatoes, salt, pepper and milk, and bring to boiling point. Mix flour with a little cold water to make a smooth paste. Add this to chowder and stir until chowder thickens. Serve at once with salted wafers. Serves 4 to 6.

NEW POTATOES IN CUCUMBER SAUCE

2 tablespoons butter
1½ tablespoons flour
1½ cups chicken stock
1 clove garlic, chopped fine
¼ teaspoon salt
Dash of pepper
½ cup sour or sweet heavy cream
Juice of 1 lemon
1 cucumber, peeled and sliced,
  with seeds removed
Small new potatoes, lightly boiled
Small sausages, if desired

Melt butter in chafing dish pan over direct heat. Sprinkle with flour. When flour is absorbed in butter, add chicken stock slowly, stirring constantly to avoid lumping. When well heated, add seasonings, cream and lemon juice, strained. Lastly add the cucumber. Cook until cucumber is tender. Serve over small new potatoes with tiny, browned sausages.

NUT CUSTARD

1 quart milk
3 eggs
1 cup sugar
1½ tablespoons flour
1 teaspoon vanilla
½ cup Brazil nuts, chopped fine
2 cups bread cubes soaked in Rum syrup
Sweetened whipped cream

Pour milk into chafing dish and heat over boiling water. While milk is heating, beat eggs well. Add sugar and flour and mix thoroughly. Add to hot milk slowly, stirring constantly until mixture thickens. Remove from fire and add vanilla and Brazil nuts. Then pour into dessert cups over pieces of bread cubes which have been soaked in Rum syrup. Serve at room temperature with sweetened whipped cream, topped with a whole Brazil nut. Serves 4 nicely.

*h, for an omelette,
so puffy and high;
made to perfection,
Not too moist or too dry!*

OYSTERS AND BACON

12 raw oysters
12 strips bacon
Salt and pepper
Paprika

Wrap a piece of raw bacon around each oyster and fasten with toothpick. Season with salt, pepper and a dash of paprika. Place in chafing dish pan over direct heat and brown on both sides until bacon is crisp. Drain on unglazed paper and serve with toothpicks. Serves 3-4.

Wonderful with drinks, and as party hors d'oeuvres!

40

ork chops fixed in sweet cream
My darling will adore;
and if I serve him pork chops,
He'll hurry back for more!

PIGS IN BLANKETS

6 to 8 frankfurters
2 cups cold mashed potatoes (seasoned)
½ cup flour
2 tablespoons butter or margarine

Cover frankfurters with mashed potatoes and roll in flour. Place in melted butter or margarine in chafing dish pan over direct heat. Brown slowly, turning often. Cover and cook 15 minutes to thoroughly heat the frankfurters. Serves 4 to 6.

Left-overs new again! Or, if you use cocktail frankfurters, they can be served as hot canapés.

41

POTATO PANCAKES
WITH PRUNES

2 eggs
2 cups raw potatoes, grated
1 tablespoon onion, grated
4 tablespoons flour
1 teaspoon salt
Stewed prunes

Beat eggs slightly and mix all ingredients (except prunes) in bowl. Heat chafing dish pan over direct heat and add butter. Drop mixture from tablespoon into chafing dish pan and press flat with spoon. Fry until golden brown on both sides, turning gently. Serve to 4 hungry persons with stewed prunes, cooked with grated orange peel for extra flavor.

PAN-BROILED
GRAPEFRUIT HALF

½ grapefruit per serving
1 tablespoon butter
2 tablespoons brown or white sugar
Maraschino cherry, or dot of red jelly

Cut grapefruit in half crosswise. Use a grapefruit knife to cut each fruit section from membrane. Heat butter in chafing dish over low direct heat. Sprinkle bottom of pan with sugar; heat slowly to melt sugar. Place grapefruit half cut side down in melted butter and sugar. Brown fruit about 15 minutes. Place cherry or jelly in center and serve piping hot.

A tempting way to start the meal for a Sunday Brunch!

PAN-BROILED SHAD ROE

2 pounds shad roe
3 tablespoons vegetable shortening
¾ teaspoon salt
½ teaspoon white pepper
4 slices buttered toast
12 slices bacon, cooked crisp

Wash the roe gently in salted water, pat dry on a paper towel. To cook it melt the shortening in chafing dish pan over direct heat. Season with salt and pepper. Cook the roe gently, turning with care until browned. Cook only about 8 minutes on each side; longer if very thick. Serve on toast with bacon strips, garnish with parsley and lemon wedges. Serves 4.

*uiet in the kitchen,
Don't disturb the mice;
The Cook is in the parlor,
Fixing Spanish Rice!*

QUINCE JELLY SANDWICH (GRILLED)

8 slices of yellow cake
  (pound or sponge)
Quince jelly
Butter

Slice cake ¼ inch thick. Spread first slice of cake with generous portion of quince jelly and place another slice on top to form sandwich. Grill sandwich on chafing dish pan in a little butter until delicately brown on one side. Turn and brown opposite side. Serve with creamed cottage cheese salad to 4 persons.

*rrf! says my dog,
as he gnaws at his bone;
would he welcome some meat
In a friendlier tone?*

RICE AND CHEESE BALLS

1 tablespoon butter
1 tablespoon flour
½ teaspoon salt
½ cup milk
8 ounces Cheddar-type cheese
2 cups cooked rice
1 egg, beaten
½ cup dry bread crumbs

Melt butter in chafing dish over direct
low heat and blend flour and salt into
butter. Stir in milk and cook over boiling
water until mixture thickens and is
smooth. Add cheese cut into small pieces.
Then add rice and turn into separate

45

bowl to cool for 1 to 2 hours. When ready to serve, heat chafing dish over direct heat with enough butter or margarine to cover bottom of pan. Form cheese balls and dip into slightly beaten egg and bread crumbs. Brown in chafing dish pan over direct heat slowly until delicate brown on all sides. Serves 4.

RED CHERRY DUMPLINGS OVER BEEF STEW

1 cup sifted flour
1½ teaspoons baking powder
½ teaspoon salt
1 tablespoon margarine
½ cup water
1 cup canned red pitted cherries, drained

Sift flour with baking powder and salt. Cut margarine into mixture until it is very fine. Add water and cherries and mix very lightly until soft dough is formed. Drop from teaspoon onto boiling beef stew cooking over hot water in chafing dish. Cover tightly and cook about 12 minutes or until dumplings are light and done. Serves 4.

Just tart enough to be delicious!

RAISIN SAUCE AND GRILLED HAM

1 slice ham, ¾-inch thick
¾ cup raisin sauce

Place ham slice in chafing dish pan and heat slowly over direct heat until slightly brown on one side. Then turn and brown opposite side. Continue cooking slowly until ham is tender when tested with fork. Do not over-cook. Serves 2.

Raisin Sauce:

½ cup raisins, washed and drained
¾ cup water
½ cup brown sugar
1½ teaspoons cornstarch
⅛ teaspoon salt
6 cloves
1 tablespoon butter
1 tablespoon lemon juice

Cook raisins slowly in water for 15 minutes. Mix sugar, cornstarch, salt, cloves, and add to raisin mixture. Stir till slightly thickened. Add butter and lemon juice. Cook slowly until ham is ready to serve. Makes 1½ cups sauce, or enough for 4 servings.

anta Spaghetti!
I worship the food!
It's good for the palate —
For the purse it is good!

SHRIMP PATTIES

3 eggs
1½ cups cooked shrimp,
  shelled and cleaned
⅛ teaspoon salt
⅛ teaspoon pepper
1 tablespoon onion, grated
2 tablespoons butter
½ cup dry bread crumbs
¼ cup sliced mushrooms

Beat eggs thoroughly. Add shrimp, salt, pepper and bread crumbs. Melt butter and fry onions and mushrooms over direct heat in chafing dish. Add to shrimp. Form

48

patties of shrimp mixture and drop into melted butter. Press flat, and brown until golden on both sides and well cooked through. Serves 4.

Excellent Lenten luncheon or Friday special!

SUZETTES (FRENCH PANCAKE)

2 eggs
1¼ cups milk
1 cup sifted flour
¼ cup sugar
½ teaspoon salt

Beat eggs in bowl until fluffy. Stir in milk and blend thoroughly. Sift flour, sugar and salt into bowl and beat with electric beater until blended and a thin batter is formed. Heat chafing dish pan. Grease pan lightly and drop batter from tablespoon. Form each pancake by tilting pan so that batter covers bottom thinly. Bake until top of pancake is no longer shiny. Then turn and brown opposite side. Butter and fill with grape jelly, cream cheese and pecans, creamed chicken, creamed seafood or tiny sausages. Roll, and serve at once. Serves 4.

STEAK IN CHAFING DISH

1 ¾-inch sirloin steak, trimmed
  (1½-2 lbs.)
2 tablespoons butter
¼ teaspoon salt
⅛ teaspoon pepper
1 teaspoon Worcestershire sauce

Pound steak well with mallet, and place
in chafing dish pan in which butter has
been melted. Add seasoning. Fry over
direct heat quickly, turning only once.
Season with Worcestershire sauce and
serve at once on hot platter. Serves 2.

SWEET POTATOES WITH MARSHMALLOWS

4 sweet potatoes, boiled and peeled
4 tablespoons butter
½ cup brown sugar
2 teaspoons orange peel, grated fine
¼ teaspoon salt
6 to 8 marshmallows

Slice cold, peeled potatoes ¼ inch thick.
Melt butter and sugar in heated chafing
dish pan over direct heat. Stir well to prevent burning. Add orange peel. Arrange
potatoes carefully in bottom of pan and

50

continue to brown slowly. Place marshmallows between potatoes and allow
marshmallows to dissolve slowly. Turn
the potatoes now and then to coat evenly
with sugar. Serve hot with Canadian
bacon, or fried ham slices.

SPAGHETTI WITH MUSHROOM SAUCE

¼ pound mushrooms
2 tablespoons butter
2 tablespoons flour
Salt, pepper, garlic
½ pound thin spaghetti, cooked

Wash, peel and remove stems from mushrooms. Cut mushroom caps into thin slices
and fry in 2 tablespoons butter in chafing
dish pan over direct heat for 5 minutes.
Add 2 tablespoons flour and mix well.
Place pan over boiling water to keep
warm while preparing mushroom liquor.
Place stems and peelings in separate saucepan, cover with water and simmer for 15
minutes. Strain. Add 1 cup mushroom
stock to the mushrooms in chafing dish
pan and bring to the boiling point, stirring constantly. Add salt, pepper and

51

chopped garlic clove if desired. Serve over cooked, colanderized spaghetti. Serves 4.

SHRIMP CURRY

1 pound fresh shrimp
2 cups shrimp stock
2 chicken bouillon cubes
½ tablespoon curry powder
Salt, pepper
2 tablespoons flour
2 tablespoons melted butter
2 cups hot, cooked rice
2 hard-boiled eggs, sliced

Cook and prepare shrimp, saving stock. To 2 cups strained shrimp stock, add bouillon cubes and stir until dissolved; moisten curry powder with a little water and add to stock with salt and pepper, mixing well. Stir flour into melted butter; gradually stir in seasoned stock and cook over low heat until smooth and slightly thickened; then add shrimp. Mix shrimp and sauce with hot rice and cook 15 minutes; garnish with sliced eggs. Serves 4.

For those who like curry, this is a wonderful one-plate supper. A cup of hot, black coffee is all that is needed to complete the meal!

The pan of hot water
Was named in Paree;
It keeps the food moist
And is called "Bain Marie"!

TURKEY HASH
WITH CRANBERRY JELLY

2 cups cold cooked turkey, diced
¾ cup cold boiled potatoes, diced
1½ tablespoons giblet gravy
½ teaspoon salt
2 tablespoons butter

Mix all ingredients except butter. Melt butter in chafing dish pan over direct heat. Arrange the mixture in the pan to cover the bottom. Brown about 5 minutes. Then turn hash over and brown the opposite side quickly. Fold hash like an omelet and serve on hot platter with cranberry jelly and parsley. Serves 4.

53

TOMATOES À LA CHAFING DISH

4 ripe tomatoes
¼ teaspoon celery salt
Sugar
Dash of nutmeg
2 tablespoons butter

Core tomatoes; cut in half crosswise. Season with celery salt, sugar and nutmeg. Melt butter in chafing dish pan over direct heat. Arrange tomatoes face down on pan. Broil slowly until skin begins to lighten and until tomatoes are done. Serve hot, face up, with cold cottage cheese and chive salad. Serves 4.

A delight for those who are diet conscious!

TUNA-HAM SHORTCAKE

1 cup medium white sauce
1 can tuna fish, flaked
1 cup baked ham, slivered
¼ teaspoon salt
⅛ teaspoon pepper
Shortcake

Prepare medium white sauce in chafing dish pan over boiling water. Add flaked tuna and ham slivers. Season. Heat 15 to

54

20 minutes over boiling water. Plan short-cake baking time in oven to terminate as tuna and ham mixture is ready to serve. Serve on shortcake biscuit cut in half with spiced pear as garnish.

Pick the left-over ham from the bone for this recipe!

TAPIOCA MERINGUE

1 egg, separated
2 cups milk
4 tablespoons sugar
Dash of salt
3 tablespoons quick-cooking tapioca

Beat egg white until foamy, add 2 table-spoons sugar slowly and beat until thick. Set aside. Mix yolk with a little of the milk, then add remaining ingredients and the rest of the milk. Place over medium heat in chafing dish over hot water, bring to simmering point, stirring constantly, and then remove. Pour slowly into beaten egg white, stirring and folding until just blended. Cool 20 minutes, stir again, and then chill. Serves 4.

A light dessert, made well ahead of time!

tterly charming
Is dinner for two;
Lighted by candles
and catered by you!

UPPER BAY MUSSELS
BAKED WITH CHEESE

4 dozen steamed mussels
Salt, pepper
1 teaspoon onion, grated
½ pound sliced bacon
½ cup Parmesan cheese, grated

Spread mussels in buttered chafing dish and sprinkle with salt, pepper and onion. Fry bacon until almost crisp; place on top of mussels, about ¼ inch apart; sprinkle cheese between strips. Cook about 15 minutes or until cheese melts. Serve very hot, garnished with parsley. Serves 6.

*Veal scallopini's
a gourmet's delight;
It makes my mouth water,
Let's have some tonight!*

VEAL STEAK IN CHAFING DISH

1¼ pound veal steak, sliced ½-inch thick
½ teaspoon salt
¼ teaspoon pepper
3 tablespoons butter

Trim steak, and season. Heat chafing dish pan over direct heat and melt butter in it. Place the meat in the melted butter and brown slowly for 25 to 30 minutes, turning from side to side until meat is tender and golden brown. Serve with oven-browned potatoes and a lively tossed green salad. Serves 2 to 3.

VEGETABLES OVER JOHNNY-CAKE SQUARES

1 cup medium white sauce
3 cups mixed vegetables
  (fresh, canned or frozen)
Salt, pepper
4 servings Johnny-cake, slit in half

Prepare medium white sauce in chafing dish pan over boiling water. When thick, add vegetables (drained), salt and pepper to taste. Serve on buttered, hot Johnny-cake squares with cold cuts. Serves 4.

Nothing like corn bread to hit the spot!

VIENNESE BLINIS

Suzettes (see page 49)
Caviar
Sour cream, whipped until thick
Tabasco sauce
Salt

Make suzettes in the chafing dish. Put a spoonful of caviar in the center of each pancake, add a dab of cream, a drop of Tabasco and a few grains of salt. Roll, place on plate, stab with toothpick and serve.

VEAL CHOW MEIN

1½ pounds veal round,
  cut into ¾-inch cubes
¼ cup butter
Salt, pepper
½ cup onions, chopped
¼ cup green peppers, coarsely chopped
¼ cup all-purpose flour
½ teaspoon Accent
½ teaspoon celery salt
2 pints heated milk
1 cup cooked celery,
  cut into 1-inch pieces
½ (4-oz.) can fried chow-mein noodles

Brown veal in butter in chafing dish until golden in color. Sprinkle with salt and pepper; add onion and green peppers. Cover; cook over low heat about ½ hour, or until tender. Sprinkle the veal mixture with flour, Accent and celery salt; stir well. Add milk; cook, stirring, until thickened. Add cooked celery. Correct seasoning. Cook covered for 20 minutes; scatter noodles on top. Cook 10 minutes longer. Serves 4.

Oriental! But you needn't make your guests take off their shoes and sit on the floor!

*Welsh Rabbit, Welsh Rabbit,
So tangy and creamy;
At midnight it tastes
Incomparably dreamy!*

WINE SAUCE FOR PUDDINGS AND CAKE

1 tablespoon butter
1 teaspoon flour
1 cup Sherry wine
2 tablespoons sugar
Yolks of 4 eggs

Melt butter in chafing dish pan over direct heat. Add flour and blend well. Add Sherry wine, 2 tablespoons sugar, and egg yolks. Stir briskly until sauce is at point of boiling. Remove from heat, dash with nutmeg and serve on plum, bread, cornstarch or steaming rice pudding. Serves 4.

ut! are you tired?
Your work is soon done;
Cook at the table,
Be gay, and have fun!

X-TRA-YUMMY-ZUCCHINI

2 medium-sized Zucchini squash
½ cup flour
Salt and pepper
1 egg, slightly beaten and diluted with
  2 tablespoons water
¼ cup butter or margarine

Wash (but do not peel) squash and cut in
¼-inch slices. Mix flour, salt, and pepper.
Dip squash into egg, then flour mixture.
Sauté slowly in chafing dish pan over direct heat 15 minutes. Turn often. Cover
and cook slowly over boiling water 5 minutes longer. Serves 4.

THIS VOLUME
HAS BEEN PREPARED
PRINTED AND PUBLISHED
AT THE OFFICE OF
THE PETER PAUPER PRESS
MOUNT VERNON
NEW YORK